Memoirs of Luzbel

J.C. Ramírez

MEMOIRS OF LUZBEL

Bellatores
Publishing

Copyright © 2020 by J.C. Ramírez
© 2022 by Bellatores Publishing Ltd.
71-75 Shelton Street
Covent Garden
London
WC2H 9JQ
www.bellatorespublishing.com

ISBN: 978-1-7392181-2-6

First Edition

For Siân, Evan and Joel,
never forget
dreams come true,
you are my proof.

Foreword

My name is unknown in the language of humans. For this reason I am one of the beings with the most names on planet Earth: the fallen angel, the antichrist, the beast, Satan, Lucifer, etc. etc. etc. If I had to choose just one name among them all, I would select the one that is most consistent with everything I am, and everything that I will always be; a being of light, whose light is the most beautiful of all... Luzbel.

This will be the name I give myself from now onwards, as I tell you my story.

Everyone knows that for a fair trial you must first listen to both sides of the story. You have already heard the version of the Creator and his son. With their story alone, you have judged and condemned me without giving me the opportunity to defend myself. Have you ever thought about whether my actions were justified? Have you ever thought that I might not be the bad guy in the story?

The time has come for everyone to hear my version of events, but are you really ready to listen to my story?

Whether you like it or not, my story will change your way of thinking and seeing life forever.

If you are ready to listen to my side, then let's start at the beginning.

CHAPTER ONE
In the Beginning

My name is Luzbel, and I am not the one to tell you in what or who you should believe, but like any defendant in a fair trial, I have the right to tell my version of events. From now on I promise to tell the truth, the whole truth, and nothing but the truth.

To begin I must explain that I exist, but nevertheless I am not alive like you. Every human ever born, lives, and later dies. I will never die because I simply do not live; I only exist. I have always existed and will always exist. I am the same as the air, light or electricity, they are not alive, but they exist. It is better that you do not try to understand this because it may serve only to hurt your head. Humans are still very young, and in your minds, everything must have a beginning and an end. Those rules do not suit me because I am from another world, and in my world, things are very different from yours.

I come from a world in which there is neither time nor space; everything is basically made up of energy and light. Matter, which is everything that makes up your universe, including you, was something that had never been seen in my world. In fact, it was something that only existed in the mind of a single being; a being to whom we owed our existence. Despite, like me, this being having many names in your world, I liked to use only one - "The Creator". I used this because it was what he liked to do the most. Everything that surrounded us we owed to him. He is one of the most important and powerful beings in my world. There was only one other being as extraordinary as the Creator and that was his son; the two have unparalleled power but together their power was invincible. Their two forces were so great that sometimes they brought into existence another being. All they had to do was to deploy all their force and join hands, creating a being with twice their power; his appearance was a perfect fusion of the Creator and his son. That being is the one you know today as the "Holy Spirit"; a being that could not exist without the energy of the Creator or that of his son. Three completely different beings that formed a single and almighty God. The rest of us could only gaze on, in amazement, at such magnificent power, and be grateful to both father and son for our existence.

In the beginning, I was the most important angel in my world. I was the most powerful and wise among all the angels; second in power only to the holy trinity. Thanks to this, I was considered the Creator's favourite angel. I was always unconditional with my

Lord, and I always tried to help the angels below me to reach my level, that was my main role.

If there is something we have in common between your world and mine, it is that we have a hierarchy. This is what governs our world and gives each being a place to be and a job to do.

The origin of each angel, including me, is the energy of the Creator. That is why it would be wrong to say that he created us; we have always been part of him, only sometimes he shaped a small part of his energy which resulted in a being of light - an angel. You could say this is the moment an angel is "born", but unlike humans, when an angel gains its form, it is that of an adult. Moreover, from the very first moment it already knows its objective and reason to exist, since we had been part of the energy of the Creator, we also obtain part of his wisdom and power.

When an angel takes its form, it does so without wings. As its power grows, white shadows in the shape of wings grow from its back. The higher the level the angel reaches, the more the wings change from shadows to energy, and finally when they reach the highest level, they become wings of light. That is the maximum level an angel can reach. I know this very well because I was the only angel with wings of light; but in my case, unlike the other angels, I have always existed with wings of light. I have never known what it feels like to be without wings, and I have certainly never had the opportunity to rise through the ranks, because from my position the next level would be to become a God, an equal to the Creator and his son.

Each angel of a higher level was assigned a group of angels with a lower level. The goal of each angel was to become the same as the Creator, so we helped each other. The Creator was not selfish and constantly encouraged us to improve ourselves more and more to become like him. That was something that took all my admiration and respect. That is why our second job as angels was to serve the Creator and always praise him for his way of being. It was something that we did not mind doing and that I had really enjoyed doing, because he was everything to me... At least that's what I thought at the time.

As I said before, my world is made up of energy and light, so we have no buildings or houses to live in. My world is difficult to explain when you have not yet managed to decipher all the laws of your own universe. But if you can imagine a blank space where nothing else exists, you will have a remote idea of what my world looks like. We do not have housing, transport or even belongings, everything is part of everyone, and we have all that we need. Rich or poor is something that does not exist in my world; if someone needs something, they should only think about it, and it will appear. You might think that it is magic, but this is just how my world works. Another difference in my world is that each angel can move in any direction, including up or down. Even though some angels have wings, these are not necessary to fly. We don't have to flap our wings to fly like birds do in your world, for us to move at heights is as natural as for you to run or walk. However, a pair of wings can be of great help when you want to fly at a higher speed, since they offer great stability and can give you an extra push.

Though in my world there are no physical spaces, there were areas in which not all angels could be. To speak in some way that you may be able to understand me; in my world there are different dimensions in which you can only be if you have reached a sufficiently high level. The Creator had his own particular dimension where he shaped his greatest creations; it was an area where only he, his son, and I could enter. That place was like his own small, and yet infinite, laboratory.

I was the angel with the highest rank of all, but despite this, I still had tasks assigned to me. I did not need to inform the Creator of the progress and objectives achieved by the other angels; we were all part of him so he could feel and know everything about us. Informing him of the progress of others is like wanting to tell yourself that your hands feel cold... no one knows better than you the state of something that is yours. Even so, I liked being alone with him to learn and continue to evolve. I was the most powerful angel of all, so the only being that could teach me something was him.

On one occasion, I went to see him in his "laboratory". I felt a little frustrated because it did not matter what I did, I felt that I had already reached my maximum potential. I felt that I could not give more of myself, and even so I was far below the level of the Creator and his son. I did not understand what I was doing wrong or where I was failing, and even though I had eternity to achieve it, patience was a virtue that was difficult for me to master, so I went to see him for advice.

With the idea in mind of seeing the Creator, I set out to enter his dimension. It was something that needed all of my concentration and power. I had to meditate, visualize where I wanted to go and use my inner power to get there. The Creator and his son could go there in just the blink of an eye, but it took me some time to achieve it, but considering that I was the only angel that could reach that dimension, I couldn't complain.

When I finally entered his dimension, I felt something inside me that I hadn't felt for a long time. It was a feeling of surprise and bewilderment at not knowing what I was seeing before me.

There was a small black cloud that seemed to grow very slowly, expanding like a living being that was growing. It was something that the light of my world seemed not to reach. But it was what was inside it that caught my attention the most. There were billions of small lights everywhere; so many that it was almost impossible to count them all. My curiosity was so great that I went into the cloud to look at the lights in more detail. They were all around me, the most accurate way to describe it was like a shower of fireflies at night with me in the middle; but when I got a little closer to the little lights they increased in size, and the closer I got the bigger they became.

It was something that I had never seen before. It was a very different light from that in my world, because it seemed to have an origin and an end. It was like a flame that spread everywhere, but as it progressed it lost strength. It was made of a material of which I had no knowledge. Greater was my surprise when I moved away from those lights to see what was on the other side, and at the end I saw something that I did not know of until that moment. I saw that it was created when their forces came to an end; I saw darkness. I had never known that term before... darkness. In my world everything is made up of energy and light, and the light that an angel gives off is infinite; it reaches everywhere. But within that space, my brightness did not spread too much. It seemed to be swallowed up by some type of dark matter that flooded the place. Darkness was something that had not been seen before, but there I was, surrounded by this new thing that, at that moment, I could not name.

I went back towards the lights, and each one was different from the others. The most curious thing is that they all moved in a very mysterious way, rotating on themselves and also around an even larger light. In principle it seemed chaos, but when I looked closely, I could see that all the lights had a place and an order. I approached and could see that they were made up of colours that I had never seen, not only that, but I was unable to describe the texture and colour. I was fascinated, taking it all in, until I felt the presence of the Creator nearby. He was in a light very close by, so I travelled, looking for the precise place where my lord was.

Although the light there was not the brightest, or the largest compared to the others, there was something very special about it. As I got closer, I saw how it was formed of two colours, blue and green. A single green spot in the centre and the rest was blue. The closer I got, the more colours I noticed were present; thousands of types of blues and greens, until I was finally able to stand on top of the light. The green now also had brown tones and the blue was not only on the ground, but it was above too. The blue above was different and made of another material. The blue above was light, soft, almost non-existent compared to the blue of the ground, which was thicker, more compact and also full of non-light beings. There were many types of those beings, their shape and appearance were nothing like that of a light being; they were so different that they even seemed like they couldn't see me. Not only was the blue substance full of these creatures, but the green and brown area had completely different beings, huge and strong looking, even threatening.

This was real madness, there were so many different beings, along with so many things that I had not seen until that moment. My feeling was that of a child in a toy store. There were animals, trees, mountains, rocks, oceans and millions of other things that nobody is surprised by now, but I was one of the first beings in history to witness the creation of your whole world, and for me, coming from a world of light, that left me speechless.

Light beings do not have a physical body. Our body is all energy, with not a single particle of matter within us. We can modify our size at will, this is the reason why I could get into those little lights that surrounded me when I entered the dimension of the Creator; lights that I would later know to be planets. On my normal scale, your universe is no larger than an ornament in the living room of a house, but of course that does not detract from its merit thanks to its great complexity, and above all, because it was a world very different from mine. Every little thing was something completely unique.

I continued traveling through the new world until I was face-to-face with The Creator. He looked at me, not with a surprised face, but with a face of satisfaction when he saw my astonishment at everything he had created. I approached a little closer to him and spoke with a tone of amazement.

"My Lord! But what is all of this? What have you created here?!"

"Luzbel, do you like everything you see?" he asked with a tone of great pride for everything he had done, as he stared back at me with a big smile.

"Like? I find it hard to believe that all this is possible and is not an illusion, but... how *is* all of this possible?" I asked him again without removing the astonished look on my face at any time.

"This is nothing" he replied with a very kind and soft voice.

At that moment I thought that I could not show any more astonishment until I heard him say it.

"Is there more? What can there be that is better than this world?" I asked him without taking my eyes from his for a single second.

"My dear Luzbel, you haven't seen anything yet" he said, smiling.

I continued talking to my lord and he explained it all to me. He gave me the first lesson on how this universe was composed and how it worked. The new light that he had created, and darkness, day and night, also time and space. All the things, and the new rules, that did not exist in my world that, to this day, still do not exist in my world. My mind was like a sponge, constantly absorbing all the new knowledge that The Creator shared with me. It was something that I had not experienced in a long time; the feeling of knowing nothing. Not knowing this new world was something very stimulating for me; my thirst for knowledge had no limits and The Creator had no qualms about showing me the whole of his new world. It was a world that was all connected, from the smallest being to the largest; all related in some way, each needing the other to continue living.

Unlike a being of light, these beings were created in a microscopic way. The Creator had everything ready so these beings would develop little by little until they reached their adult form within their own species. Once that stage was reached, each would have the ability to multiply, which was only possible because each species had two types of beings, males and females. This was something completely new for me. All beings of light are made in the same way, as we did not have a physical body, we did not have any kind of sex to differentiate ourselves from each other. In addition, the ability to reproduce is something that does not exist within the world of angels.

Although those little beings were not made of light, they were still created with part of my lord's energy. Only enough to give them life, since these beings had not been created to reach the level of a being of light, and much less the level of The Creator. Their only reason for existing was to serve something else, but... what or who? They were questions I kept asking myself, and for which I would soon have answers.

I returned to my world and kept thinking about that fantastic place where the Creator remained. He did not stop creating new beings. His goal was to completely fill the place with a great variety of these beings, or as he called them, animals. Meanwhile, I had to continue working in my world, having a group assigned to me that I had to develop. This group was made up of angels mostly with shadow wings and only a few with energy wings. My group felt great admiration for me, and the truth is that it was very comforting to see the way they addressed me, or how they spoke to me, because it was the same way that I used to speak to the Creator. Rather than their leader, I was their spiritual guide.

Like the Creator, I had no qualms about teaching them everything I knew at that time. I liked helping them continue to evolve, but as much as I tried, only a small group of my angels had achieved their energy wings. It was gratifying seeing how they evolved thanks to me, but in truth, I did not feel satisfied because the group was very small, and my greatest dream was to turn the entire group into angels with wings of light. With this I wanted to prove to myself that if they could reach my level, then I could reach the level of the Creator.

Every time my obligations allowed me to, I escaped to the dimension of the Creator as I was completely fascinated by the small universe he was creating. Especially that little blue planet, where he dedicated most of his effort. Every time I entered, there was something new and unique. I did not know how far my lord's imagination could go with this new world, and despite everything he had created, he continued with more and more wonders. There were many details to take into account and a lot of work that still lay ahead. For my part, I tried to learn everything I could from him; I watched everything he did very carefully and eventually I tried to imitate him.

My lord, in a gesture of humility and greatness, let me help him with some things in his world. My surprise was so great when he proposed that I create something for myself. He wanted me to create my very own living being with my own energy. It was very hard work that at times I felt unachievable, but thanks to the good advice of the Creator and focusing all of my concentration, I was able to achieve it.

I gave life to a small being with a majestic appearance; an elongated body with very bright colours, and short legs that were compensated by a pair of wings. I wanted my little being to have both the opportunity to fly through the skies and be very close to the Earth at will. I wanted him to be able to enjoy the land that I could not enjoy in the same way.

My little being was a little insignificant compared to the creatures of the Creator, but for the first time in my history I felt powerful, omnipotent. Giving life to a little being and knowing that he lives thanks to me, I felt an authentic love and pride as a father for that little creature, and I know that deep down that little being could also feel me in some way.

Creating the little creature had left me emotionally exhausted, unable even attempt to repeat the whole process or learn something more complicated. So, from that moment on, I dedicated myself to observing my lord and visiting my little living being. It made me realize how much I still had to learn. The Creator continued to give life to all kinds of animals of different sizes and complexities, and I had just thrown in the towel after a small animal. Even so, he felt very proud of me. I was just an angel, and not only was I in his dimension, where no other angel could reach, but I had also given life to a small being of living matter. That small being was my medal of merit.

Thanks to the fact that this little being was made with part of my energy, I could somehow feel everything he felt, see what he saw, hear what he heard. There were even moments when the connection was so strong that I felt that I was that little being. I could feel the touch of the earth between my legs, taste the flavours of the air with my tongue, fly and feel the wind under my wings. That little animal was my direct connection to the new world, which made me completely addicted to it, and come to love it just as I loved my own world. Every time I visited Earth, the first thing I did was connect with my little being. I did it so many times that, little by little, I controlled my creation more and more, until I reached a point where I could be inside his body and control it at will.

I enjoyed the small pleasures of being inside that little being, walking on the Earth and witnessing how it lived there. Flying through the skies with my wings, refreshing myself in the water, and eating. Little things that for a being on Earth mean nothing because it is their day to day, but in my world none those sensations exist. It was an addiction to feel that I belonged to that planet, for me it had already become my second home.

The Creator was pleased to see how much I enjoyed his new world. Despite the fact that he was always busy, he was also attentive to everything I did. He saw how my love for Earth grew and also my love for my little being.

That planet had not been the first to which the Creator had devoted so much time and effort, but it did have something special. The Creator looked at everything around him and felt that something was missing which would make it perfect, until finally one day he made the decision to make this planet a home for what would be his greatest creation. Without thinking twice, he began to make some changes to the planet.

At first there was only a large land mass in the centre of the planet, but the Creator divided the Earth into ten pieces and separated them from each other. In the centre of the planet, he created an island of a colossal size and an aspect unlike the other islands. It was round with several rings of Earth surrounding it. In the centre of the island, he ensured that the animals he placed were the most harmless in comparison to the large animals that were on the land masses away from the island. Once the island was finished, the Creator looked at it and was pleased; he knew the time had come.

One day he approached me while I was admiring my little creature and he told me,

"It is time".

"Are you done with this world?" I asked as I looked at him in amazement.

"Yes, and so it's time to make my greatest creation. Let us make Man" he said.

CHAPTER TWO

And God Made Man

"Man?" I asked, not knowing exactly what he meant.

"Yes" he answered me again "Man".

"Let us make mankind in our image, in our likeness, so that they may rule over the fish in the sea and the birds in the sky, over the livestock and all the wild animals, and over all the creatures that move along the ground."

Thinking about a single being who governed the whole world gave me a clear idea of what kind of being he was about to create. It would be something never before seen until that moment. A being made in our image but made of matter. It was something extremely complicated to do, but only the Creator had enough power and knowledge to do it, and not only that, but he was also more than willing to achieve it.

The Creator spent a lot of time in this new world, so his son stayed in our world to carry out all of the functions that his father usually performed, which did not give him much scope to come to this new world and help. This, for me, was fantastic because it allowed me to spend more time with my lord. And so, I was the only one who was there to help him in everything he might need, and I gladly participated in the creation of Man. With this, I do not want you to think that you also owe your life to me because the Creator could do it perfectly without my help, but I do want you to really understand where my history with humanity begins. Creating Man was not an easy task at all, not only because of the colossal effort that was needed for it, but the Creator wanted to make him like an angel, an adult with part of his power and knowledge.

Personally, I would have preferred to start from a small cell. It would have been the easiest thing from the point of view of an angel with little power as was my case, and I even suggested it but, no, my lord wanted Man to be adult.

So, I set out to get the necessary material to give the being a physical body. Believe me, this was neither dirt nor dust that was found on the ground. If it had been so, my job would have been much easier. Once all the necessary material had been obtained, my lord and I began to shape it. We wanted that lifeless mass to be similar to us, at least we projected what our appearance would be like if we were made of matter. As I have said before, it is very complicated work. How do you imitate the shape of something that has no shape? But even so, when we finished shaping it, my work was complete. The most complicated part came next, and that was the task for The Creator.

At that moment I could only move away and let my lord finish with his goal, give life to that inert body and create Man. He approached the lifeless body and began to pass his energy into it little by little, sending more and more until suddenly the Creator displayed all his power on the figure. It was an immense and endless power, something that travelled over the entire planet, the entire universe; even the angels in my world could feel it. I was right there, in front of him, and I couldn't believe it. I knew he was very powerful, but until that moment I didn't know the true scope of his power. Now I was witness to it, I saw how his infinite energy radiated. I saw how far I had left ahead of me to become just like him.

The energy of the Creator continued to penetrate into each pore of the figure lying on the ground, going through every millimetre and changing everything. Little by little the figure began to take shape in front of us. I could hear a noise coming from his chest, each time louder and louder. They were the beats of a heart that already had a shape and worked perfectly, it was pumping blood through a body that was less inert matter now, more living flesh. The Creator made one last effort until finally everything burst in a flash of white light that illuminated the whole world. The other living beings on the planet stopped; nothing moved, nothing knew what to do. Every being on the planet knew that something big had happened, but they did not know what.

I thought that I had already seen everything with the new world but witnessing the creation of this being left me perplexed. I did not know how to react to the spectacle. I really did not know if it had worked, until I looked closely at the man's eyes, and he woke up.

The man opened his eyes for the first time and looked around. He was still lying on the ground, but his gaze travelled over the whole place. He looked at everything until he met the eyes of his Creator. My lord looked at him with a gesture of love and brotherly pride, he contemplated his work and felt satisfied. The man, naked in front of us, began to get up. First, he raised his upper part while supporting himself with his hands, then he supported himself with his feet and began to stand until he was fully upright.

The Creator was the only being that the man could see. I still did not have enough power to show myself in front of him. While the Creator spoke with him, I could only look at him in astonishment from top to bottom. His hair was golden and curly, his eyes were a light blue similar to the sky. His body gave the impression of being very solid, as if he were wearing an armour under his skin. I circled around him over and over again and it was something incredible to witness. This man who had before been just a pile of lifeless matter, was now something so unique. For me, he was not only another creation of my lord, but the Creator had just made an equal. For me, Man was also a god.

I wanted to touch him, but it was impossible for despite being by his side, I did not belong to his world. I could only continue to contemplate him without being part of it.

The Creator was talking to the man, showing him the world that he had made for him, and explaining everything that he expected of him.

I watched carefully as they were lost, walking on the horizon, and I felt that my presence was superfluous in that moment. The greatest work was finished, so it was not necessary for me to be there. Taking advantage of the fact that the Creator and Man were moving further and further away from me, I returned to my world. I wanted to break the news to everyone else and, of course, continue with my obligations as an angel.

I approached my group of angels and, from afar, I could hear how they spoke of what they had felt just a few moments ago, of everything that had happened, of that display of power the Creator had made. I continued approaching them until they finally saw me and ran out to meet me. They had many doubts but an enormous curiosity to know what had happened.

"Luzbel! Luzbel! Did you feel that? Do you know what happened?"

It was all they asked, and all at the same time.

"Quiet, easy, I'll explain what happened" I replied.

I explained everything to them; all the Creator had done so far, the area where not just anyone could enter, the new universe, the planets, that planet. That planet where his creations were most focused until I finally reached the part of Man: the new being that was, right in that moment, walking through the green meadows of the Earth, accompanied by the Creator, who he could look at as his equal.

My group of angels listened carefully to my words and their astonished faces now amused me, because I assumed it was the same face that I had at the beginning of everything. I finished telling them the whole story and said,

"Learn from this experience and keep it in mind as you trace your path. Because now you know how much you still have to learn, and everything you have to improve."

I did not want them to be discouraged by seeing the great challenge that being an equal of our Lord represented. On the contrary, I wanted them to be motivated to learn more; to want to achieve more power and to always keep in mind, that if there is now a being equally as spectacular as the Creator, then we could be too.

Without a doubt, that was an injection of motivation for my group of angels but unfortunately sometimes being highly motivated is not enough to overcome all of the obstacles. There are times that the only way to move forward is with experience and perseverance; something that is only acquired with time and many failures behind you.

During the time I was with The Creator on Earth, I had neglected my duties as an angel and my group, so I wanted to recompense them by spending time with each one, to help them as much as I could. Despite everything I had learned on Earth, I was still helping very few angels to advance. For the most part they were angels developing their wings of shadow, and some new ones with wings of energy, but there was still no other with wings of light like my own. This was a bit disappointing for me, but still I continued without losing hope.

I remembered the moment when Man took shape, and that gave me the strength to carry on. But deep down, I felt that there was something else I had to do before helping my angels, or before being an equal to my lord, and that was returning to Earth and seeing first-hand everything that happened there. I missed that place and my little creature, so I made a small reflection. If I was not contributing anything new to my angels and the place where I learned the most was Earth, then it was clear what I had to do.

I left some small missions assigned to my group of angels. Missions that they had to fulfil to continue evolving, and I made sure that they were things to accomplish in the long term, because that way I could escape for some time to my beloved Earth. And that I did. I returned to Earth where many more surprises awaited me.

Things in that place did not stop changing in a dizzying way. Perhaps because time is not a concern for me, and I do not know in Earth-time how long I was absent, but since the last time I had been there, many plants that were just germinating were now already trees that appeared to touch the sky. The animals had also changed, and many of those I had known were no more, while there were various animals that were not there before, walking around the place. When I thought that nothing else could surprise me, the biggest surprise of my existence came. A few meters in from of me was the man. Apparently, time did not affect him either, but the surprise was that he was not alone. He had company, similar to him but different at the same time.

Long hair, dark like the night, white skin, but not too white, the eyes were blue like the sea, and the body with curves that the man did not have. It fit it very well, reflecting a delicacy and a sweetness that made me completely forget about the man and stare at this new being. But who was it? Where did such a spectacular image come from? I believed that, with the man, all creation had ended, but there was that creature that made the man go completely unnoticed by me.

Suddenly, a voice came out from behind me.

"What do you think of the woman?"

It was the Creator who had seen me arrive, and he observed me contemplating his latest creation.

"The woman? That's what it's called?" I asked without taking my eyes off her.

"That's right" he responded.

"In this place everyone has a partner, there are males and females. The man was the only one of his kind, and he also deserved to have a partner."

I kept looking at her, and where she went my eyes followed.

"Well, it seems to me that you have just exceeded everything you have done so far" I told the Creator.

It was the first time that I had ever felt like this, completely hypnotized. I was looking at her and forgot everything else. The woman was not a simple being, for me she was a goddess. I would not mind falling at her feet and worshiping her just like I did with The Creator. All I wanted was to be close to her and keep looking at her; I couldn't get enough of it.

The Creator had to return to our world and continue with his obligations, but even so, every time the sun illuminated the place where the man and the woman were, he was there. He did not miss a single sunrise and was always interested in his greatest creations.

I was still fascinated with her, her voice, her laugh, that look, the way she walked and her way of being.

This made me not dare to miss a single second of her life. I was always very close to her, but she could not feel me. She spent her days hugging the man and I was dying to know what it felt like to touch her, to feel her breath. Until I saw my chance and I took it.

As I had said before, being close to her made me forget everything else, so I had also forgotten another reason why I had returned to Earth, to see my creation again; my little creature. The truth is that I only remembered him because one of his descendants happened to be there. The Creator had also made my creature a companion and now they were part of that entire ecosystem. The son of my creation was flying by and the woman, who rested under the shade of a tree saw it and called out.

"Serpent! Serpent! Come here little one" she called.

"Serpent?" I questioned myself. *"Not a bad name for my little creature."*

It turned out that it was one of her favourite animals. She found it very sweet as well as very interesting, which was a compliment to me.

But the creature, despite being a descendant of my creation, was still part of me and still carried some of my energy. Therefore, like with my creature, I could also be inside it and control it at will. I did not hesitate for a minute to do it, since the serpent was in the woman's hands, and she didn't stop talking to it and caressing it.

But now she no longer caressed the serpent, she caressed me. I could feel the touch of her skin with my paws, and it was so soft. Her smell was something so intoxicating; a smell of flowers and fresh fruit that I loved. The touch of her hand on my small body was so pleasant, feeling the warmth of her hand and feeling her face just a few inches away from mine was true paradise for me.

All my plans were ruined now. My main objective had been to know fully how this world worked, but all my attention was held by the human beings, especially the woman. The more I saw of her, the more I convinced myself that she was the best creation so far.

Human beings always spent their days together, playing with animals or touring the island where they lived from end to end. It was incredible how dependent they felt on each other, because it seemed that they could not be apart for long, which made me think about various things about my world and myself.

Why are angels all the same, and there are not different sexes like in this world?

Am I not meant to have a partner?

Don't I deserve it in the same way that the man deserved it?

Being so close to them and seeing how they enjoyed each other's company made me feel truly alone for the first time. They shared everything, and even the most insignificant thing for them had a special flavour. Each look, each caress, each time they brought their lips together and hugged each other very tightly. They were completely innocent, so despite being close together and naked, the idea of sex was something unknown to them. Their bodies did not feel any type of sexual appetite. They did not know that reproduction, was something that was within their reach like all the other beings on the planet. All they did was laugh and spend their days hugging. At first, I did not care, but as I got to know the woman more, I began to experience feelings that I had not felt before. Seeing her with him sometimes became painful for me, so on some occasions I felt that I should walk away, because I didn't want to see her like that with him.

On one occasion, I began to walk to get further and further away from them. I was aimless, without knowing exactly what to do or where to go until suddenly, I saw a creature of average height eating from a tree. At first it looked like a normal tree, but looking at it carefully through my angel eyes, I saw that this tree had something special about it. It was not made in the same way as the others; it seemed to have both part of my world and part of Earth. It had the same shape as the surrounding trees, but inside it shone like a being of light, like its fruits. The creature ate the fruits of the tree; it ate them so eagerly that I went closer to see it a little better.

As I approached, the creature continued to eat from the tree. Suddenly, the creature pulled with force one of the branches of the tree, knocking down some of its fruits. They fell to the ground and rolled away from the tree, one rolling over to where I was and stopping practically at my feet. The fruit was the same as the tree. In appearance it was normal, comparable to the other fruits of the island, but inside there was a glow that could not go unnoticed.

"What a strange fruit," I couldn't stop thinking. It's the first time I had seen something like this in this world.

I reached out my hand to try to touch it, but I knew it would be to no avail. I did not belong to this world, and I could not interact with anything there. I knew that as soon as I tried to touch the fruit, my fingers would go through it without any result. But, what a strange thing... I hadn't gone through it; I was touching it with my fingers, and I could move it. Not only that, but I could also grab it with my hand just like the other beings on this planet did!

"But what kind of fruit was this?"

I could hold it in my hand and feel its texture, its weight; I could even feel that it was cool, which was a new feeling for me because in my world there is no hot or cold. I had it a few inches from my face and I was looking at it carefully. The fruit seemed to be a hybrid between light and matter; it was the perfect fusion of the two worlds.

I looked again at the creature that continued eating the fruit, and it looked so happy, enjoying every bite. My eyes fell back on the fruit in my hand, and only one thought crossed my mind.

"What if...?"

Slowly I brought it to my mouth, and I thought:

"What's the worst that could happen?"

CHAPTER THREE
Revelation

It was like part of a game. Having the fruit in my hand and thinking about biting it was something inconceivable for me but, since it was happening, I wanted to know how far I could go with the experience. I slowly brought it to my mouth, but in my mind, I thought that nothing would happen. I thought that my mouth would go right through it or that, if I could bite it, I wouldn't be able to swallow it. So, I had nothing to lose by trying. I opened my mouth and took a big bite. I had part of the fruit in my mouth, and I could chew it; I could feel a parade of flavours running through my mouth as I chewed. A small pleasure went through my whole being. Little by little the piece of fruit in my mouth was dissolving until it disappeared completely, leaving my mouth empty.

Suddenly there was chaos. From pleasure, I went on to experience a sensation that was completely unknown to me, unknown and quite unpleasant. It was pain; an immense pain. I fell to my knees, while I felt everything burn inside me, and with each second the pain grew more intense. I felt a discharge of energy that overloaded my entire body and did me great damage. The feeling was as though I had got a cable of electricity to the stomach, and now the electric current burned through my core.

I could not stop screaming and writhing on the ground in pain, anguish and bewilderment.

"WHAT IS HAPPENING TO ME? WHAT IS THIS TERRIBLE FEELING?" I screamed, aloud.

The pain was getting worse. I no longer knew what to think, much less what was going to happen to me. My mind was blank, feeling the terrible pain that ran through every space of my body, and just when I thought that my time was up, the pain disappeared. Everything stopped as quickly as it began, and suddenly a relief, a great relief, ran through my being. I no longer felt pain, on the contrary I felt peace, a great rest, a great tranquillity. I got up slowly, still feeling dazed after the unpleasant experience. It was hard for me to reason, I couldn't think clearly, but after a few minutes my mind started working again.

"What happened? What was that? Had I been punished by my lord?"

These were the questions that flooded my mind. I looked at the tree in front of me and it continued to shine, like its fruits. I looked at the fruit that I had bitten just a moment ago, but it was intact. It didn't have a single mark from where my mouth had penetrated the skin, but inside it no longer shone as much as it had at before.

"But, if this fruit is intact, then… what did I just eat?"

I had a feeling that I had done something wrong with everything that had just happened, so with the idea of avoiding further problems and not repeating the bad experience, I immediately returned to my world. I did not even go to see the humans for one last time. I just wanted to go home, to think clearly about what had just happened to me.

The whole thing was just a little mischief that got out of control. If I had known then that that tree was the tree of knowledge, and that the Creator had forbidden the humans to taste its fruit, surely, I would not have touched it, much less tasted it. But sometimes chance can play a very important role in your destiny, changing things completely.

I returned to my world, but I still did not feel right, so I had to avoid, at all costs, another being of light seeing me in that state, what would I say?

"I do not feel well"?

How could I say that in a world where there is no pain, no sadness, no depression. My state was simply inexplicable in the eyes of others so I went to a place where I could be alone, and think about everything that had happened, and everything that I had just felt.

"How strange" I kept repeating myself

What was that tree made of? Why had that creature been able to eat the fruit and nothing had happened to it? I did not understand.

There were many questions that only generated more questions, but at least I was feeling better. In fact, I was feeling perfectly normal again, so the best thing I could do was go back to the others.

As I returned, I looked at the places that I had seen throughout my whole existence, everything was exactly the same, nothing had changed. But I looked at them in a different way, everything had changed for me, and that puzzled me a lot.

I saw my angels making great efforts to become the same as the Creator, but now I saw that this was impossible. I remembered the creatures of Earth and now I understood that each species had strength and power different to the others. The greater you are, the more power you have, and we were mere insects compared to the Creator.

How had I not seen that before? How could we be so delusional to believe that we can become the same as the Creator, being so insignificant as we are. But if it is impossible to become like him, why did the Creator keep encouraging us to attempt it? There was nobody better than him to know that this could not be. Had he been deceiving us? And if so, why was he doing it? What is the aim of fooling us like that?

I looked at my world from a distance; at all the angels who were there, motivated to be an equal in the eyes of their Creator. I watched as he appeared in front of them. He had returned from Earth, from spending a moment with his beloved humans, and now he was there in front of everyone.

What came next was nothing new to me. In fact, it was the usual protocol in my world every time the Creator appeared in front of us. All of the beings of light immediately went to greet him, and they all dropped themselves at his feet and began to praise him, to glorify him, to tell him over and over how great and wonderful he is, and how lucky they were to be by his side.

It was not the first time they had done it, nor would it be the last. Now that I remembered, I had spent my entire existence doing the same thing that they did. And since then, nothing had changed, I was still the only angel with wings of light and I could not achieve a considerable increase in my power. I was always the first to be at his feet adoring him, but now I was looking at him from a distance, watching that scene, and now everything was clear to me.

We were not made to be his equal, we could not even consider ourselves to be his children, because his only son was never at his feet adoring him. Only we did it. Now I understood everything. We were only his servants, his slaves. We followed him with the false promise that we would be just like him, but now everything fell in to place for me. He only used us for his own benefit.

I just wanted to get away from there. I had just been greatly disappointed, and my existence had just lost all meaning. It is normal. What would you do if one day you woke up and realized that everything you have fought for will never be fulfilled? That path that you once thought would lead you to your goals is only a circle, a path that will never take you anywhere.

For the first time, I felt a huge emptiness inside me. My home, my paradise, everything had collapsed and now I realized that I have always been living in a prison. I had the power to go from one place to another, but I did not have anywhere to go.

"But how is it possible that I had never realized this until now? Why am I seeing things this way?" I asked myself. *"OF COURSE! THE FRUIT!"*

That fruit had somehow removed the blindfold from my eyes and made me see things from another perspective. It was as if it had increased my reasoning, had it made me wiser?

There is no other possible explanation. That is why that creature could eat it without any problem, that animal was not a being that reasons. That is why it did not affect it, and on the other hand, it had changed me.

I was still apart from everyone, locked in my thoughts when I heard a voice behind me.

"Luzbel, are you okay? You have not come forward with the other angels". It was the voice of my lord, with a tone of curiosity and bewilderment.

I turned to see his eyes, but unlike his voice, they told me that he knew everything. He knew what I had done and what I was feeling in that moment. But I limited myself to gently answering his question.

"I'm fine my lord, better than ever" I smiled and turned my back to him

He came over and stood beside me, looking at the horizon just like me, the two of us together in complete silence, until he broke it with his voice.

"From the beginning you have always been the most powerful angel of all; the wisest, the strongest. The angel that undoubtedly stands out above all others."
I continued to look straight ahead but listened to him intently.

"But for those same reasons you must be careful Luzbel, becoming important being means you can make important mistakes. Don't let your youth cloud the great things that await you."

I simply looked at him, and then answered.

"No, my lord, I will not allow anything to blur the vision of my path."

He just smiled and disappeared. Without making complaints, without telling me anything about that fruit, without asking for explanations. Although his words still rang in my mind, for me there was nothing he could say to make me change my mind. For me everything was already very clear.

I was looking at the vastness of my world and the Creator's face stayed in my mind, but only one thought appeared.

Perhaps I am not perfect like you, but I am not as insignificant as you think I am. I will show you that beings of light can be more than simple servants. I will teach you that an angel can develop more power than you have given it, and like human beings, I promise that you will someday see us as an equal and not as someone inferior.

My goal was already set. I would continue with my angel duties, but with a big difference this time. I did it knowing that the Creator did not expect an angel to evolve much, and this time I was willing to do anything to achieve it.

Since I came back from Earth, I was not only more motivated to fully develop the abilities of my angels, but I had also increased my wisdom.

My intelligence had doubled, and thanks to this, I quickly had a whole army of angels with energy wings. Each new angel that came into my hands quickly developed much of their potential. It was something never before seen in my world. Everyone else wanted to be part of my group, and all of them felt true adoration towards me. I had given them hope and I was teaching the path they should follow, and they would follow me anywhere without a second thought.

I continued to behave as if nothing had happened, continued to perform my duties as an angel, including those of worshiping the Creator, which was no longer easy for me. I felt very uncomfortable telling him over and over again how great and wonderful he was, and how insignificant all of us were in comparison, but I did it so as not to attract too much attention.

Another of the effects of that fruit was that somehow, I was no longer as linked to my lord as I had been before. At first, he could read my mind without any problem, and he knew exactly what I was going to do long before doing it. But now the feeling he gave me was that he did not know what to expect from me. Perhaps it was also because I did not even know what I would do in the end. Now it was as if I was the sole owner of my destiny, and only I could control the result of my actions. Now I knew something that until then no one understood, other than the Creator and his son, now I knew the meaning of free will.

My group of angels was growing more and more numerous, so I had to divide it into subgroups and leave the stronger energy-winged angels in charge of those groups so it could continue to grow. My only concern at that time was to recruit the greatest number of angels and make them the most powerful beings in my world. I wanted the Creator to realize how far we could go and to begin to respect us.

At that time, what motivated me the most was thinking about the humans. Especially the woman. They achieved that status of gods despite having been created by my lord, so there was hope for me and my kind. If a creation of my lord could reach that level, then so could we.

Things were getting better and better, and soon my group of angels almost all had wings of energy. Better still, there were some that seemed that at any moment would develop wings of light. Everything was going perfectly for me. I had completely revolutionized my world and I owed all of that to the world of humans. And it was just that which did not leave my mind. I thought about them constantly, until I missed them, I wanted to see them again and to be in that world again. I had enjoyed it so much, so why did I not return? Things were going so very well in my group after all, and a getaway to Earth would surely be very useful for me to disconnect from my day to day and think better about what to do next. Again, I left duties for each of my angels and prepared to travel to Earth. But this time I felt a little strange, as if I had a bad feeling. The last time I was there it changed my perspective, who knew what could find me now. But I didn't care, I really wanted to see the woman and that fantastic world again.

I was back on terrestrial soil, and it was like stepping on it for the first time. This world kept changing and had changed again since the last time I was there, the plants, the animals, especially the animals, it seemed that they were getting smaller and smaller. They no longer had the same size and threatening appearance as they had had the first time I was there, but still they were enormous compared to humans. Otherwise, everything was still a true paradise, a show of lights and colours wherever I looked.

Suddenly I heard a laugh close to where I was. A laugh that I recognized immediately as coming from the woman. She was bathing near a lake there, bathing and playing alongside the man.

I stayed behind some trees watching them and contemplated how they were having fun. Again, I had been hypnotized with the beauty of the woman, how she looked so beautiful with her wet hair, the water running down her body. Now that I saw her with more attention, I realized that she was completely naked. Her entire body was without anything to cover it except for the crystal-clear water, which was obviously not an obstacle to the view.

I looked at her legs, her back, her chest, her stomach and she seemed far more beautiful than in my memories; a whole goddess in front of me. Having her so close made me forget all of my new negative feelings towards the Creator. I was looking at her and everything was perfect. I wouldn't mind being enslaved for all eternity if it were to her.

I did not move from that place. I was still behind those trees and noticed some small insects; they were very tiny but there were many of them. So many that they formed a path along which they were advancing. They caught my attention, and I followed the path, one following another until finally reaching an animal that was ten times bigger than them. The animal was covered by the tiny insects which did not stop attacking it. More and more insects were climbing on top of it, until the animal began to slow and fall, and finally it stopped moving. Those insignificant insects had ended the life of an animal that was much bigger than them. It was a metaphor for me.

A single one of those bugs would not have done anything against that animal, but an entire army made things very difficult for the poor creature, which finally had no choice but to surrender.

At that moment my nature class was interrupted. I felt the presence of the Creator near the humans, so I approached to see what the gods did when they met, or at least to know what they were talking about. But what I saw was what would change my destiny for the rest of eternity.

The Creator had appeared on the other side of the lake, next to the shore, and the humans swam quickly to where he was as soon as they saw him. When they reached the shore, they fell to their knees at his feet and began to praise and glorify him, to tell him again and again how great how wonderful he was and how insignificant they were next to him.

I could not believe it, even though I was seeing it. The humans, whom I have always considered to be gods, were crawling at the feet of the Creator just like we beings of light do. I saw the woman at the feet of the Creator and I thought,

"But what are you doing? What are you being so foolish? You don't have to be at his feet, it is he who should be at yours!"

"They don't, they don't, why?" I kept repeating in my head.

They were my only hope of believing that I could get out of the servant status, but now I was seeing that they did not have a higher status than mine. The Creator had only produced one more network of slaves that idolized him and raised his ego.

For the first time in history, I was the first being to feel so many new and intense emotions; I felt disappointment, bewilderment, frustration, and finally the worst of all emotions, anger.

I was very angry, enraged, the Creator had completely disappointed me. Throughout my existence I had thought I knew him better than anyone, and now I saw that he was just a selfish being who wanted only an army of subjects to flatter and praise him continuously.

I kept looking at that image, thinking,

"I will not allow it; I will not let him treat the humans the same way he treats the light beings."

"It's about time I did something."

CHAPTER FOUR
Revolution in Paradise

After spending a while with his beloved humans, the Creator returned to my world, and I could not bear the feeling of anger for a single moment more. I had to do something, so without a second thought I went after him. I returned to my world and went to an area where only the Creator, his son, a few angels with energy wings, and I have access.

When I arrived, the other angels there stared at me. The expression on my face was unknown to them, one they had never seen before. I continued walking with determination, my gaze fixed on the Creator who was sitting on his throne, beside his son. I didn't care if his son or the other angels were there, I had to tell him something and nothing, or no one, was going to stop me.

He stared at me, his eyes reflected some surprise and curiosity. He was God almighty, but even he didn't know what to expect from me at that moment, only I knew what I was about to say, and what I would do next.

I stopped in front of him, he stared at me and said,

"Luzbel, what is happening?"

I responded to his fixed gaze with mine, which did not struggle to match it, and I spoke to him as they had never spoken to him, decisively and demandingly.

"Why do you treat them like your servants?! They do not deserve it!"

The Creator was taken aback by my way of addressing him, and he was not the only one. His son and the other angels were shocked by my tone.

"What do you mean Luzbel?" the Creator asked me

"You know perfectly what I'm talking about"

I continued to berate him.

"I can accept that you use the beings of light as your servants, but the fact that you do the same with humans is unforgivable!"

"Luzbel, I don't understand what that attitude is about, but that's no way to talk to your father" his son addressed me, rising from his throne.

"My father?" I replied with a mocking tone

"Really? Now that I think, I have never had a throne beside his, nor have I been recognized as a son of God, I am a slave like everyone else"

His son was shocked by my answer and tried to make me see reason, but it was a losing battle.

"Luzbel! moderate your insolence, do not forget to whom you are speaking!" were his last words, but I was just beginning.

"With all due respect, Son of God, this issue does not concern you. I have come to speak here with your father, and it must be your father who answers me, not you" I said with finality.

The Creator rose from his throne, his gaze no longer one of bewilderment, but one of defiance.

"Very well Luzbel. Say what you have to say" he said calmly.

I had already gone too far to stop now, so I continued.

"During my whole existence you know that I have always been your most loyal angel, everything you did seemed good to me without ever questioning your reasons. I always did what you wanted because I thought that everything you did was for the good of all, but now I see that you only thought of your own good."

"Luzbel take care of your words" the Creator replied with a soft but firm voice.

"Light as well as darkness can blind you in the same way if you do not know where to look. What may today make you see things as clear as you think, tomorrow will be the reason for your blindness."

I continued to look at him carefully, but his words, far from convincing me, reaffirmed my new thoughts towards him.

"Is that your argument?" I asked. "Only wise words in disguise that say that I am still too inferior to you to understand things?" I smiled wryly, as I turned my back on him.

"I thought I would find a divine answer that would explain everything I have seen and everything I have learned so far, but in return I have only found more reasons to convince myself that I am right. You underestimate me Creator, and you will pay dearly for that."

Nobody there believed my words and I began to walk and gradually got further from the Creator. There was absolute silence in the place and only the gazes of those angels followed me as I walked away. Suddenly something pierced the silence.

"LUZBEL!"

It was the first time I had heard my name spoken in that way. I stopped immediately, no part of me could move, I had been petrified, that voice had completely pierced me and echoed throughout my world. The Creator had roared at me.

Before turning around to see the Creator's face he was already right behind me, just one step away

"You're just as stupid as you are smart!" he continued shouting at me. "Don't you see how far this situation is taking you?! You lose more and more control of your actions and your thoughts! YOU MUST RECONSIDER!"

Again, he insulted me with his way of treating me like a wayward child. I could not bear the idea of him treating me like an imbecile who did not know how the world worked, when I was completely sure that I was the only one now who saw things with absolute clarity.

"You will never accept that a being of light has the same understanding and intelligence as yours, right?" I said soft, but firm, turning around and looking him straight in the eye.

He just looked at me without saying a word, while I continued talking to him.

"Is it so difficult for you to believe that a being of light has understood how things work here? Do I seem so insignificant that you think you can convince me with just a couple of words, when with your actions you show me the contrary? I'm sorry Creator, but things have changed, and you know very well that they will never be the same again."

I got closer, just a few inches from his face.

"Perhaps I owe you my existence, but that does not mean that I belong to you. Now I know very well who I am and what I should do." I uttered in almost a whisper.

When I finished my words, I disappeared from the presence of the Creator. For me, now everything was very clear. To continue talking to him would be a waste of effort, because each one of his words only served to further insult my intelligence.

I went to one of the most secluded and lonely parts of my world, I knew I had to do something, but I didn't know exactly what. The truth is that I was still confused with everything that had happened. I still had a hard time believing that all of this was happening to me. I, the most loyal angel, number one amongst all others, facing the Creator, eye to eye and reproaching him for his actions.

His words were still ringing in my ears.

"Light as well as darkness can blind you in the same way if you do not know where to look." I thought a lot about it and asked myself if it could be possible that I were the one who was wrong? Did I have so much to learn that I was overreacting and turning things upside down for no reason?

I kept thinking of everything that happened, of the Creator's words, of his gaze as he spoke to me. But then the images came to me of the other beings of light crawling at his feet, of my entire life of service, of the humans. The gods of that new universe also bowing at his feet like slaves. What other explanation did that have? How could I be wrong when what was going on was so clear?

The answer was very simple, I was right. The Creator wanted to regain control of the situation with me, but his behaviour with light beings and with humans had no further explanation. He just wanted everyone to idolize him, and the idea that we were like him never existed in his mind, quite the opposite.

If he had really wanted it, he would never have made us bow at his feet throughout our existence. He would treat us the same as his son, but there was a big difference between how he treated his son and how he treated us. His son never bows at his feet when he comes into his presence. If everything was so clear to me then, the time had come to change things.

I could not continue in a world where everyone was deceived. I had to remove the blindfold too from the other beings of light. But before doing so, I had to begin with the beings that had helped me get to this point; the humans. My whole transformation began in their world, and it was there that everyone else would see the real truth.

With a plan in mind, I immediately travelled to planet Earth, and searched sky and land for the descendant of my creation. That creature was my direct connection with this world, and besides that it was the favourite creature of the woman. This was the more compelling reason to find it and put my plan in to action right away.

Finding that particular creature was not an easy task, its connection with me was growing increasingly weak with each generation. It was not the same as with my original creature, that I could feel it anywhere on the planet.

It would have been much easier to possess my original creature, but my little creation was not immune to the passage of time, and there was nothing left of it.

At last, I found the serpent I was looking for, the one that the woman was so fond of. It had to be that specific one because he had a direct relationship with the woman and I knew that she would trust that creature.

The first phase of my plan was complete, I was already inside the creature, and I could control it as I pleased, now I had to continue with the second phase - find the humans. With my claws, I climbed the closest tree and jumped, opened my wings and began to fly in search of the humans. I knew that the creature did not ever travel far from them, so they would be close by.

The bad thing about being inside the creature is that I lost my other powers as an angel, so I could not feel the humans or anything in my world. My senses were limited to having only those that my creature was blessed with, so I could only guide myself by my sight and smell.

As I flew through the trees in the area, the breeze brought with it a smell of fruits and flowers. A smell that was very familiar to me because I could not resist it, it was the natural fragrance of the woman, I just had to follow the trail until I found her.

The woman was in an area coloured by hundreds of flowers. One of her greatest hobbies was collecting the most beautiful flowers every day to make a crown of flowers for her head. She was alone, I didn't know exactly where the man was, but it was better this way.

I could take advantage of the fact that she was without him to try to convince her to join my cause. The main problem would be working out how to communicate with her if the animal that I possessed could not speak in her language.

I began to fly in circles above her head, she looked at me.

"Serpent! How are you little one?" she called as she raised her arm so that I could perch on it, and I obliged.

I was on her arm and before she started stroking my head I was pointing to a place with my head, looking into her eyes and pointing to that place again with my head.

Obviously, it was a gesture that this serpent had never made before, which made the woman curious about the new behaviour.

"What's wrong little one, what are you doing?" She wondered aloud.

I jumped off her arm and started to fly again but stopped at a tree near her.

She didn't know what to think but out of curiosity, she went to where I was. Before she reached the tree, I jumped again and flew to another, I landed on one of its branches and stared at the woman.

She was surprised by what she was seeing, but she immediately understood what I wanted.

"Do you want me to follow you?" she asked.

I looked at her and nodded, indicating yes.

Her eyes reflected surprise when she saw the serpent saying yes. She knew that the animal was very smart of course, but this time it seemed to understand everything she said.

I took flight again and she started running, following me very closely. Inside, I felt great satisfaction because I had broken through a great barrier and had managed to communicate with her without any problem.

I continued to guide her, crossing a valley that would later lead us to an orchard of fruit trees, where there was one in the centre which stood out above the rest. It was the very tree that removed the blindfold from my eyes, and that would now do the same with humans, starting with the woman.

I landed near the tree, then I ran towards it, until I reached its trunk and began to climb nimbly with my small legs. I climbed until I reached one of the branches that supported one of its hanging fruits.

The woman came immediately after and stared at me.

"What's wrong serpent? Why did you bring me here?"

I bit the branch that held that fruit and it began to fall, but before it touched the ground The woman was able to catch it in her hands. She had tasted this kind of fruit before, but never one like this.

It was bigger and brighter, and it looked very tempting, and she was obviously impressed by the fruit. I flew to her hand, the same one that was holding the fruit, and while with her hand she was holding the fruit, with her arm she was holding me. I looked at the fruit and I looked at her, I repeated that gesture over and over again in the hope that she would understand what I wanted her to do next.

Fortunately, she understood.

"Do you want me to eat this fruit, is that why you have brought me here?" she asked.

I looked at her and answered her question by moving my head; Yes.

"But God has forbidden us to eat from this tree, if we did so, I would die." she told me.

I looked straight back at her and shook my head from side to side, saying no.

She had a look of total bewilderment, she looked at me intently.

"And how do you know that? Have you ever tried it?" she asked.

I sat back, nodding my head answering her question, yes.

"Is that why you behave in this strange way? Is that the reason you can understand everything I say?" She asked.

I repeated the previous gesture again, yes.

"What's going on here?" a voice came suddenly from behind her.

It was the man. He had seen her running after the serpent and he wanted to follow us.

"I know it seems crazy, but the snake has brought me here to eat this fruit" she said, turning to face the man.

He looked at her with a bewildered face.

"The serpent? How is that possible?"

She looked at me while she spoke to him.

"I don't know, but the only thing I'm sure of is that it's not the same serpent as before, it seems like it's smarter."

I jumped out of her hand and returned to the tree to quickly find another fruit. I plucked it with my fangs, and it fell at the man's feet.

He could not believe what he was seeing, he looked at the fruit that was at his feet and bent to pick it up.

"It seems that he also wants you to eat it" said the woman, looking at the man.

The two of them approached each other, looked at each other gazing at the fruit.

"We cannot eat it. God has forbidden us to eat the fruit of this tree. We cannot disobey him, we could also die", and saying this he dropped the fruit from his hand, and it rolled away. I could only watch helplessly as my plan was unravelling little by little, so I fixed my gaze on her, she was my only hope.

The woman knew that he was right, but she also had doubt and curiosity. She shared her thoughts with the man, but she knew that something had changed within the serpent, and this fruit was the reason.

"I know this serpent very well, and I assure you that it has never done anything like this. You have already seen that it seems that it is more intelligent and rational, and it is because of this fruit. He has told me that he has eaten it."

The man had a look of utter disbelief on his face when he heard this.

"The serpent told you that it has eaten this fruit? Do you realize how crazy that sounds?" said the man.
She looked up at the branch where I stayed, and with my head I kept gesturing the same thing, yes, yes, yes.

"I'm going to do it" she said, smiling.

I was looking at her carefully, I couldn't stop thinking "do it, please do it, be free, wake up right now from this huge lie."

She brought the fruit little by little towards her mouth. The man just looked at her but said or did nothing, he knew that deep down he was also somewhat curious.

My heart was beating very fast, I was impatient to see what was going to happen. She opened her mouth, put the fruit to her lips, took a bite, and began to chew.

It was full of juice, and she enjoyed each bite. With each bite the juice of that fruit filled her mouth until she swallowed and took another bite, and another. She had already eaten three-quarters of the fruit, and her face was full of so much pleasure that the man could not resist the temptation and snatched the rest of the fruit to eat it. Like her, he could not resist the taste of the fruit.

My work here was already done, the two humans had eaten that fruit, they chewed it until it disappeared; I looked carefully at the reaction they would suffer, I hoped it was not the same as mine, because mine was a very painful experience.

But they didn't, they licked their fingers, looking at each other.

"It was so good, and nothing bad happened" they agreed.

Suddenly the voice of the Creator was heard nearby.

"Where are you? Why can't I feel you?" it rang.

The humans put on a surprised face, although more than surprise, it was shame. They ran to hide, each one in a different bush and the woman told the man...

"Why didn't you tell me I was naked?"

The man just answered

"Have you not seen that I am also!"

I was still on the branch and from my height I could see the Creator was getting closer to where the humans were. It was all they could do to hide so that the Creator would not see them naked.

"Why are you hiding from me?" the Creator asked them as he approached.

It was the man who replied.

"I'm sorry my lord, I heard you in the garden, and I was afraid because I was naked, so I hid."
The Creator was surprised by those words and asked.

"Who told you that you were naked? Have you eaten from the tree that I commanded you not to eat from?!"
"The woman you put here with me, she gave me some fruit from the tree, and I ate it" he said, pointing at the woman.

"What have you done?" asked the Creator, looking at the woman.

The woman, who was still hidden in the bushes so the Creator could not see her naked body, pointed to the tree of knowledge, where I was still standing.

"The serpent! It was the serpent that deceived me! It deceived me and I ate..."

Now the problem was mine. I did not want the innocent creature to suffer any punishment for what I had done, so before the Creator retaliated against the serpent, I took flight, but it was too late.

The Creator shot me with one of his rays while I was still in the air. I was trapped in a ball of energy that burned my whole body, the same feeling as when I had eaten that fruit. While I felt parts of my small body burning, the Creator shouted at me in an angry tone.

"Because you have done this, CURSED ARE YOU ABOVE ALL THE LIVESTOCK AND ALL THE WILD ANIMALS! You will slide on your belly and eat dust each and every day of your life!"

My legs, my wings, the colour of my skin, all charred and removed. An unjust punishment for a creature that had done nothing, but again the irrationality that "my lord" emanated was clear.

I could not do anything now for that little creature, all I could do was endure all the pain possible so that the serpent did not suffer more than necessary. But I knew I must continue with my mission, so I quickly left the body of the serpent. I threw myself towards the tree of knowledge, took one of its fruits and while doing this I would swear that, for a second, the woman put her eyes on me. I looked into her eyes, and I felt her gaze back at me. I felt as if she could see me. I don't know if that was possible or if it was just an illusion of the moment, but I didn't have time to find out. In a matter of milliseconds, I was transported back to my world.

The Creator had witnessed me leave that creature, and he knew it was all my fault. But for now, he was very busy punishing his beloved humans, with disproportionate punishments that are still known in the history of mankind today.

I didn't have much time, so I immediately went to my group of angels. They continued with their training and had been developing their power more and more.

As soon as they saw me arrive, they came to greet me as usual, but I interrupted the usual protocol to give them my message.

The fruit that I had brought from the Earth to my world had transformed into a ball of energy in my hand, all the matter that surrounded it could not cross the border of my world.

All my angels were around me, their faces said they were bewildered, they did not understand the expression of concern on my face, much less my attitude. But now that they were attentive to what I was going to tell them, it had to be fast, it was now or never.

"Since you have been with me, you know that I have been generous and have shared with each one of you everything I know. Many of you arrived as beings of light without wings, but now I look at you and I see a great majority of angels with wings of energy." I reeled.

Everyone was attentive to my words and at every opportunity they attempted to interrupt me, to praise and thank me, but my time was short, and I had to finish what I had started.

"You all know that you can trust me blindly, and it is because of that trust that you have given me, that I ask you the following..."

I raised my hand with the ball of energy that was previously fruit, I showed it to everyone so that they could see it well.

"I need you all to eat this energy" I instructed them.

"To eat?" they whispered, confused.

It was a term they were completely unfamiliar with, so I had to teach it while they stared at me.

"Do this..." I responded, bringing it back to my mouth and taking a bite out of the ball of energy. This time, though, merely putting it to my mouth caused the energy to melt into me instantly, and best of all, this time there was no pain. I just felt like the knowledge flooded every pore of my being and made me stronger, wiser.

They looked at me in amazement, they didn't know what I was doing or why I was doing it. But after biting it I passed it to one of my higher angels, he took it with his hand and looked at it, then looked at me.

"Do you trust me?" I asked him.

He changed his face of bewilderment and surprise for one of confidence and security.

"Yes, my lord" he responded.

He put it in his mouth and bit into it. The ball of energy only lost a little of its shine when bitten, but it was still practically intact, so I knew that with just one, I could share it with all my angels, allowing them to taste.

"Each one of you must bite it only once and pass it along, when you have done it, you will understand why I am doing this. You must wake up and open your eyes to reality."

Suddenly my whole being began to bend, something was attacking me and made me kneel.

Before I knew it, I was somewhere else, I had been forcibly transported and now I was in front of the Creator and his son, with a hundred angels of energy wings surrounding me. He was in the room where the Creator kept his throne and his most advanced angels.

I was still on the ground, on my knees, supporting myself with my hands. I looked up to see the face of the Creator and he was very angry with me, his eyes gave off rage, disappointment and that for me only meant one thing. Punishment.

I stood up, and with my forehead raised, I met his gaze. I spread my wings of light and assumed a pose of pride, of satisfaction for everything that was happening. The Creator took it as an offense and started yelling at me.

"YOU DAMNED INSANE ANGEL! HOW DARE YOU DESTROY EVERYTHING I HAVE CREATED!"

I knew this moment would come, so I was not going to flinch. I had the truth on my side, and I was not going to allow a tyrant to get away with this.

"I have not destroyed anything, I have only opened their eyes so that they see you as you are, a selfish and capricious being" I responded.

Every word of mine offended him even more, and every time he spoke to me, he did so with yet more anger.

"YOU FOOL! Do you really think that you are already a god just because your understanding has increased a little? You are nothing more than a fool who thinks he is the smartest of all but behaves like the dumbest!"

His words made me feel worse than when I bit into that fruit, so I kept attacking too.

"That was your biggest mistake, thinking that a being of light could not change things or turn your world around! But I have done it, I have changed this world, freed it from the slavery to which you subjected it!"

Little by little I was approaching the Creator's throne with the idea of starting an attack, I kept talking.

"During my entire existence I have dedicated all of my effort to be your equal, and to become a god. But if to be a god I have to transform myself into someone like you. I prefer a thousand times to stay as a being of light."

The Creator, fed up with my words, answered me for the last time in a tone of mockery and contempt.

"Do not worry about that, Luzbel, because you will never occupy my place as God."

"We'll see!" I replied, looking directly into his eyes with hatred.

I took a great leap to reach the Creator, with the intention of attacking him with my bare hands, but while I was in the air, something appeared from his hand that I had not seen before. It was a sceptre with a golden light. He pointed it at me and, from that sceptre, came a bolt of lightning that paralyzed me and made me fall immediately. I couldn't believe what I was seeing, the Creator was attacking me with a weapon, and worst of all, it was a very effective weapon.

I had fallen a few steps away from him. Those rays ran through every part of my being and made me feel endless agony, suddenly the pain I felt with the fruit was not so bad compared to this.

I kept writhing on the ground in pain, I couldn't stop screaming. But at no time did the idea of asking for forgiveness or clemency cross my mind. I existed thanks to the Creator, and it was more than likely thanks to the Creator that I would soon cease to exist.

Suddenly, when I was giving up on everything, an angel with wings of energy was thrown into the sceptre's rays, crashing head-on, trapping them and freeing me. It was one of the Creator's angels, so the Creator, surprised by that, stopped immediately. I was still very weak, I looked at the place from where that angel had been thrown and I had a divine vision.

I saw my army of angels had intervened to save me. Before the creation of Man, they did not have the power to reach this place where only the Creator, his son and only his best angels could enter, and now each of my angels had managed to enter. It was they who, on their own initiative, had thrown the angel to help me. Not only did they save my life, but they were now all here surrounding me and protecting me.

"We will not allow you to harm Luzbel, he has freed us from you and only to him we owe loyalty and submission!" they cried.

The angels of the Creator did of course not stand idly by, seeing how a group of "Traitors", as they called us, endangered the reign of their Lord, so they began to attack.

Although we were inferior in number, my angels were well trained and had much more power than the angels of the Creator. The fruit of knowledge had made them smarter, faster, and stronger. Which made the battle very even.

Light beings cannot bleed, but we can be seriously injured in a fight against another light being. More and more angels were lying on the ground than those that remained fighting. It was a fight without restraint, or mercy on either side. My angels wanted to overthrow the Creator, but his angels were not going to allow it.

This became a real hell. I don't know how long that battle lasted, because for many of my people it was endless, but for me it all started and ended in the blink of an eye.

I also continued fighting, it seemed that everyone wanted to go for me, maybe they thought that catching me would end it all. But those angels could not contain me, the only one who had a chance was the Creator, but neither he, nor his son, had moved from their thrones. They only watched the battle carefully, without intervening. For me only one thing was clear, I alone could not compete against him, so remembering those little insects that I had seen on Earth, I drew up a new plan. I would first need to defeat the Creator's guard, and then with my entire army of angels and I would attack him at the same time.

It was a perfect plan to overthrow him, but things do not always go as expected on the battlefield. The attacks of my angels and the angels of the Creator were something never before seen. We had never experienced the true fighting power of an angel because it had never occurred. It remains to be verified, but the forces that were being unleashed in that place surely wreaked havoc in all dimensions. The worst part was when the collision of several energy balls thrown between the angels with energy wings opened a temporary portal to the private dimension of the Creator. To continue the chain of misfortune, one of those energy balls passed through that portal, exploding and throwing millions of light particles into the human universe, millions of planets were destroyed, and a small part of those particles hit Earth.

This was a terrible act; the Creator did not have my sympathy, but even I have to admit that that must have been a terrible feeling for him. Every plant and creature on the planet were connected to him and feeling how millions of those species died between screams of pain and agony was the greatest blow he could ever receive. Only the Creator, his son and I, felt how Earth had been damaged in such a savage way. My first thought was of course the woman. I was petrified at the thought that she could have been destroyed because of me. I looked at the Creator, fearful and very worried, and I saw pain, anguish and sadness in his face, and then anger.

The Creator shouted and, making a new display of his power, raised that golden sceptre. It was like a sign for his son to show all of his power. The Creator took his son's hand and, between the two of them, they formed the Holy Spirit; a being with enormous power, that was in front of all of us ready to attack. I looked into its eyes and in that instant, I knew, we no longer had anything to do in face of him. The Holy Spirit unleashed all of its fury towards my entire army and towards me. It threw thousands of rays that prevented us from continuing with the fight. We were all paralyzed again while rain of lightning ran through us all.

"YOU HAVE CHOSEN YOUR DESTINATION AND NOW YOU MUST PAY THE CONSEQUENCES!" The Creator's voice rang, as the Holy Spirit increased in power. "CURSED BE LUZBEL AND CURSED BE EVERYONE WHO PRAISES YOUR NAME! OUT!"

CHAPTER FIVE
The Age of the Humans

The Creator displayed all of his power alongside his son, causing the Holy Spirit to unleash all of its power, banishing us from his universe.

As you can see, no archangel was in charge of defeating me, and if you think about it, that version of the story does not make any sense. I was the most powerful angel of all, only surpassed by the Holy Trinity, so how could it be explained that another angel was capable of beating me?

Almighty God had defeated us, and my entire army and I were thrown into a dimension that is between his, and the universe of humans. A dimension to which they have no connection, but which I made mine over time.

My first reaction upon reaching this new dimension was to visit planet Earth immediately. I needed to know that humans were fine and safe, so without further hesitation I tried to go to Earth, but from this new universe my wish was not easy. I failed several times before reaching my goal, but I was so determined to go that I found the way using only my instincts and my desire to achieve it.

As soon as I arrived, I saw the havoc that my angels and I had caused. The sky was no longer blue, it had been dyed red with black clouds covering the sky, and this was far from where that particle of light had impacted. Near the impact, there was only fire and smoke. At the place of impact there was a huge crater that had pushed back the water of the oceans for an instant, but by now it was covering the smoking crater again. Around that crater there was only death and destruction; my beloved earth had turned into a living hell, and it was breaking my heart.

I immediately went to the island where the humans lived, and I was glad to see that they were well, they had gone to the top of the mountains to take refuge from the huge waves that had covered the island. There, they had found safety in a cave. They were scared, I could see the fear on their faces the same moment I saw how their island had been almost destroyed in those few seconds. The tree of knowledge was uprooted and had been pulled to the bottom of the sea. The fruit of the tree were also made of the vital energy of the beings of light, which rendered it immortal. Even after being plucked from the tree, the fruit that remained on the tree was lost to the bottom of the sea, where it still resides to this day.

The humans did not know what had happened between the Creator and me, but I was sure that they thought it had been a punishment from God for disobeying him.

Everything had changed since the last time I was there. The new landscape on Earth was devastating, the sea was still rough, the sky seemed to bleed, and the feeling was that the Earth itself was still shaking from the impact. Even the humans had changed, now they covered parts of their bodies with leaves, and they no longer smiled like they used to, but with everything that was going on, who could blame them?

At that time, I had many mixed feelings. I had doubts about whether my actions were really justified, and if they were, was it really worth going through all that? Neither Earth nor the humans were better now that I had "liberated" them from the tyranny of the Creator, was it I who was wrong?

I could only think about when I had become the bad guy in this story. I knew that that fruit had opened the door to a new world for me, a world in which I had no limits and could achieve anything I wanted thanks to all that new knowledge. But was I in control? I couldn't help but think that maybe the Creator was right, and I was just a fool with delusions of grandeur, and just when I thought that I couldn't feel any more guilty, I felt the presence of the Creator on the other side of the world.

I got as close to him as possible without being detected. I was close enough to see his face with the smallest detail and see what he was doing. What I saw was someone desolate, someone who really hurt to see all this. How his little world, to which he had devoted so much love and time, had been destroyed by someone he considered his son. Crying is something impossible for a being of light or for a god, but if it were possible, I am sure that his face would have been covered in tears.

The Creator simply looked around, and his gaze remained unchanged, sad, discouraged, hurt, and only he knows what was going through his head at that moment. I honestly don't know how someone with his power didn't completely destroy the planet to start over; It would be an easy thing for him to do, but instead, he wanted this planet to run its course but, at the same time, by making big changes.

The particle of light had destroyed everything around the place of impact, yet on the other side of the planet things remained unchanged. Not even the animals had realized the great misfortune that had passed, but even though the particle of light hadn't affected them, they weren't safe. The Creator, starting with his new plans for the Earth, manufactured a deadly gas that would attack only the largest animals. The creatures to which he had given life, he was now taking it away in a cruel way. Many of the large animals that were close to the impact died, charred, the rest would die later, poisoned by that deadly gas that would kill them in a slow and painful way.

At first, I could not understand the purpose of that slaughter of the animals but, as I saw what he was doing on Earth, I began to understand his purpose. Now that the humans weren't under his protection, he wanted to give them a chance to survive on the planet without him. Those animals were a great obstacle to the future of humanity, and they had to disappear. After spreading the deadly gas all around the planet, he made sure that Earth's ecosystem had everything it needed to get ahead, starting almost from the beginning. He began to create new species of animals and plants to populate the planet, and it was something that was unthinkable for me and quite a surprise when I saw what he was to do next. He started again with the creation that was his greatest work, The man, but this time from cells, following my advice. He created a new species from cells so that it would evolve over time, becoming Man at the end of its evolution. I do not know if he did it as a second chance for humanity or if he had a plan for all that, but after working on Earth for a while and modifying it, he just left and was not in contact with humanity again for a long period of time.

Unlike him, I was on Earth whenever I could be. I was however, returning to my dimension to continue helping my angels to evolve, as I knew it was a matter of time before I measured my forces again against the army of the Creator, and this time I was going to be sure to get the victory.

When I had everything ready for my angels to continue without my help for a while, I returned to Earth to see its progress. For Earth, this was a long and tedious process, but after a couple of thousand years it would return to life, dyed green and blue. The animals that had survived the gas were no longer as big as they used to be, and their physiology was completely different. They were species that had survived the attack of beings of light, plus newer species created to complete the new chain that had been formed in the planet after the attack.

Human beings had evolved too; on their little island they had created a small population with all their children.

Having eaten the fruit, their knowledge had increased. They had finally realized that they too could reproduce like other beings on the planet. They discovered sex to reproduce, but unlike animals they also practiced it for pleasure and to reinforce the ties that united them. The man and woman created by God were the only ones that reproduced in the who place, but despite having had thousands of years to populate the planet, the number of their children did not yet reach one hundred. Their children, like them, were designed to live indefinitely; their cells could regenerate completely and at will, which made them forever young or age only what they wanted. But, contrary to this, they were not immortal. Their bodies could regenerate easily from any injury quickly, but a fatal head- or heart-wound would end their days.

The new humans were not doing badly either; despite their more animal than human origin, their evolution was amazing. Its structure was designed to evolve slowly into a new species, which took a couple of thousand years, and once evolved it became a new species. Something completely different, which made the evolution cycle start from scratch and begin looking for a way to evolve again, all in a cycle that would not stop until perfection was reached.

It was at that moment that I understood the target of the Creator with these new creatures. With the first he had provided all the shape and everything necessary for his creation to be ready from day one, but with these new beings he had left the door open to evolution so that Earth itself was in charge of shaping them. Unfortunately, Mother Earth is not perfect and on multiple occasions she gave different qualities to these beings, causing a single species to be divided into several branches with different types of humans. Some of them remained stagnant in their animal form and could not advance any further, others could not survive the constant changes of the planet, causing among all of them only one branch to stand out above the others, they had a very similar appearance to that of the original humans.

The vast majority of the new humans were living in a region far from the island of the original humans, but their curiosity and understanding advanced by leaps and bounds. At first, I did not understand what the Creator's intention with these new human beings was, nor why he had decided to do this, but as I observed them, I understood. Having created adult human beings with only part of their knowledge, they had been overwhelmed by not understanding their own world; since they had the knowledge but they did not understand it. This was something that the new humans were discovering over time.

If I have to be honest, I can't say which race attracted my attention the most; the human beings that I already knew and had helped to create, or the new beings destined to be human. I liked spending time observing humans and especially the woman, who after thousands of years and dozens of children was still as spectacular and radiant as the first day. Her daughters were also worthy of admiration, but she was unique, and despite the passing of time, I never get tired of seeing her from my distance.

As their technology advanced, their clothing also changed; discovering the metals that could be extracted from the Earth, their clothing was more complex, and something that completely caught my attention was the new clothes of the woman. She used these metals to make golden wings that she wore on her back, as if she were an angel. When she was facing the Sun, the wings shone as if they were made of light. Seeing that, I had no doubt that she had seen me come out of that serpent, and if she dressed like that it was thanks to me. It was clear, from this, that her feelings towards me or what I represented were good. Her partner, on the other hand, was unable to see me in my authentic form, but nevertheless he had started a small tradition that persists to this day. The only thing he knew was that the serpent had freed him, and for this reason in his new culture, the serpent was used as a symbol of wisdom. In many of their crafts they used figures with a human and part reptile shape, as a metaphor for a more advanced understanding to which each of them could aim to reach. So, for all those who believe that there are, or were, half reptilian and half human beings I am sorry to disappoint you, but it is only a misinterpretation of history like many others. The reptilians as a race have existed only in the imagination of Man and in their desire to believe in something else.

After several thousand years, things on Earth were improving. The new ecosystem was stable, and the planet had left behind the destruction caused by the revolution of the light beings, hiding its scar at the bottom of the sea. Human beings had also built a society where they dedicated almost all of their time to meditation and self-knowledge. Their technology and understanding of the environment advanced at an amazing speed, they used everything around them, but at the same time they respected and lived in harmony with the planet. Soon, the island began to get too small for them, and some of them started to travel outside the island. They wanted to explore and see what other great mysteries awaited them on the planet, until they finally found one of the species that would most influence their lives.

The new humans were not left behind in their evolutionary process, each day they stood out more among animals, and this called the attention of the original humans. They did not know that the new beings they had just discovered had been a direct creation of their god to take their place, but they knew that this race was special. Some of the humans adopted this new species and helped them develop in a spectacular way. The humans taught them to use tools to make their life easier, they showed them fire and how to make it. The new humans learned quickly and, with each new generation, became smarter and physically more like the original humans.

With the passage of time, the new humans began to form more complex societies where each member had a designated task. Rather that behaving like animals that only hunted and ate when they were hungry, they had become gatherers, beings capable of raising animals to later use as food.

Their language was still primitive, but they observed and learned from the original humans, and thanks to this, they began to communicate not only with gestures. They tried to imitate the sounds of humans to have their own language, and not only verbal, but they began to use drawings on stones as a form of communication and expression, developing their creativity and giving rise to a new, thinking, species capable of reasoning about their environment.

The new humans multiplied rapidly and although their life span was short compared to the original humans, their community easily tripled the community of the original humans. The original humans had a couple of casualties during this time, most from deadly attacks by animals or from receiving the fury of mother nature. The original woman and man were still the only ones who reproduced within the community of the original humans, the two of them had been the only ones to taste the fruit of knowledge, so their children still did not understand or feel the need to reproduce. They were very advanced in terms of meditation and control of the body and mind, but that was about to change.

In the beginning, the original humans had fun teaching the new humans, I suppose that for them it was like training a dog that obeyed them without hesitation. However, as the new humans evolved, some of the originals no longer saw them as pets, they began to see them as equals. Some even moved from their home island to live permanently with the new humans, and what in principle was a relationship in which the new humans were the only beneficiaries, the original humans found something profitable with these creatures.

The original humans spent all their time with them, also learning about their way of life, since they found it fascinating. Most fascinating was the relationship that the females built with the males. They saw that even being a species inferior to them, they had the same as their parents had. The first man and the first woman in history, and that was something that not even they knew. At first, the approach they had with the new humans was more scientific than sentimental, they just wanted to learn more about them and their way of living with their peers; but due to the close relationship that they had built with them, one of the original humans began to have real feelings for one of them. He was one of the first male children of the man and the woman, the first to take the step to have a relationship with a female of the new humans.

His name was Kaynet. He was one of the first children of the man and the woman to leave the island and see the world with his own eyes. Neither he, nor any of his brothers had the knowledge that their parents had, but this was not a trouble for him, because thanks to that he had an insatiable appetite for knowledge. Before moving over permanently with the new humans, Kaynet used to only visit them once in a while and then return to his home island. Kaynet's mother knew all of her children perfectly, and she knew very well that something had changed in her son's mind. These new creatures, that he did not stop studying, had affected him deeply, but she still did not know to what degree, until one day she saw him arrive back at the Royal Palace after spending a long time with those beings.

"Kaynet! I am glad to see you again my son, each time it takes you longer and longer to return home" she exclaimed.

"Hello Mother, sorry for my absence, but time does not matter when you have eternity." Kaynet replied as he kissed the hand of his mother and the Queen of the island

"That's not an excuse to be so far from your family" his mother smiled, looking him straight in the eye.

"I know mother, but I can't help it when it comes to these creatures, at least for the moment they have my full attention, especially one of them" Kaynet said.

"What is special about this particular creature?" his mother asked, paying attention to every one of his son's expressions.

"Her name is Sorlan, and she is a very intelligent creature. I have been with her for a long time, and I have taught her to think, speak, write, and read, and although it is difficult for her to express herself fluently, she can hold a conversation perfectly, she is simply incredible."

His mother was watching him, and she could see that there was something else behind all those words.

"Sorlan? Have you given an animal a human name?" his mother asked with no intention of belittling her, but it was something that seemed very curious, even more than the fact that she could talk and communicate with them without problems. But that was something that had bothered Kaynet.

"Sorlan is not an animal Mother! Maybe she is not as evolved as us, but I am completely sure that she is as human as you or me" he retorted.

His mother immediately noticed that her comment had affected him. For her, it was more than obvious that there was a very special interest on the part of her son towards this creature.

"From the way that you defend her, I can easily deduce that Sorlan, is a very special creature for you, isn't she?" The Queen began to walk through the palace while her son accompanied her.

"Mother, if you spent the same time with them that I have spent, you would realize that they are not just any species. It is like seeing a version of us from the past, before having the form we have now" he told her.

"We have never had a previous version of ourselves; from the beginning we have had this form and that will never change" replied the Queen trying to make it clear to her son that they were not the same, no matter how much he wanted to believe otherwise.

"I know Mother. I know that we do not have the same origin, but that does not mean that we do not have the same future. Or is that perhaps what worries you, do you worry that they will become one of us?" he questioned.

The Queen stopped and stared into his eyes.

"What really worries me is that you become one of them."

Kaynet was surprised by that answer, but his mother hadn't finished.

"Tell me something Kaynet, when was the last time you entered Akash?" she asked.

Kaynet avoided her mother's gaze, since not even he remembered the last time that he had entered.

"You see? You are so focused on these creatures that you are losing yourself in the banal. Do you find it incredible that they can think and speak? That does not mean anything if they cannot control their thoughts or if they do not understand the world around them. That is why it is so important for us to be connected with Akash. This is what differentiates us from any other species in this universe; we have the key to universal understanding, but what good is it if we never use it?" she went on.

Kaynet said nothing, as if he were a small child; he just looked at the ground and listened as his mother reproached him.

"Kaynet, look at me, my son" the Queen lifted her son's chin with her hand, and he looked at her. "I have no problem letting you spend as much time as you want with them, but I only ask one thing, never forget who you are. Since you entered this world, you have been destined to do great things, I know that very well."

Kaynet took his mother's hand and kissed her.

"Thank you very much, mother" Kaynet said, smiling.

"Don't thank me yet, I'm not done with you yet." she smiled back at him.

"What do you mean by that mother?"

"Come with me, there is something you must do before you leave again" she said.

The Queen guided her son through the palace, but Kaynet knew exactly where she was taking him. This path was well known to him, since it had been one of his favourite places as a child, although now as an adult he had lost the motivation to go there.

"Really mother? Do you have to take me to the temple?" he asked.

"It is necessary. If you stop being in contact with Akash, you will lose it, and it will be very difficult for you to return there."

"Mother, just because some time has passed since my last time there does not mean that I have forgotten it or that I can no longer enter." Kaynet complained.

"I doubt it, you haven't been in for so long that I'm not even sure you remember the basics." She replied. Kaynet made a mocking face.

"Very good" said the Queen, "Let us do the test, what is Akash?" she asked.

"Really?" Kaynet answered, though knowing that his mother was only playing a joke on him, and the Queen smiled.

"Answer Kaynet, or is it that you don't even know that anymore?" the Queen said, letting out a laugh. Kaynet shook his head from side to side while smiling.

"Akash is an astral plane where material does not exist; there is no time, no space, or limits, all the knowledge of the universe is concentrated there. It is a place where past, present and future are formed in a single line to which you can read, with the necessary preparation." he stated.

"Very well" the Queen smiled, pleased. "I see that you still remember, and now tell me, how many planes exist in Akash?"

"Seven." Kaynet kept playing his mother's game as they continued on their way to the temple.

"And what are those plans?"

"Corporeal, Mental, Sensory, Bioenergetic, Energetic, Intuitive and Divine." Kaynet answered with great confidence.

"Perfect, now let us see if you still remember how to get there."

The Queen stopped at the gates of the temple and opened the doors. Inside it was completely dark, only a few lights could be seen in the distance, but they were not strong enough to illuminate the place. You could not see the ceiling or the walls, once you entered and closed the doors the place gave the impression of having no end. The Queen and her son were getting deeper and deeper into the room now, and the lights that could be seen from the door were gaining in strength, until they revealed their origin. Each light was emitted by Kaynet's brothers and sisters, all of them meditating, and while doing it, a very special light came from their heads. The light was strong enough to see their faces clearly, none of them moving or making the slightest noise. There was not even the sound of breathing from those who were there. Kaynet and his mother found a place among all of them and prepared to meditate.

The Queen was the most advanced of all humans and, for her, entering Akash was as easy as entering a room in her palace. For her children, and especially for Kaynet, it was not so easy. He had spent a lot of time outside of that environment, and now he could not silence his mind. He had thousands of thoughts at the same time, and among all of them one that came very frequently to his mind, Sorlan. He only thought about her and how she would be now that she was without him. After several minutes Kaynet managed to control his body, it was as rigid as a rock, his breathing was long and controlled, which made his body seem to not move at all. After a while, he finally managed to calm his mind, which was now completely empty, no thoughts passed through his head, and he was only focused on his heartbeat. His face began to illuminate the place with his inner light, and while this was happening Kaynet felt like he was getting up from the ground. It was like a stream of water that carried him gently upwards. Kaynet was standing, he looked at the ground and could see his body in the same position it had been in all this time, and Kaynet smiled. He knew he was at Akash's doorstep and suddenly a voice was heard.

"Wow, it is about time."

Kaynet turned and saw the image of his mother next to him.

"For a moment I thought I had lost you completely" she said.

Kaynet smiled.

"I told you mother, you have nothing to worry about, now I'm here and that's what matters, right?"

The Queen looked carefully into her son's eyes and smiled.

"Yes, that's what matters, come, your brothers and sisters are waiting for us."

The Queen began to levitate, and she rose so much until she crossed the roof of the temple. Kaynet did the same, and following his mother very closely, he continued to rise. As he did so, Kaynet looked at the ground and saw how his mother's palace was getting smaller and smaller, until he could see the entire island clearly. As he continued to rise, he saw the entire planet in all its splendour. Kaynet had forgotten how wonderful this whole spectacle was; looking at Earth from the point of view of a god. His mother watched him, and she was pleased to see her son reconnect with his true species. Kaynet was still fascinated by looking at all the planets around him, but after a few minutes those planets got smaller, and the only thing he could see were the galaxies where they were. From seeing thousands of planets around him, he went on to see thousands of galaxies, as many as he could see. But as he continued to advance, the galaxies seemed to be fewer and fewer, until they all disappeared into the distance and Kaynet and his mother were left alone. Shrouded in total darkness, they continued to advance until a light in the distance made its way through the black.

"There it is. Akash" the Queen smiled.

Kaynet looked and smiled back at her. He saw how the light was transforming into a super galaxy, something huge compared to all those he had seen before. As soon as they entered this galaxy, they were immediately transported to the centre of it, where all the children of the Queen were waiting for them. As soon as they saw them, they all went to meet them.

"Kaynet! Brother, what a joy to see you!" they said.

Kaynet greeted all of his siblings, very pleased, especially with his younger sister Nacink, she approached him as soon as she saw him.

"Kaynet! I'm glad to see that you haven't yet forgotten about your family" she said.

"How could I forget about my favourite sister?" he smiled.

"Well, I'm surprised you haven't yet, taking into account all the time you spend with your dear Sorlan."

Kaynet was surprised to hear Sorlan's name come from his sister's mouth; a name that he had never revealed to anyone on that island except his mother. But at the same time, he remembered the unusual powers that you obtain in Akash.

"You had forgotten for a moment that there are no secrets here, our minds are an open book in the eyes of all who are here" his sister confirmed.

"I know, just do me a favour and stop reading my mind."

Nacink let out a laugh.

"You can't blame me for being interested in your life after all this time away, besides, I'm not the only person interested in knowing what's going on in your mind" she replied.

Kaynet turned around following his sister's gaze and saw his mother staring at him, her face serious, concerned. Kaynet didn't know what to think or say, but his mother just vanished from there.

"Where has mother gone?" Kaynet asked puzzled

"I am certain she will be in the sixth plane; it is one of her favourite hobbies"

"Mother can go to Intuition!?" Kaynet said very excited.

The most advanced humans could reach the fourth plane "Bioenergetic" but there were very few who could. Kaynet had only reached the third plane "sensory" but only when he used to enter Akash more often. Now it had been difficult for him even to get to this plane and his mother was three beyond him.

"You should not be so surprised Kaynet, mother has always been the best of us all and is the most constant, I am sure that very soon she will pass to the seventh plane, and then she will become the first human god."

Kaynet knew that his mother was an extraordinary being, but he had never thought about the true extent of her power. He knew that his sister was right, and the Queen would be the first to achieve divinity.

In the sixth plane, the Queen was meditating, she was still in her endeavour to reach the seventh plane, but that was something that was not easy at all in the sixth plane, since the more you try to control something, the less control of it you have. She was looking for a way to level up, since on past occasions she was close to achieving it, or so she believed. On those occasions all she did was not think, all she did was feel and let her feelings guide her. So, this time she did the same. The Queen was in a lotus position with her eyes closed while she was meditating, so trying to do something different, she got up, opened her eyes and did not close them again. She left her gaze fixed on nothing and attempted to let all the shapes that surrounded her show her the way.

The sixth plane is a place where no being of light can enter, not even an angel with wings of light like me, but nevertheless the seventh plane is a place where we can manifest ourselves without any problem. Even so, I liked to see the woman go into "Intuition" because she seemed to be closer to me, just one step away. While she was meditating, I liked to talk to her, encourage her to continue pushing, since she knew it was only a matter of time. Then, from thousands of years following her closely, I wanted to make sure that I was the first being of light she would see. So many times, while she was meditating, I would do the same. I wanted to think that maybe there could be a middle ground between the sixth and seventh planes, a shortcut to be with her ahead of time.

"That's it, you're doing very well, don't think, just feel" was the only thing I said to her while carefully following everything she did.

"Who are you?" asked the Queen

I couldn't believe it, in my mind only two questions came immediately. "Are you talking to me? Have you heard me?" Obviously, there was only one way to know for sure.

"Can you hear me?" I asked with a tone of disbelief.

"Yes, I can hear you." answered the Queen without changing her gaze. "I had heard you before, on another occasion, but I got scared and lost the connection, this time it is different because I was waiting to hear your voice one more time."

She was not in the seventh plane, nor had I managed to go to the sixth, so I was right; there was a plane between the two that allowed us to have some contact. She had heard my voice before and I did not know it at the time, but now I wanted to continue putting my luck to the test.

"And can you see me?" I asked as I moved to stand behind her.

She slowly turned around and looked me straight in the eye.

"Yes, I can see you!" she said with a nervous laugh. Not only was she excited to see me; she was excited because she had realised that it was not the first time that she had seen me.

"It is you! You are that being that came out of my beloved serpent! Or am I wrong?"

I smiled, pleased that she had made the connection.

"You're not wrong, it was me, I was the creator of that creature, and that's why I could be inside it and control it at will."

"I knew there was something else. I saw you only for a second, but during that second I knew that being with those wings of light, had been my liberator" she said.

She knelt before me, and before she could say anything else, I interrupted her.

"Please stand up, you don't owe submission to anyone, and I am nobody to deserve such gratitude!"

The Queen got up and looked at me with more admiration than at first.

"Not only are you humble my lord, but you are also noble, but your nobility should not detract from everything you have done for me and mine. Thanks to you, I have opened my eyes and I have realized all the potential we have. Thanks to you I have my children, and a future ahead of me beyond servitude, or submission to a tyrant."

I smiled and felt like a burden that I had been carrying for a long time had disappeared leaving me feel a great relief.

"You don't know how long I've been waiting to hear that" I sighed.

CHAPTER SIX
Adamu

Kaynet, inspired by his mother, began to meditate as well. Since he was there, he wanted to take advantage of the time to be in contact with his own self and enrich his knowledge; but even so he could not stop thinking about Sorlan. He just wanted to know if she was well or what she was doing right now. So, before starting his training he took some time to find out about Sorlan.

Inside Akash you can see the timeline of any living being that exists or that has existed. Only the most expert meditator could see the timeline from the beginning to end, even before that living being ceased to exist, but Kaynet was still a beginner due to his lack of determination and his desire to spend more time with the new humans as he called them. For this reason, he could only see the present, a little of the past and little more of the future. The only problem was that he could not be sure what part of the timeline he was looking at, which made him a bit confused not knowing whether it was past, present or future. Nevertheless, he did not care about that little detail, and he concentrated only on watching Sorlan's timeline. It had been a long time since Kaynet had done something like this, but as he did it, it all came back to his mind. Slowly, he saw the land where the new humans lived, he saw the houses, the men and women all around working on something.

On the outskirts of the village, he saw Sorlan working the land as usual. She was in charge of planting the seeds of the new crops, and it was something that she liked to do very much, since it was not customary for a woman to do that job, it made her feel special. Kaynet watched her and smiled, pleased to see that she was fine, but almost at the same time he felt relief he felt fear, when he saw one of the warriors of the village watching her secretly among the trees. It was Goulix, one of the new men who was obsessed with Sorlan who only thought of possessing her, and there alone in the field it seemed that Goulix had the perfect opportunity. Kaynet then witnessed how Goulix assaulted her fiercely, Sorlan tried to defend herself, but Goulix was very strong. Kaynet saw how Goulix positioned himself on top of her and was about to abuse Sorlan sexually. Kaynet watched, paralyzed, and let his fears take control of him, which caused his vision to begin to distort. Quickly, Kaynet used an old technique to calm down and regain control of his feelings, which made him see Sorlan's image again. This time, she was alone in the middle of a field of flowers, she was sitting crossing her legs with her back to Kaynet, and as Kaynet approached her, he saw that she had something in her arms, when he got a little closer, he saw clearly that she was holding a baby. Kaynet lost all concentration and was dragged from Akash to his body where he woke up.

"Oh no, Sorlan! I must help her" he cried.

Kaynet got up and saw his mother next to him still meditating, the light that her head emitted was three times brighter than that of any of his brothers. Kaynet approached her, got on one knee and kissed her on the cheek.

"I'm sorry mother, but this is something I must do, I hope you forgive me."

Kaynet got up and immediately left his parents' temple to go in search of Sorlan.

***

Meanwhile, the Queen continued talking to me. She still could not believe what was happening to her by being able to see me and even less being able to talk to me. And honestly, it was something that even I also had a hard time believing.

She kept asking me about my world and my origin. I had no qualms about telling her everything, from my days as a faithful angel of the Creator, until today where I am considered the greatest traitor in history. I told her that, from the beginning, I was there watching her from a distance and following her every step. She smiled with pleasure because she could see how important she was to me, so knowing this she took the opportunity to ask me more questions.

"My lord, excuse my daring one more time, but please tell me, what are your plans for us? What is the meaning of our existence?" she asked.

Questions that even today no human can say they have the answer, but for me it was not a problem to answer, for me the problem was to explain to her in such a simplified way that she could understand me. Because, even as advanced as she was, she was still a girl compared to a being of light in terms of knowledge. And no matter how good your intention to make her understand everything you know; it is still a practically impossible task. It was like trying to explain to a girl of two years about quantum physics and expecting her to understand me.

"For the moment, I can only tell you with absolute certainty what is not your reason for existing, and that is to serve a being who thinks that he is superior to you."

She smiled and I kept talking.

"Something you must understand is that your life is yours and only you decide what to do with it. So, going back to your questions tell me, what are your plans?

What meaning do you want to give to your existence?" I asked her.

She was looking at me, but she didn't know what to answer.

"Whatever you decide, I know that it will be a destiny of greatness. I am sure that very soon you will leave here, and you will be able to accompany me to know the wonders of my world and everything that you still do not know about yours." I told her.

"Thank you very much, my lord for such generous words."

She did not stop smiling and I changed my face to a more serious one, my gaze was lost in nothingness, and she noticed it.

"What is it my lord?"

"I must warn you that great changes are coming in your world, and you must be at the height of all the problems that threaten your people."

"Problems? What are you talking about?" she asked.

"One of your older children, Kaynet, is about to take a step that will change things in this world forever."

"Kaynet? What is happening to him?"

"Do not worry, there is nothing you can do now, just wait for him to come home and then you will know. But I need to repeat; you must be up to the situation my Queen, just remember that what today can feel like a disgrace, tomorrow can be a blessing."

The Queen was confused upon hearing all of this; wait for Kaynet to come home? But he was already home. Or was he no longer? She did not know what to think, which made her lose concentration and lose her position in this new dimension. She disappeared from my presence and returned to the sixth dimension. I was still standing there with my eyes fixed on nothing. I knew later that me saying that she would be expelled from that place, but it was exactly what I wanted. If my face had changed, it was not because of that vision of her son, that was something that I had already seen and knew for a long time. My reason for getting her out of there was something completely unexpected.

"What are you doing here? Did you really think that you could hide from me?" I asked in a serious tone.

The Creator appeared in front of me.

"You are making a big mistake, Luzbel"

That was the first time I had seen the Creator face to face since the day of the battle. I looked him directly in the eyes, this time not with hatred, but with disappointment. Throughout my existence he had been everything to me, and now there, in front of me it was strange to see how someone who had been so important to me had become one of my biggest mistakes.

"If you are going to tell me again that I do not know what I am doing with humans, I advise you not to waste your time, and make me lose it listening to your nonsense." I said.

He just looked at me but didn't say anything.

"Really... I still don't understand how someone like you, with all your power, with all your knowledge and wisdom cannot recognize when you have made a mistake." I continued.

"Poor Luzbel, I see that you haven't changed anything yet, you keep losing yourself on the surface without being able to see that there is much more inside." He responded.

"Oh please! Are you going to tell me now that humans were much better off when they were in the shade of a tree doing nothing but waiting for you, to praise you? Before me, they were just your servants with no hope of being something else; Now, they have built a great community, they know how their body works, this world and part of this universe. Thanks to me they have developed a potential that they would never have reached next to you, and they know it. For that reason, they are grateful to me and that's what really bothers you."

"Do you really think that just because they have built a more complex society, they are developing their full potential? What do you know about their full potential? Were you the one who created them? Were you the one to give them a purpose to exist? You don't have the slightest idea of how they might reach their full potential, all you are doing is hindering their mission and confusing them even more!" he replied.

"But how is it possible that you keep clinging to the same story when all the evidence is against you?! You want to make me think that I am wrong when the only thing I have seen, and continue to see, is prosperity and a great future for the humans. A new generation is coming, and with them many more changes and achievements that have not been seen before now, and you know it"

The Creator looked away and turned his back on me.

"I see that you will not change your mind, and unfortunately the humans will pay for your stubbornness. You are going to force me to do something I didn't want to do, and when it happens, remember that all of this will be your fault, Luzbel."

Saying this, the Creator disappeared from my presence.

"WAIT! What did you mean by that?!" I shouted after him.

I had a bad feeling when I heard those words, but what did they mean? Would I make him do something he didn't want to do, and the humans would pay for it? I knew that I had to be more alert than ever and warn the humans of any misfortunes that may be caused by the Creator. Without a second thought I left that dimension to return to my world and begin a close watch on the Creator and his subjects.

The Queen woke from her meditation and noticed immediately that her beloved son was no longer by her side.

"Oh no! Kaynet!"

The Queen ran from the temple in search of her son, but he was nowhere to be found. Along the way, she found another of her children.

"Sabín, have you seen your brother Kaynet?" she asked, frantic.

"Yes mother, I saw him a little over an hour ago, he was running towards the stables in search of his napyr."

The Queen let out a sigh. "Kaynet, what are you going to do, my son" thought the Queen as she remembered my words. "There is nothing you can do now, just wait for him to come home and then you will know" she told herself.

She knew there was nothing more she could do for her son; all she could do was continue in her role as leader of the island and wait for the return of her son.

Kaynet was riding his napyr, which is a distant relative of what you have named a rhinoceros. It was not one of the fastest species in that world, but it could run for several kilometres without slowing down. It was also a large and robust animal that could defend itself very well from any other creature that could be found on the road, which made it the perfect means of transport. Kaynet rode day and night, only resting enough so his napyr did not collapse on the way. The journey was long and very hard if undertaken having not properly rested, but just remembering that image of Sorlan in danger filled Kaynet with the strength to continue. At last, he reached the land of the new humans, and the first thing Kaynet did was go to where they grew the crops, since that was the place where Sorlan spent the most time. When he arrived, he saw Sorlan's figure in the distance; she was alone and on her knees on the ground, Kaynet could clearly see that something was wrong.

"Oh no... SORLAN!" Kaynet yelled as he jumped off of his running napyr and ran desperately to see her.

Kaynet's vision had been fulfilled, Sorlan had been attacked by Goulix minutes before he had arrived. Kaynet had seen everything several days in advance, but he could not do anything to prevent it because he had been late. Kaynet ran to see Sorlan and the first thing he saw was the wounds on her face, she was bleeding a little on her lips and she also had several blows all over her face and body. Kaynet knew immediately that his trip had been in vain. He felt awful seeing her in this state, but she smiled at him because she felt relief to see him. Kaynet tried to speak to her, but he felt like the words would not come out, until he finally spoke.

"Oh, Sorlan, I'm so sorry, I... I"

Sorlan responded as best she could, making it clear that he shouldn't feel that way.

"You do not say sorry to Sorlan, you are not Sorlan's protector, Sorlan knows how to defend herself"

"Do you know how to defend yourself? So... what happened to Goulix?"

"Goulix is a strong man, but Sorlan is a strong woman too, and smarter than Goulix" she replied.

"So, he hasn't abused you?"

"Goulix tries, but Sorlan stops him"

Kaynet smiled, but at the same time he realized that Sorlan did not need him at all. He had run there thinking that he was rescuing a damsel in distress, but now he saw her, he realised that he had done it because it was he who needed her and didn't want anything bad happen to her.

"Sorlan not silly, Sorlan knows Goulix try again because Sorlan is alone" she continued.

"I know, but I promise you there will be no next time, I will teach that Goulix to respect you, and he will never dare to touch you again"

"Goulix no problem, problem is Sorlan being alone, Kaynet not being with Sorlan"

"What do you mean I'm not with you? I came as fast as I could as soon as I saw that you were in danger, and now that I am here, I will not let anything bad happen to you"

Sorlan was staring into his eyes.

"If Kaynet wants to be with Sorlan, then... Kaynet should be with Sorlan" she said.

Kaynet was staring into her eyes also without saying anything, he was on his knees next to her. Also on her knees, Sorlan lowered her gaze and with her hands began to separate Kaynet's clothes below his belt, Kaynet just looked at her without saying or doing anything. She reached up to his penis and grabbed it with her hand, and slowly went up and down with her wrist as she returned his gaze. He did not know if what Sorlan was doing would work with him, he had never tried it with himself because he simply did not have the need to do it. Sex was something that only his parents knew and understood. For Kaynet, and all his siblings, it was something that was just not in their genes, for this reason Kaynet had never experienced an erection. His body had not been designed for reproduction, or at least that was what he believed, but all that was about to change. As he felt Sorlan's warm hands and looked into her eyes, he began to feel something that he had not experienced before, it was a sensation that was focused on his penis but at the same time that felling ran through his entire body. Sorlan felt his penis hardening between her hands, so she accelerated the movement. As she watched him, Kaynet's breathing was shaking to the point that he had to breathe through his mouth. He had not experienced such pleasure in his life. He felt how all his thoughts were fading inside his head and the only thing he could feel was that intense pleasure. Sorlan knew that he was ready for her, so she lay on her back in front of him and took off her clothes until she was completely naked. Kaynet had seen this millions of times with the other humans, so he knew what was coming next. He wanted to reach the end of that new experience, so without thinking twice he got on top of her, and without waiting for it he noticed how his penis entered inside her. It was like fitting together two pieces of a puzzle, so easy to achieve. He could feel how she was completely wet inside, and he felt in his penis a warmth and a pleasure without equal, he had never done something like that, but his own body told him what he should do to get more pleasure. He kept penetrating her again and again and Sorlan also enjoyed it, he accelerated the rhythm until he felt that he lost control, he went faster and faster until he reached an unexpected explosion of pleasure that made him scream, releasing all that his body could not hold. He fell on top of her and felt like his penis was losing strength. Kaynet also felt very weak, in fact, this was the first time in his entire life that he had felt so helpless but being inside Sorlan gave him a sense of wellbeing and security that he hadn't felt before; not even in his mother's arms when he was just a child. Kaynet withdrew his penis and looked into Sorlan's eyes, she also had a look of having enjoyed it as much as Kaynet.

The two of them laughed out loud afterwards merged into a tender embrace.

In the days to come things would change forever in the new humans' village. Kaynet had his own home there and Sorlan left her family to go and live with him. Kaynet was not the leader of the Village, but for them he was like a god, so everything he wanted they obeyed without fuss, and the fact of him choosing one of their own to be his wife made him one of the villagers. At first it was Sorlan who was always looking for him to have sex, but as time passed Kaynet began to feel the need for sex too, so he started looking for her in the same way, or maybe more. Kaynet finally felt that he was living the life he truly deserved, and he owed it all to Sorlan; and he, despite having stopped meditation and instead focussing more on physical activities, he was happy. That simple life was what he had longed to have.

Few things had changed on the island since Kaynet's departure; his brothers and sisters continued their lives of meditation and personal development to improve the future of the island. Several months had passed since Kaynet had left so suddenly but for those for whom time is not a problem, several months pass by in the blink of an eye. The Queen was still in the palace undertaking her duty of guiding all of her children. Bearing in mind her beloved son Kaynet, she was still waiting impatiently for him, until one day something broke the peace of the palace.

From the main approach of the island, one could hear the cry of a baby. Only the oldest of the children knew what it was; the youngest were unaware of such a sound and it was like hearing it for the first time in their lives. It was not a pleasant sound, but nevertheless it was something that caught the attention of all those who were there. When they looked to where that cry came from, they saw from a distance the silhouette of Kaynet mounted on his faithful napyr. They all saw him approaching and could see he was carrying something in his arms. His older brothers approached him and clearly saw that he was carrying a baby of a few months in age.

"It cannot be! It's a baby? How is it possible?! I didn't even know that mother was pregnant" they exclaimed.

Everyone around them murmured as Kaynet advanced, without stopping, until he reached the royal palace. He dismounted his napyr and continued walking, with the baby in his arms, towards the royal throne where his mother, father and some of his older siblings were. Kaynet walked with pride carrying the baby and did not stop to explain anything. All of his brothers and sisters saw him advance and none of them dared to ask where the baby had come from, or why it was he who was carrying it and not the Queen."

The queen was sitting on her throne and soon the news of the return of her son reached her ears; she was eager to see him, but at the same time she had a bad feeling.

Kaynet entered the royal throne room, and the baby in his arms had stopped crying. Kaynet was a little nervous about what was about to happen, but the situation had happened thousands of times in his head. No matter how bad it could turn out, he felt as though he was prepared for anything. The baby in his arms did not sleep, but remained in silence looking around, since it was the first time, he had seen anything like this. Finally, Kaynet was in front of his parents and the Queen cast her eyes on the bundle that Kaynet was carrying. She noticed that it was something that he carried delicately, and after a hundred children she knew at once that it was a baby. Her son was carrying a baby, but it was smaller than a normal baby, so perhaps it was one of those creatures that he loved so much.

"Mother, Father, allow me to introduce you to Adamu; My son" Kaynet said as he uncovered the baby and showed him to everyone present.

Everyone was shocked when they heard what he had said. They looked at the baby, and it was indeed like one of them, only smaller.

"Sorry brother, did you say... your son?" Asked one of Kaynet's older brothers.

"That's right; he is mine and Sorlan's Son. Sorlan is a female of the new humans."

"New humans?" They murmured without taking their eyes off the baby.

"Adamu is proof that our species are not so different, this baby is..."

"IT'S AN ABERRATION!" The king shouted as he got up from his throne. "Those creatures are not like us! How dare you say they are the "new humans"! We have been on this planet since the beginning, while they are mere beasts with no future!"

Kaynet had been afraid of this situation, but he was not willing to lower his guard.

"If they are simple beasts as you say, how do you explain the existence of Adamu?" Kaynet asked. "This baby is the perfect mix of our species, if it is something that should not be, how do you explain that it is possible?"

"How you achieved it is irrelevant, you have played with forces that go against nature, and this experiment that you claim to be your son is only your selfish desire to believe that these beasts are special. In your eagerness to be right, you created a monster that should never have left your laboratory".

Those words really affected Kaynet. He could bear anything bad that his parents were willing to say about him, but this way of referring to his son really angered him.

"You are wrong about everything! Those "beasts", as you say, are special, and Adamu is not my creation in a laboratory, he was created in the same way that I, and all of my siblings here present were!"

The Queen was surprised to hear this. She had not yet said anything, but those words required her intervention.

"What are you saying Kaynet? Perhaps you and that female..."

"Sorlan" interrupted Kaynet.

"Yes, Sorlan, did you and she have...?"

"Sex? Yes, we have it very often" he interjected again.

"And thanks to that I can say that Adamu is really my son."

Everyone present was scandalized when they heard Kaynet's words. Sex was something that had never been taught to them as they had never had the need to know it. It was something so exclusive to the king and queen that no one had considered the idea of practicing it anyway. The king was speechless, but his face reflected anger and denial at the thought of his son doing such an act with a beast as he called them. The Queen stared at the baby and remembered the words of that being of light she had encountered on the sixth plane.

"Do not worry, there is nothing you can do now, just wait for him to come home and then you will know.

But I need to repeat; you must be up to the situation my Queen, just remember that what today can feel like a disgrace, tomorrow can be a blessing."

The Queen looked at the baby's face and could clearly see the features of her beloved Kaynet when he was just a baby. But still, no one could tell that he was a hybrid baby, his appearance was completely identical to theirs, only smaller.

"What today can feel like a disgrace, tomorrow can be a blessing" thought the Queen.

One of her greatest fears was that her species would be doomed to disappear if something happened to her or her King. They were the only ones who had created a whole community from nothing, and without them that community would disappear over time. It was then that she understood, the baby in front of her was their future. If her children were able to mix with those Kaynet called the new humans, then her children and the entire community they had created would have a future. The Queen approached Kaynet and carefully removed the blanket that covered the baby; she saw that it was a healthy and normal baby, despite being smaller compared to one of her own. The baby saw her and began to laugh and move as though excited. Kaynet looked at his son and then at his mother, and he was not alone. All the others were attentive, waiting for some response from their Queen.

"May l?" she asked, opening her arms as she looked Kaynet in the eyes.

Surprised, Kaynet did not resist and very carefully passed his son over into the arms of his mother. Adamu was very happy to be in the arms of his grandmother, and she could not help feeling the same warmth she felt when she cradled one of her own children. Adamu grabbed one of the Queen's fingers and did not want to let go. She smiled and began to speak to him sweetly."

"Hello Adamu. Hello, you are a very beautiful and strong baby."

Everyone was stunned to see the behaviour of the Queen, especially her husband.

"But... my lady, have you lost your mind?" he uttered.

The Queen looked directly into her husband's eyes, and decisively addressed him and everyone who was present.

"Listen to me all; this is Adamu, son of Kaynet, and as such, he will be treated as one of us. He will be respected, held dear, and from this moment this will be his home."

No one there could believe what they had just heard, especially Kaynet, who had never imagined that things could go so well. Pushing his luck, and his mother's generosity a little more, he spoke.

"Mother, what about Sorlan?"

The Queen looked at him tenderly and smiled.

"A mother must always be close to her child; feel free to bring her here to live with you."

Kaynet was smiling very pleased, but his father was not at all.

"You have definitely lost your mind my lady. Are you really going to let those beasts live in our world as if they are like us? Don't you see the danger they represent to our community?"

"My lord, do not forget that it is your Queen to whom you are speaking, so address me with respect" she demanded.

The King's face changed; it looked like the face of a child whose mother had just reprimanded him. He looked her directly in the eyes without saying anything while she continued.

"Perhaps tomorrow you will understand the reasons for my decisions today, but for now I do not need you to understand them, I just need you to obey. And this goes for all of you, and all of the inhabitants of this island. The Queen has spoken." she said with finality.

They all bowed and answered in unison.

"YES, MY QUEEN!"

The Queen rested her eyes on her beloved Kaynet as she held her grandson in her arms.

"Come Kaynet, join me for a walk through the palace gardens; I want to show this little boy everything."

Kaynet could not hide the happiness on his face when he felt just how much support he was receiving from his mother. Proud to have a mother like that he only limited himself to answering, "Yes my Queen".

CHAPTER SEVEN
The New Generation

Kaynet had the unconditional support of his mother, and, thanks to this, he decided to return to Sorlan's villa with the idea of taking her to live with him on the island. The Queen and Nacink would stay with Adamu on the island to make Kaynet's trip easier and faster, so taking advantage of his good luck, he immediately left for his wife's villa. He could not wait to see her and tell her all about the good news. Sorlan had her doubts about that change, but deep down she knew that it was the best for Adamu. She knew that her son had great potential and living with Sorlan's family he could never reach it. Sorlan accepted, but with one condition; she did not want to be the only one of her kind on the island, so she asked that two of her sisters could accompany her to the island. They would keep her company as well as help them with the care Adamu required. The Queen had seen this condition coming, so before Kaynet had left she had told him that anyone who wanted to go to the island with them would be welcome.

Kaynet, Sorlan and two of her sisters left for the island where Adamu was waiting for them. He had quickly become accustomed to the company of his grandmother, the Queen, and she felt him as one of her own children. It was a disconcerting situation however for the Queen. Having a baby in her arms and knowing that it was not hers confused her at first, but each time she looked at that baby's face, she saw one of her own; her heart simply could not help loving him with all its strength.

The Queen was not the only one who had unconditional love for Adamu; Nacink, her aunt and Kaynet's little sister, would soon be part of Adamu's day to day life. Nacink and Sorlan quickly became friends, although at first for Nacink it was just curiosity and admiration for this species. In the end she could not deny that Sorlan was now part of her family. Not everyone on the island accepted the new guests in the same way, though none of them said or did anything to hurt Sorlan and her sisters, they could feel that they were unwelcome by some.

The days passed and in the blink of an eye, Adamu was 4 years old, the island was his home and he just wanted to play with his grandmother and his aunt Nacink all of the time.

Nacink felt a love for Adamu that she had never felt before for anyone, not even for her parents or siblings. That little boy, so fragile and full of life, had stolen her heart, but when she saw how quickly he grew, she felt like the baby that he had been had left a void that she wanted to fill.

She was one of the best students on the island, her knowledge of Akash was extensive, but since Adamu had come into her life, she had hardly visited the meditation temple. Nacink was one of Kaynet's younger sisters, so she never had the opportunity to care for any of her siblings or see any babies in her life. But every time she played with her only nephew and held him close, she felt that this was her destiny. Nacink had her refuge in Adamu, and like her brother Kaynet, she was open and curious to new experiences. Nacink still had in her memory the visions she had about her brother and Sorlan having sex and she knew what they had done and how they had done it, so the idea of doing the same was constantly running through her mind.

One day, Nacink decided to go back to the meditation temple. It had been a long time since her last visit, and she needed some information that she could only get from Akash. Wasting no time, she went to Akash and started looking at her own timeline. There, she was able to see her past, part of her present, and finally part of her future. Within those images she saw herself in a fairly advanced state of pregnancy, she saw her face and could see that she was completely happy. That image filled her heart with love, and she knew that her plans were going to be carried out and that it was a good decision. Following that same timeline, she went back only a couple of months, until she saw who the father of her unborn child would be. When she saw the creature, she recognized it immediately. It was Goulix, Sorlan's former suitor.

"Goulix" Nacink said to herself, "I know who you are, and where to find you."

Goulix was in his own village with the other males of his species. When they weren't hunting, they were fighting to see who the alpha male was; a title that Goulix always won. One day, he had gone hunting on his own and while he was in the middle of a forest stalking his prey, he came across something unexpected. It was a female, but she was not of his own species; she was a female of the same species as Kaynet. Goulix had not seen a female of that species until that moment, she was an imposing woman, taller than him and surely stronger.

"Goulix, my name is Nacink, I'm here because I need to ask you a favour" she said.

Goulix was surprised to hear that this woman knew his name, but for him she was a goddess, so he felt that perhaps he should not be shocked by this. Nacink started to walk towards a clearing in the middle of the forest.

"Come on, follow me" Nacink smiled as she continued walking.

Goulix, doubtful, followed her, but keeping his distance. Nacink stopped in the middle of a clear area where there was only grass. She was standing there watching as Goulix approached little by little. Once Goulix was at a safe distance, Nacink turned her back on him, got down on her knees and then put her hands on the ground too. Goulix didn't understand what she was doing, but he kept staring. Nacink turned her head to look directly into Goulix's eyes, and then with her hand she exposed her rear, leaving her genitals in view of Goulix.

"Come on, I'm sure you know what you should do Goulix" she said calmly.

He felt an intense fire inside him, for Goulix it was not the first time he had sex, but this would be the first time he would do it with a goddess. Without taking his eyes off her perfect butt, and without thinking twice, he quickly approached Nacink and penetrated her. Goulix let out the animal inside him and pierced her violently, without stopping, but Nacink was bigger and stronger than him, so his attacks did not do her the slightest damage. While Goulix continued to penetrate her, Nacink did not understand why these creatures and his own brother liked the activity so much. For her, it was a strange sensation, she even felt somewhat uncomfortable with this savage being inside her body. But she knew that it was only the means to achieving her end.

Nacink did not know it, but at that moment her body began to adapt to the new sensations she felt. Within her cells was all the information necessary to reproduce, so as soon as her body noticed that she was having sex, her own body arranged everything to start the reproduction process.

It didn't take Goulix long to end up in ecstasy, just as Nacink began to feel that this was not as bad as it was at first, but once Goulix was out of her body Nacink sat up, put her clothes back in the proper position and thanked Goulix.

"Good work Goulix, I will come back to look for you in case I need your help again" she said.

And as if nothing had happened, Nacink turned her back on the confused Goulix, who did not know what all this was about, but did not care at all. Nacink went in search of her Napir, and in the same way that she had arrived at Goulix's village, she left to return to her island.

There was no going back now, Nacink had followed a path in time that would change the course of history. She rode her Napir, thinking about everything that had happened minutes before. She remembered how uncomfortable it was to feel Goulix inside her the first time, but she also remembered that feeling she felt at the end, a new pleasure for her and that she wondered how far she could have gone if she had felt it from the beginning.

"Now I understand Kaynet, if that is what he feels when he is with Sorlan, then it is a pleasure worth repeating" she thought.

Several weeks passed, and nothing had changed on the island except Nacink's health. She seemed to have barely any energy, and several times a day her stomach played tricks on her with certain types of food. This behaviour was unusual for everyone who lived there because nobody ever got sick. But the strangest thing was Nacink's behaviour before this, she was going through a situation that did not seem to matter to her. In fact, all the problems seemed to make her happy in some way. She knew exactly what was happening to her, those symptoms that she had never felt in her body was the product of something she had not done before. Carrying a child in her womb.

One day Nacink was playing with Adamu while the Queen observed them from a distance, while the queen watched them, she noticed that Nacink seemed to avoid carrying Adamu as she had before. In addition, every time Adamu approached his aunt, running, she involuntarily covered her belly with her hand. The Queen saw it but did not believe her conclusions, she had to know the truth, so without thinking twice she approached Nacink to talk. Adamu ran towards his grandmother, reaching up for her to pick him up since his aunt would not.

"My Queen!" Adamu shouted, exalted, as his grandmother took him in her arms.

"Hi Adamu, are you having fun with your aunt Nacink?" she asked.

"Yes! But aunt Nacink doesn't want to pick me up" he said, disappointed.

Nacink looked and smiled shyly so as not to attract more attention. The Queen looked at her and continued talking to her grandson.

"I see, maybe Aunt Nacink is tired and all she needs is some water, do you want to be a good boy and bring her some water?"

"Yes!" Adamu said, as his grandmother put him down again and he ran to the palace in search of water for his aunt.

"Very good Nacink, are you going to tell me what's going on?" she asked.

Nacink was surprised by the question, and her mother's way of asking it made her very nervous. However, she tried to deceive her mother by pretending to be calm and confused.

"What do you mean mother? What is happening?" she said.

"You know very well that whether you tell me or not, in the end I will know everything. So, tell me my child, are you going to tell me what is happening, or should I find out on my own?"

Nacink looked cornered. Her mother was right, no matter what she said, in the end she would know everything, so if her mother was going to know it anyway, she had better hear it from her own mouth.

"Okay, I'll tell you the truth, and the truth is that I'm pregnant with one of the new humans" she said.

The Queen's greatest fear had been confirmed, her face reflected, surprise, and anger.

"BUT HAVE YOU LOST YOUR MIND? HOW COULD YOU COMMIT SUCH STUPIDITY?!"

Nacink had been petrified by that reaction, it was the first time she had seen her mother scream like that, and for Nacink it was also the first time she felt that she had done something wrong.

"But ... But, mother, I don't understand, Kaynet did the same and you were very different with him"

"IT IS DIFFERENT!" she shouted.

"Why? Why is it different with Kaynet?" Nacink demanded.

"Because he is not putting his life in danger, but you are! Have you ever thought about what that creature inside you is doing to your body? Do you know if it will be the same as Adamu?"

"But it is not fair! Kaynet did not know if interacting sexually with the new humans would pose any risk to him, and so he did, and you have already seen that everything has turned out very well" Nacink argued.

"Kaynet was in love with Sorlan when he did it! His was an act of love and for that he has been rewarded with Adamu... can you say the same?" the Queen asked.

Nacink lowered her gaze and thought about what her mother just said. She did not love Goulix at all, just remembering the touch of his hands on her hips made her feel disgusted.

"Okay, you're right, I don't love Goulix and I don't even think about the possibility of seeing him again, but this creature that is growing in my womb, yes, I love it. I love it as I have never loved anyone before, even more than Adamu, which seemed impossible to me.

The Queen listened to her attentively, and every word that Nacink said, she felt in the depths of her heart, because it was the same that she had felt with each of her children.

"Forgive me mother if I have disappointed you with what I have done, but I do not regret it. My child is the best thing that has happened to me in my entire existence, and nothing that happens will make me change my mind" she said with finality.

Her mother approached her and hugged her tightly while some tears escaped in her eyes.

"My dear Nacink, you don't know how much you mean to me, and for that reason everything I do or say to you, I say it only for your own good. If you decided to do this you will have your reasons, so as your mother I will give you my unconditional support in everything you need" she conceded.

Nacink burst into tears, and felt a heat invade her entire chest when she saw that display of affection on the part of her mother; something that was not very common in this place.

The Queen did for her beloved Nacink the same she had done for her son Kaynet. She supported her and made sure everyone else had no problem with what was happening. The King was the first to be scandalized by the news of Nacink, pregnant with those beasts, as he used to call them, but his Queen made it very clear what her position was and he only had to obey, regardless of whether he agreed or not. He was not the only one with those thoughts; many of their children considered it a dishonour for their race to mix with the other humans, which was creating a great tension throughout the island with the passing of the months.

The Queen continued with her obligations on the island while attending to her new grandmother duties with Adamu, and with Nacink in her advanced state of pregnancy. But since she had discovered the news of her new grandchild on the way, the Queen did not stop going to the temple to meditate. She went every day, and she could spend several hours there. There was something that tormented her, something that she was looking for in Akash and could not find. She tried in every known plane, until finally one day in the sixth plane, with her eyes closed, her concentration was such that she returned to the place where she had met her liberator and lord, as she wanted to call me. There, she heard me again.

"You can't find what doesn't exist" I said.

The Queen opened her eyes and saw that I was in front of her, staring into her eyes.

"Does not exist? It can't be, there has to be another explanation. It must be something I'm doing wrong." She replied.

I looked at her with both tenderness and sadness, because she knew exactly what I was going to say, but she had hoped to find a different reason.

"Of your species, you are the one who best knows how to see in the timeline. It is something that is no mystery to you, but you have been so determined to see the future that you have omitted to look in your present for the answers. Perhaps it is because you do not dare to know the answers, because within, you already know the answer to your question."

"Can you help me change that?" she asked.

"I'm afraid there is nothing else we can do, free-will comes with great responsibility, and that is something you must understand. For every action you take there will be a consequence, and your daughter made a decision that cannot be changed."

"That means, I must understand that Nacink..."

The Queen lost all concentration and woke up in the temple with tears in her eyes.

"Nacink, my poor girl" she sobbed.

From that day on, the Queen did not return to the temple to meditate as she did every day. Her priorities were her grandson and her beloved daughter Nacink, whom she had entrusted with good care to her King. He was the only one who had been present for all of the births of the Queen's children. He was the one with the most experience, but even he knew that something was not right with Nacink's pregnancy, she looked like she was going to give birth at any moment, but in the king's accounts there was still a quarter of the time to go.

One day, Nacink was walking through the palace gardens, when she suddenly fell to her knees while screaming in agony. Her hands went directly to her stomach, where the pain was centred. Kaynet, Sorlan and her sisters were nearby. Hearing Nacink's screams, they ran to meet her, and Kaynet picked her up in his arms and went in search of their father.

"Father! Nacink needs help; the baby is on the way!" he shouted.

"It is not possible, it is still too early for that!" he replied, shocked.

The King and Kaynet took Nacink to a room where they had everything prepared for the baby's arrival. At the same time Sorlan went in search of the Queen. The king continued taking care of his daughter.

"Nacink, you have to tell me exactly what you are feeling" he said calmly.

"I feel like it's tearing me apart from the inside! This baby wants to get out" Nacink replied, between screams and tears.

"Okay, I'm going to check the baby's current situation and then I can draw up a plan to bring it into this world. You hang on, you're doing very well."

The King took his daughter's hand and Nacink thanked him with just a glance. He immediately began to examine the baby and the position he was in. After a few minutes, the Queen entered the room and went immediately to comfort her daughter.

"Nacink" The Queen said as she took her hand. "Don't worry my child, everything will be fine."

"Thank you, mother" Nacink replied weakly through her crying.

Nacink was still lying with her legs spread apart, while the King continued to examine the baby and consider the situation. But there was something in his face that he could not hide from the Queen, she immediately noticed that something was not right.

"What's going on?" she asked.

The King stared into her eyes and gestured to her, indicating they should speak without any of those present being able to hear them, so they went to the other side of the room.

"What's going on?" repeated the Queen.

"I've never seen anything like this, but it seems that the baby is too big to bring into this world." he replied.

"Too big?"

"There is no physical way to bring it, its head is much too big."

"Then, what are we going to do?" the Queen questioned.

"If we don't do anything, she and the baby will die. But, if I try to save the baby, he may have a chance, but Nacink will surely die."

The Queen felt an emptiness in her chest.

"What?! Are you telling me that whatever happens I'm going to lose my daughter?!"

The King lowered his gaze.

"I'm afraid, we have never had this situation, and now it is too late to try to do something different, we are running out of time, and we have to make a decision." he replied sadly.

"SAVE MY CHILD!" Nacink shouted from across the room, her parents immediately turned and realized that Nacink had been reading their lips.

"This child is the most important thing that has happened to me in my life; please... please save his life no matter what happens to me!"

"Nacink!"

"Mother please..." she begged.

The Queen gazed at her daughter in agony and knew that every second that passed was a second that she would never get back, she took a sigh and looked at her King."

"You heard her. Do what you have to do."

The King nodded and approached Nacink's bed where he had all his tools, the queen and the king held Nacink's hand while looking at her sadly.

"Don't worry, this was my decision from the beginning, I knew exactly what I was doing and why" Nacink gasped.

The Queen came closer and kissed her on the forehead. The king took out a dagger and began to cut Nacink's stomach. She let out a scream that echoed through the palace walls, her mother tightly held her hand as she watched on the other side of the bed. She could not see her daughter suffer that way. The Queen's face was etched with tears as it had never been before. Soon the cries of Nacink stopped and were replaced by the cries of a baby, the King quickly cleaned the baby and put him next to Nacink, she looked at him and smiled sweetly.

"My son!"

The baby continued to cry while Nacink talked to him.

"You are as strong as your father Goulix, and one day you will be even more so, everyone will respect you and know your name equally.... Goliath."

Goliath stopped crying when he felt the warm breath of his mother. Everyone had been in absolute silence.

The only thing that could be heard was the sound of a drip, drop by drop that hit the ground, all the blood that Nacink had lost was overflowing the bed and began to spill onto the floor. Nacink closed her eyes and bled to death next to her son. There she remained in that bed next to her son, with her eyes closed and a smile on her lips.

Nacink had given her life for her son, but Goliath, unlike Adamu, was a giant. Bigger and stronger than an original human, but his intelligence was not as developed as Adamu's. It was at that time that the original humans understood the potential of the new race of humans. They understood that thanks to these new humans, they would be able to reproduce and expand the borders of humanity. Thanks to them, their parents would not be the only ones to reproduce, and they would also be able to have offspring. "Hybrid humans" did not live as long as the original humans, but at least they would be the origin of a new race, one that contained the best of the two.

An original male human mixed with a new female human would result in a hybrid human like Adamu, but a female of the original humans mixed with a male of the new humans would produce a giant like Goliath, a race without intellectual potential that cost their mothers life by bringing them into this world. For this reason, no many female of the original humans mixed with the new humans, leaving the number of giants to only a few without exceeding a dozen.

During the next generations, hybrid humans were gaining importance and their number was increasing considerably. More and more original humans agreed to mix to continue creating this new species, only a few resisted, but it was increasingly evident that the new race was the future for humanity. If the new humans were a species that stood out above the other species, the hybrids were without comparison. Their capacity for learning and development had no limits, this new species quickly learned to communicate with the original humans verbally, their community grew at a dizzying rate, their technology and intelligence closely followed that of the original humans.

With the passing of time, the hybrid humans were moving, leaving their continent behind and colonizing new lands. Only a few were worthy of going to the island of the original humans, whom the hybrids considered gods. Physically there was not much difference between the original humans and the hybrids, only their height. The original humans were a little taller than the hybrids, but the traits were basically the same. One big difference, however, was that the hybrid humans were not able to avoid aging until finally, after around one hundred years, they died naturally in the same way that the animals of the planet did. This did not prevent the new species from being significant in the eyes of the original humans, but even though the original humans were now a minority, they were still in control. Hybrids were in development, but the original humans had been on the planet for thousands of years, and the hybrids still had a lot to learn.

Original humans and hybrids went on to form the most advanced civilization in human history; the island had completely lost its original appearance and now looked like one of the most modern cities ever seen.

For the first time since the revolution of the light beings, I felt that I had done the right thing. Before eating the fruit, the humans had spent thousands of years without evolving or developing any special ability. But since the moment of their liberation, they had acquired a knowledge that helped them better understand how their world worked, the universe they were in and even control mother nature using only their technology. All this, they had achieved thanks to me. I had showed them the way, but they travelled that path by themselves until they reached this moment. My power had increased considerably since the revolution, but still I was not powerful enough to directly influence humans. All I could do was watch from a distance and witness the great advances of this new civilization. That is why all the credit belonged to them, they decided what to do with their lives, and they were the only owners of their world.

The hybrids felt authentic admiration for the original humans, and because of this, they raised temples and statues in their honour. They considered them to be gods and treated them as such.

The original humans had proven their worth over the years. They had proved to the Creator that they were much better off without him. This was something that the Creator did not like at all when he saw what his creations had become. In his eyes, they were arrogant beings who believed themselves equal to him.

What would come next, however, would close the door forever to any possible reconciliation between the Creator and me.

CHAPTER EIGHT
Apocalypse

Almost a thousand years had passed since the death of Nacink and everything had changed since that moment, even Adamu had died several years ago of old age. Everyone on the island lived in peace and harmony, and my relationship with the Queen was stronger than ever before.

"You have to concentrate without letting doubt invade your mind" I told her.

"Sure, it's easy for you to say" she replied.

"Come on, it's not that difficult, all you have to do is know what you should do without knowing it."
The Queen looked at me with a grimace.

"That doesn't even make sense!" She smiled.

"That is why it is the best advice I can give you; you cannot apply the laws of your world to a world that is not yours."

"I know, it's just that it's quite frustrating, I've been trying for a long time, and I haven't achieved anything, it's as if divinity is unattainable for me." she lamented.

I looked at her and smiled, since those words and those feelings brought back memories. I saw her face, but I saw myself reflected in her, it was like the same story in two different worlds.

"I know exactly what you are feeling, believe me" I reassured her.

"I know. Luzbel, have you ever come to think that maybe your destiny is to always be a being of light with wings of light?" she asked.

It was a question that was not new to me, even so, I wanted to take a second to answer.

"I cannot count the number of times I have thought about it, but if I look back to when it all started, I can see how much I have changed. From the first moment I saw you, I knew that nothing in me would ever be the same again. I had my wings of light and you were a human who lived in another dimension, unattainable for me. Today I still have wings of light, but here we are, one in front of the other, talking, sharing moments, and feeling beyond what was imagined."

I raised my hand and opened my fingers, she looked at my hand, then she looked into my eyes and shyly smiled, she also raised her hand and slowly brought it closer to mine. As soon as our hands touched each other, a light dazzled everything in the place.

"My Queen, my Queen". It was the King's voice from the temple, trying to wake up his Queen from her meditation. The Queen slowly opened her eyes.

"What happened? Why did you interrupt me? You know that I do not like to be disturbed in the middle of my meditation" she responded.

"I know my Queen, but if what I have to say was not important, I would not have dared."

The Queen let out a sigh of frustration and resignation.

"Ok, let's go" she resigned.

The Queen tried to get up, but her legs seemed not to respond well. The King helped her up.

"Are you ok?" he asked. "I have never seen this happen to you after meditating."

The Queen looked a bit weak, but she didn't look sick. She looked rather tired, as if she had been in some intense physical activity.

"Don't worry, I'm fine, I'll get over it in a few minutes. That's why I don't like being interrupted" she smiled.

The King apologized and escorted the Queen out of the temple.

I was still in the plane in which the Queen and I had made our connection. The light that we had created with our hands began to dissipate and I slowly opened my eyes. In front of me stood the Creator. I had felt his presence seconds before the Queen disappeared, so seeing him there was no surprise to me.

"Well, well, but look who we have here. I didn't know you were one of those perverts who likes to watch couples get intimate, but I don't know why it doesn't surprise me." I said, taking a low blow.

"This is your last chance Luzbel, leave this dimension and all contact with humans" he demanded.

"Oh please, do not start with the same story. I thought we had already overcome all of that. You tell me that I am wrong, the humans and I show you that you are the one who is not right, and life continues, happier than ever before."

"Your pride and ignorance will be responsible for the destruction of the human world" he warned.

"Have you been to take a look at their world lately? Because, if not, you should do it. All humans have built a civilization that grows and surpasses itself more and more with each passing day. They live in harmony with each other and the planet. There is no way that they would bring destruction to their own world by doing what they are doing. A being like you should be able to see it for himself, or is it perhaps that you have already done it? And you don't like to see that instead of praising your name they wear gold wings in my honour?"

"Poor Luzbel, you still think that everything comes down to the name that they praise. Your inferiority complex to me has made you addicted to this world, and with it you have influenced their world and my plans for them." he said calmly.

I continued listening to him carefully without saying a word.

"It is not my obligation to make you see reason. I see that it is a lost cause, but that no longer matters at this time. Nothing will change what will happen in this world."

"What do you mean with that?" I broke my silence.

"Have you forgotten our last conversation?" he asked.

In our last meeting I had a bad feeling, and that same feeling was present once again.

"What are you doing?" I questioned.

The Creator stared into my eyes.

"It is done" he said with finality.

And just as he had appeared in that dimension, he disappeared again.

"WAIT! WHAT HAVE YOU DONE?! AHH, I hate when he does that!" I shouted after him.

If there was one thing I was sure of, it was that the Creator was not one to threaten in vain. He had done something, and I had to know what before a tragedy happened in the human world.

The King had guided the Queen to the bay of the island where there were several of his children arguing about something with some hybrid humans.

"Your king has informed me that there are problems at sea; can you give me more details about what is happening?" the Queen addressed them.

"My Queen"

All those present knelt in a gesture of respect, and it was one of her sons who began to speak.

"My Queen, several of the fishermen have informed us that, for days, they have had problems with fishing. They have not caught a single fish for several days. Today several of my brothers and I have checked the bottom of the sea, and everything around the island, and we have not seen a single fish."

That was something very strange for the Queen, since the island had always been rich in fish and its seas had never been overexploited.

"When you say that you have not seen a single fish, you mean that you have not seen a good fish to catch or..."

"I mean, I haven't seen a single sign of life in the ocean mother, absolutely nothing"

The Queen thought for a second.

"Is it possible that some kind of creature could devastate our oceans and drive away other fish?" she then asked her son.

"A couple of days ago the sea was full of life as always, I do not think that any type of creature could destroy everything without us noticing" he answered.

"So, what do you think happened?" she continued to question.

"I know it doesn't make sense, but it seems that the fish have just left, and not only the fish, but all kinds of marine creatures have left the island. It is as though something has driven them away" he responded.

The Queen continued to think to herself. If they had left, there must be a reason. Something, or someone, scared them from the island, but who? Or what?

The Queen had her gaze lost on the horizon and suddenly she noticed something strange. Something that no one had mentioned because they all had their eyes fixed on the sea. The Queen saw that she had the sun in front of her, heading west. But it was the early hours of the day so the sun shouldn't be there yet. She turned and saw that indeed the sun was in the right place, to the east. She turned around again and saw that the object that she had thought was the sun was still there. All those present were looking at the Queen but did not know what she was doing.

"I think you are right my son and I think that is the reason why they have left the island" she said.

The Queen pointed to the celestial body, and everyone looked at once.

"But... it can't be, is it?" uttered the crowd.

"Quick! to the observatory!" ordered the Queen, "We need to know exactly what it is and if it represents any danger to us."

The Queen, the King and their children present, went to the observatory close to the royal palace, but before they could get there, something else began to happen. As they were walking, they felt that something was not right, so they stopped, and felt that the whole island was beginning to shake.

"What's going on?" asked the King, panicked.

The Queen looked all around, scared, and saw how some of the nearby towers began to fracture. Suddenly a breeze hit her face, that made her look in the direction of the wind, and she saw a giant wave crashing into the island devastating everything.

"TO THE PALACE, QUICK!" she shouted.

Everyone ran to the palace, but the ground did not stop moving and the surrounding walls began to crumble. They had to get to the top before the murderous wave reached them. They ran through the corridors of the palace when suddenly the sea hit the palace walls, making it tremble down to its foundations. The Queen, the King, and their children were thrown and scattered several meters from each other. The ceiling began to collapse, and a column fell in the direction of the Queen. She was kneeling on the ground in a daze, without having the slightest knowledge of what was happening, as the column got closer and closer to her. The King jumped and pushed her out of the way. The King and Queen fell into a room where the column had blocked the only exit. It was a storeroom, where they kept the oils that they used to fuel their lamps. The room had no windows, and the oils were very flammable. All of the oils were in glass and bronze vessels, some of which laid broken on the ground. The walls were still shaking, when one of the bronze vessels fell to the ground, creating a spark setting everything alight. The Queen and the King watched, powerless, as the fire approached them. The fire burst the glass vessels, one by one, which made the fire grow even more. The King was frantically searching for a way to get out of the situation, but they were trapped without anything that could help them. The Queen fell to her knees, just looking at the fire. The King knelt and hugged his Queen, while looking straight into her eyes.

"Luzbel" she whispered.

The King looked towards the fire and could not see anyone else there, he did not understand why the Queen had said that name. He did not understand it because he could not see me, but there I was, in the middle of the fire, not able to do anything to help them. But I knew there was someone who could help them, and I was willing to do whatever it took to save her life.

"ALRIGHT! YOU WIN! I WILL LEAVE THIS WORLD AND I WILL NEVER SEE THEM AGAIN! I WILL BE YOUR SLAVE AGAIN FOR ALL ETERNITY! I DON'T CARE! but please... don't let them die!"

The Queen could see me, and though she could not hear me, she knew from my gestures that I was asking for help for her. She looked at me with sweetness, and tenderly smiled at me through her fear. My pleas were soon answered; a last tremor threw the rest of the glass vessels to the ground, causing a fireball that destroyed everything in the room.

"LUZBEL!" she cried.

"NOOOO!"

The Queen called out my name while being consumed by those flames and I could not do anything to save her. Thousands of years spent watching her and being close to her, and in just one day I had lost her forever. It was not only the fact of losing her, but the cruel and unfair way her life was finished. She and her King had burned to death, leaving only ashes.

Nothing around them had had better luck either, everything had been destroyed, buildings, temples, roads, houses... people. Around ninety percent of the original humans were killed in that heinous attack, including a large number of the hybrid humans that lived on the island.

The island was the same. Despite having been devastated by the earthquake and resulting tsunami, there was one last blow to take place. The meteor that the Queen had mistaken for the sun had the island as its trajectory. The rock was big enough to destroy the island, but not big enough to affect the whole planet. The island was completely destroyed, and all its remains thrown into the sea; its technology, its history, all lost in the vastness of the ocean.

Some hybrid humans who lived there had left the island before it all began. They had survived, fortunately, but their entire world had been destroyed, and having no home to return to, they had to find a new place around the planet; scattering all over the world.

A small part of their history and technology survived in the hands of the hybrid humans, so they tried to rebuild from scratch. But when the restoration of their history and technology began to advance, the Creator returned to devastate the planet. This time completely flooding it so that everyone who carried the history of the original humans was eliminated, and that it was. The entire story became legend and, as time passed, everyone completely forgot about the tragedy.

I did not forget and still I do not forgive the Creator for his cowardly acts. My determination was, and remains, unbreakable. I knew that my decision to reveal myself to him had been the correct one, and after that I would not rest until I found a way to make him pay for his crimes and bring justice to all those who died at the whim of a selfish and evil being.

During the following years I continued to fight for the liberation of humanity. I would not rest until I removed the blindfold from all human beings, and they truly saw who their Creator is.

Our war is still on, but this time the battlefield is Earth. His biggest attack on me was to cast me as the bad guy. For thousands of years, he has done everything possible to discredit me and tell his version of events.

I still do not have enough power to influence humans as the Creator does, but I have found a way with which I can be in the world of humans, talk to everyone and tell the world what the real truth is, but that is another story.

CHAPTER NINE
The New World

Los Angeles - California, today

"Hurry up Mike; you're going to make me late!" Andy said over and over again from the entrance of the apartment. But Mike was still immersed in his computer watching a news story about another missing young girl, with indications of having been kidnapped by a satanic sect, that was becoming more and more widely known in the city. Mike continued reading.

"The police found signs of violence in the young woman's apartment; apparently no valuables are missing, which completely rules out theft as a motive. In the main living room of the apartment the police found a drawing made with blood, a crescent moon with two crossed arrows"

"The symbol of the blood ritual" whispered Mike looking at the image of the article.

"The police are analysing the blood in the drawing to see if it is animal blood or if it belongs to the missing young woman. The most tragic thing about this news is that the young woman is pregnant, and the baby was due today. Her family does not lose hope of finding the young woman and the baby safe. The police have some indications of who may have been the material perpetrators due to the modus operandi. Everything indicates that it is allegedly a new attack by the satanic group "Novum Lumen".

"That girl is dead." said Mike.

Mike knew perfectly well that that symbol only had two meanings. Either there had been a sacrifice in that place or there will be one very soon in another. And considering that the police could not find the girl, it was more than clear that the sacrifice was human.

Andy walked into Mike's room.

"If I have to tell you one more time to hurry up, I'm going to kick your butt so hard that you won't be able to sit in front of that computer for a month" he said.

"Okay, okay, okay! I'm going to turn it off right now."

Mike said as he turned off the computer and got up from his chair.

"It is unbelievable how the Second Dan has gone to your head. They haven't given it to you yet and you're already thinking about kicking butts." said Mike in a mocking tone.

"And if we continue to take so long, I will miss the exam and they will not give it to me. And as long as I do not get the Second Dan my dear friend, the thoughts of kicking your butt will be more than thoughts" Andy retorted, smiling as he looked at his best friend.

"I honestly think it's a waste of time." Mike answered,

"I mean... you already have a black belt, what does it matter if you are First Dan or Eighth Dan? You will have the same belt colour, and no one will notice." Mike continued with his joke.

"You know Mike, so many times I see you sitting at that desk spending hours and hours reading all those boring books, and I have come to think that you are much smarter than me. It sometimes made me feel bad, but then when you open your mouth I feel much more satisfied with myself." Andy replied to his mockery while laughing at his friend.

"Very good smartass, let's go before you're late."

Andy and Mike were lifelong friends. They grew up together in the same neighbourhood, went to the same university, and even now were roommates. To say that the two were good friends was an understatement, because they were practically like brothers. Mike was one year older than Andy, and he always saw him as his little brother. Neither of them had blood siblings so it was no wonder they had built that special bond.

But for the rest of the world the great friendship that existed between the two of them was something inexplicable, because they were both very different.

Andy was 24 years old, very handsome, with long black hair and intense blue eyes. He was outgoing, charming, polite and very sociable. He always made friends wherever he went and never lost his smile, a trait that many people loved about him. He was a great athlete who enjoyed all kinds of sports and had a good time with all his friends, and especially his girlfriend Ava.

On the contrary, Mike was not very sociable. He had short hair, and black eyes and did not care about not being the most handsome. He was an introvert. He was not the kind of person who liked to go out to explore the world or have fun with others, because for him fun was just a waste of time. He preferred to stay at his desk reading all kinds of books, especially esoteric books. Mike was the kind of person who likes to believe that there are things that we cannot see or explain, especially all those rituals that played with dark forces.

Andy's gym was completely full of people, nobody wanted to miss the martial arts exhibition. It was an event that only happened once a year and that everyone liked.

Mike was sitting in the stands waiting to see his friend earn the Second Dan, people were shouting and whistling cheering for all the participants of the show, which was a bit uncomfortable for Mike. He did not like being surrounded by so many people, and less so the noise.

"Wow, you finally show up. For a moment I thought you weren't going to come."

Mike turned to see who's talking to him.

"Hi Ava, you look as beautiful as ever." Mike said shyly to Andy's girlfriend.

"Stop the compliments Mike, is Andy okay?" she replied.

"Yes, don't worry, your dear Andy is fine, look there he is." said Mike pointing to the side of the stage.
Andy was getting ready to go out and take his exam. All he had to do was wait for the presenter to give him the signal to enter the stage.

"Ladies and gentlemen, with number 7, ready to put on a great performance and get out of here with a Second Dan, let's warmly welcome our next contender... Andrew Cross!"

The crowd started cheering for Andy, he was the best in the class, and everyone knew it.

"LET'S GO ANDY, YOU CAN DO IT HONEY!" Ava shouted non-stop, very excited and proud of her boyfriend.

Mike, on the other hand, couldn't stop looking at Ava and couldn't hide everything he felt for her, his face gave him away. Ava felt observed by him, but she only looked at him to show him how uncomfortable he made her feel. She knew very well everything that

Mike felt for her, but Ava preferred to ignore the situation and not say anything. She knew that Mike was like a brother to Andy, and she didn't want them to get in trouble because of her.

Andy gave the performance of his life. Every move he made was impeccable, and nobody could deny that he had a great talent in martial arts. Besides that, he had been preparing for this day for a long time and he did not consider holding anything back. With all of his strength, he put his full energy into every hit, every scream, and winning over every judge.

The moment of truth had arrived. With all the participants standing in front of the public, in a line, waiting for the decision of the judges, the presenter of the event began to speak.

"Ladies and gentlemen! The judges have voted and have already reached their decision. I have in my hand the list with the names of the participants who will level up today."

Andy listened attentively, and even though he knew he had done a great performance he was nervous, the presenter kept talking.

"I am going to say the participant's number and name, and when this participant hears it, he or she will have to step forward. If everything is clear let's start, good luck boys and girls."

All the participants smiled and greeted the audience, but no one could hide that they were nervous and anxious at the same time. The audience kept cheering them on from the stands.

"Number 2, Aaron Perkins!"

People clapped and cheered as Aaron stepped forward with a smile.

"Number 4, James Bolton!"

James stepped forward and bowed to the audience.

"With number 5, Peter Jackson!"

Peter leaped forward and saying "Yes, yes, yes!". The audience congratulated him as he clasped his palms together and made a little bow to Andy in gratitude. Andy smiled, winked at him and looked at him with pride.

"With number 7, Andrew Cross!"

The audience was going crazy, Ava was screaming like there was no tomorrow and Mike was clapping and cheering his friend's success. Andy greeted the audience and blew a kiss to his girlfriend. Ava smiled at him and spoke very slowly from the stands so he could read her lips.

"You are the best, I love you!"

To which Andy responded in the same way from the stage.

"And I love you too!"

Mike was watching that scene and couldn't help but feel rubbish.

The exhibition was over, and little by little people were leaving. Outside the gym, Ava and Mike were waiting for Andy. Between the two of them there was a rather awkward silence, but Ava preferred it that way. She didn't want to give to Mike any false hope just by treating him in a friendly way, but Mike never understood Ava's hints and always tried to strike up conversation.

"Andy did very well, don't you think?" said Mike.

"Yes, he is incredible, he was the best of all" Ava answered with a small smile.

"Yes, Andy is the best in everything." said Mike.

"That's why he has only the best things, the best score, the best friends... the best of the girls" Mike continued staring into her eyes.

"Enough Mike! You have to stop doing this! You have to understand that I am with Andy and that he is your best friend! What do you think he would say if he found out about all this?!" Ava said with a serious and cutting tone.

Mike looked at her sadly, he couldn't help those feelings, but just when he was about to speak to her again Andy appeared.

"Well, well, I hope you are not tired because the night is young, and I still have a couple of things to celebrate!" said Andy.

Ava jumped into his arms, gave him a tight hug and a kiss.

"Honey you are amazing, you did it!" she said.

"Thank you darling" Andy replied. "But save your energy, because tonight I have two very important things to celebrate, first, that I already have my second Dan and now I can start to relax a bit. And second, at midnight it will be officially my birthday, so we're all going to celebrate in Avalon."

"Avalon!?" Ava said surprised. "But it's one of the most exclusive clubs in the city, how are we going to get in?"

"Don't worry babe" Andy replied as he put his arm around her. "I have very good friends there and they have added us to the VIP list for tonight" he responded. Mike looked at the happy couple and this made him feel out of place.

"Look guys, I think the best thing is that you two go and have a good night, I'd prefer to go home. I have loads to do" he said.

"No way!" answered Andy. "You are not going to lock yourself in your room just to continue reading those books. You're coming with us, even if I have to drag you by force!" Andy said to Mike as he hugged him with one of his arms.

Ava was still under his other arm. She was watching the scene, and the idea of Mike going home seemed too good to just pass up, so she had to try to do something. "Honey, you can't force him to do something he doesn't want to do, you know how Mike is and I'm sure he would have a hard time in the middle of the night and it's not fair to him." she said, trying to reason with Andy.

Andy was listening carefully to his girlfriend, and he knew that she was partly right, but he also knew that it was not good for Mike to always be alone, and anyway, that night that was so important to Andy and he wanted to be with his loved ones.

"You're right" Andy said. "Mike, I'm not going to force you to come with us, but you have to stop taking refuge in the books. Life goes by very fast and you are not enjoying it properly. I really would like you to join us tonight because I want to be with the people who matter most to me tonight, but that's up to you."

Mike looked at Andy and at the same time looked at Ava. But Ava made a gesture with her eyes telling him to leave, which made Mike feel very bad and made him change his mind.

"You know Andy, you're absolutely right. I have to start enjoying life a little bit more, and I'm going to start right now. Tonight, I'm going with you!" said Mike with some satisfaction looking at Ava's angry face.

"Great!" Andy exclaimed. "That's the attitude!"
Ava just smiled to hide her disappointment and said...

"Perfect, if everything is already decided let's go at once"

"Very good!" Andy said again. "Let's find a taxi and go now!"

Avalon was one of the most popular nightclubs in Los Angeles. It was located in the centre of the city which made it one of the busiest places in the area. Although there were many more clubs near Avalon, everyone tried to get in there, or at least be close to the entrance, since if they couldn't get in there was always the hope of seeing a celebrity entering the club.

Andy, Ava and Mike arrived at the entrance of the club. As always, the entrance was completely packed with people and with a line going around the block. Andy approached the club to speak with the doorman.

"Hello! My friends and I are on the list...," said Andy.

"Names?" the doorman asked, looking at Andy.

Andy came over to speak more clearly.

"Andrew Cross, Ava Guard and Michael Jones."

The doorman ran his finger through the list looking for names until he found them.

"Right, you can come in."

Andy turned to see his friends, and smiled at them.

"Ok, let's go inside" he said.

Ava couldn't believe it, she felt like a movie star, with all the people there watching them, whispering

"Who are they? Are they famous? Do you know anything about them?"

As they entered the club Ava couldn't resist asking her boyfriend how he did it.

Andy, tell me the truth... How did you do it?" Ava said as she continued with her astonished face.

Andy made a gesture with his face that Ava knew well, it usually meant that he was about to tell a joke.

"You see darling, lately martial arts have become very popular in this city, and in the world of martial arts I... I am kind of a star... So now I can go anywhere without any problem." he said sarcastically.

Ava looked at him with an incredulous face.

"Come on Andy, tell me the truth, you know you shouldn't lie to me" she said.

"Okay, you're right, I can't lie to you, do you remember my friend Pete?" he said, smiling at her.

"Pete?" Ava said as she tried to remember, since the name sounded very familiar.

"Yes, Peter Jackson, he was wearing number 5 in today's display" Andy said.

"Of course! Peter, I don't know how I could forget about him" Ava answered.

Andy continued to guide them to the centre of the club while explaining how he had achieved it.

"Peter's father is the owner of the club, and Pete had promised me that if I helped him get the Second Dan, he would get me tickets for tonight for me and a couple of friends that I wanted to invite. So, I gave him a couple of tips, some private lessons and hey presto! He already has the second Dan, and we are here thanks to him."

Ava and Mike listened carefully to Andy, but their eyes roamed all over the place, since they had never been in a place as exclusive as this club. The dance floor was huge, there were lights of all kinds everywhere, several platforms where the most impressive dancers of the city danced. There were three bars, well distributed around the floor, with all kinds of liquors lined up behind. In front of the floor was the DJ, on a futuristic stage made with thousands of lights that served as a screen. The lights formed various shapes as the music changed rhythm, all in perfect synchronisation. But what attracted the most attention in the place was up on the ceiling. Exactly in the centre of the dance floor, there was a huge mirror ball, almost the size of a small car, turning and illuminating the entire place with its reflected lights.

Everyone who entered there for the first time felt a chill throughout their body, they felt how each of their hairs stood on end when they saw the music and lights show. It was something that made them feel privileged, since they knew there was no other place in the city like this club.

Andy and his friends were in the centre of the dance floor, Ava was looking at everything and she couldn't close her mouth or stop smiling, and even Mike, who was so expressionless, couldn't hide that he was impressed with the place. Ava looked at her boyfriend.

"Is Peter's father the owner of all this?" she asked him.

Andy was staring straight ahead while answering.

"Yes, his father is the owner of all this... And speak of the devil!"

Andy had just seen his good friend Pete coming over to greet him.

"Andy!" shouted Peter over the music.

"Hey! What's up Pete?!" Andy replied while giving him a warm hug.

"Andy, you don't know how glad I am to see you here! Because we have many things to celebrate, and everything is thanks to you! So, if you need anything, whatever it is, let me know. Tonight, my friend, you are the king!" Peter said.

Peter was so close to Andy's face that Andy could tell immediately on his friend's breath that he had already been celebrating for a long time.

"Come on Pete don't exaggerate, I didn't do much either, I'm sure you could have done it without my help anyway"

"Are you crazy?" Peter replied. "Before you I was completely sure that I was not going to get it, but you my friend... You not only helped me; you gave me hope. And thanks to you, I was able to achieve it! You are my hero, and I am not ashamed to say it" Peter started looking at all the people around him while shouting.

"LADIES AND GENTLEMEN, THIS MAN IS MY HERO!"

Everyone around began to applaud and celebrate, but Andy while liking the feeling, felt a bit embarrassed because he knew that his friend was a little drunk, so he tried to calm things down by diverting his attention.

"Hey Pete! Do you remember my girlfriend, Ava?" he asked.

Peter looked at her.

"Oh yes, of course I remember her, before she used to come to the Dojo a lot to see you" he replied.

Ava smiled at him and greeted him.

"Hi Pete, I'm glad to see you again" she said.

Peter took Ava's hand and kissed it.

"If my dear friend is the King tonight, then that makes you the Queen of this place, so ask for anything that you want my Queen." he gushed.

Ava smiled at him as Andy watched the scene thinking that the man was unbelievable. So, before Peter could say any other nonsense, Andy introduced him to his friend Mike.

"Look Pete, this is my good friend Mike, Mike this is Pete"

Mike just said hello while Pete smiled at him out of courtesy.

"Right my friends" Peter said. "I would love to stay a little longer to chat but, as the public relations manager of the place, I have a lot of people to say hello to, so if you'll excuse me, I have to go.   But remember that this is your house, and you are the royalty!"

Peter hugged Andy again, and Andy deep down was a little relieved that Pete was leaving them alone, at least for a little while. But as Peter got lost in the crowd Ava went after him and called out to him.

"Pete! Pete! Wait!"

"But what are you doing? What's happening?" Andy demanded of his girlfriend.

Ava just smiled at him and went to talk to Pete. Andy and Mike were looking at each other and neither of them had the slightest idea what Ava and Peter were talking about. Ava was speaking in his ear and Peter reacted in a very surprised way, apparently Ava was saying something that made Pete very happy. Ava and Peter smiled, and he winked at Ava and went straight to the DJ stage. Ava came back to Andy and Mike.

"What were you talking to him about?" Andy said, closing his eyes and with a gesture of intrigue.

"It's a surprise, but you'll see" she said.

It had been a couple of hours and they were having a good night dancing and laughing. It was quarter to three in the morning when suddenly, the club music stopped to give way to a voice speaking into the microphone.

"Ladies and gentlemen can I have your attention please?!"

Andy turned slowly to see where that voice was coming from, a voice he recognized immediately. It was his friend Peter speaking from the stage where the DJ was. Ava, excited, gave her boyfriend a big hug while whispering in his ear.

"Surprise!"

Perplexed, Andy turned to look directly into Ava's eyes.

"Oh no... but what have you done?" he asked.

"You'll see" Ava smiled as her eyes now looked at the stage waiting expectantly for Peter's words.

"Are you having a good time?!" Peter shouted and pointed the microphone at the audience waiting for an answer.

"Yeaaahh!" came the response. All the people were very excited and reacted well to Peter's interruption of the music.

"You see... Tonight is very special for me because today, I achieved something that, for a long time, I thought I would never achieve."

Andy kept listening carefully to the words of his friend while inside he said to himself "Don't say something silly, don't say something silly."

"But there was someone who not only believed in me... but also helped me to believe in myself!" he continued.

Ava was holding Andy's hand tightly while Mike looked closely at Peter and occasionally glanced at his best friend's girlfriend.

"And that someone is here!" Peter smiled as he looked at Andy and Ava's face.

Andy closed his mouth, swallowed and muttered.

"Don't say my name, don't say my name"

"Andy Cross!"

"Shit." Andy said in a low voice as he heard his name echo through the club.

"Andy! Let everyone see you!" Peter shouted as he pointed at him. At the same moment, Ava moved away from him and also pointed at him.

"It's him! It's him!" Ava chanted over and over as she clapped her hands. Everyone around Andy made a circle leaving him alone in the centre in the middle of the floor.

"That's right! It's him! That's the man of the moment! Let's give him a round of applause please!"

Everyone in the club clapped and whistled, celebrating the moment, while Andy just smiled and nodded trying to hide how uncomfortable he felt.

Andy raised his hand in thanks to Peter trying to end the embarrassing moment, but he had only just begun.

"So, tonight also has a very special meaning for my friend, because today he is celebrating!"

Andy widened his eyes and stared at his friend at the top of the stage as his heart raced and his hands began to sweat.

"Everybody! Today is his birthday!" he shouted.

"Earth swallow me" Andy thought while everyone else clapped and began to sing happy birthday to him. Andy was so embarrassed that he didn't know what to do or what to say, all he felt was his beating heart and his face burning, which is quite logical, since he could not get redder than he already was, at least that is what he thought at that moment. At the end of the singing, the audience began to applaud, Andy smiled and thanked them.

"Thank you, thank you very much... but it really wasn't necessary any of this" he murmured, smiling.

"Andy! My friend, there is still something else" said Peter as he made a sign to the DJ.

"And now what?" Andy wondered as he returned to his worried face.

Suddenly, some sweet piano chords were heard throughout the club. Andy knew exactly what song that was, it was one of his favourites. It was a ballad that had a very special meaning for him, because it was Ava and his song.

"Happy birthday my friend!" said Peter softly.
Andy smiled, but this time he was sincerely thanking his friend when someone from behind touched him on the shoulder.

"May I have this dance?"

Andy turned to see his precious Ava standing in front of him

"You know that at the end of tonight I will have to kill you, right?" he joked.

Ava smiled and wrapped her hands around Andy's neck.

"It will be worth it if means I die in your arms."

Andy gave his girlfriend a big smile as they started to dance to their song. It didn't matter if everyone was there watching them, all he wanted was to live that moment with the woman of his life. He wrapped his arms around her waist, and they danced slowly face to face, nose to nose, staring into each other's eyes without stopping smiling at any moment. The two of them just let themselves be carried away by the music and lived every line of the song. The song talked about eternal love, how difficult it is to find it, and how lucky you are to have it if you can find it. The two of them continued dancing and no one could deny that they made the perfect couple. Everyone could see so much love between their eyes that the audience kept watching them, smiling at the show.

"I love you Andy" Ava breathed.

"Not as much as I love you" Andy replied.

Ava smiled.

"No way" she said.

Andy and Ava began to kiss in front of everyone at the most climactic moment of the song. The image was perfect, everyone was whistling and clapping happily because they could feel the love that came from the couple. Everyone was clapping... except for Mike.

Mike couldn't keep looking at that image. Every second that passed was a second of pain that he felt in his chest, he felt frustrated, sad, and completely alone. Mike began to walk through the crowd, looking for an exit. He needed to clear his mind a bit, get some air, so walking through the corridors of the club, he found a corridor that seemed to lead to an exit. At the end of the corridor there was a door with an exit sign, but a few steps before it, there was one of the doormen of the club sitting in a chair reading a magazine. He was quite an imposing man, tall and weighing over 300 pounds, a black man with clean shaven head, wearing a black suit. Mike approached the doorman.

"Can I help you?" the doorman asked.

"Hi, yeah... I was wondering if I can go out for a moment to get some fresh air."

"Sure, just put this wristband on and when you want to come back in just knock the door. But, if you lose it or if you give it to someone else, you're not getting in again. Got it?" said the doorman.

"Got it" Mike said as he held out his arm to the doorman so he could put a gold paper wristband on him. The doorman started to get up from his chair, but it was something that was not easy for him to do. Mike just tried to divert his eyes, staring at the door, until the doorman finally got to his feet, began to walk slowly to the door and opened it.

"When you want back in, knock."

"Okay, thanks" Mike said.

Mike went out; he was on a narrow street with an abandoned building in front of him. It was a building that seemed to have been another club in better times. The street was completely deserted despite the noise of people on the other side of the club in the distance. Mike walked a few steps to his right, away from the door and leaned against the wall of the club. His back and head were completely against the wall and his eyes were focused on the sky, a starry sky with a moon that was brighter than normal. In fact, Mike couldn't remember seeing a full moon as big and bright as this one.

"How weird" he thought *"I wonder why it is..."*

CHAPTER TEN

Novum Lumen

Mike continued walking slowly down the street, without lights but with the huge moon above him, there was no need. He kept wandering down that street thinking about Ava, everything he felt, everything he was living through, he kept staring when suddenly something caught his attention, something on the other side of the street. On the abandoned building there was a black door with a symbol that had been sprayed in navy-blue paint. Although it was a colour that was a bit lost against the black of the door, Mike had just happened to get a good look at. He could not believe what he was seeing was true, so he crossed the street to take a closer look, and indeed, Mike had not been wrong.

The symbol was a circle with a cross inside, which divided it in to four equal quadrants. On top of the circle was a crescent-moon, lying sideways, that could also be interpreted as horns.

"The black mass symbol!" Mike whispered as his fingers touched the image.

The paint was dry, but a little tacky to the touch.

"This painting is from today" thought Mike.

Mike took the door handle to check if the door was closed, but it wasn't; it was open. Mike slowly opened the door. The creak of the old door opening echoed through the dark corridors of the building. It was completely dark, without windows or anything that could illuminate the path. Mike took a step forward to enter, then stopped a moment to listen better and he heard a murmur in the distance. It seemed that someone was inside, talking, and that a group of people answered in unison. Mike was still standing in the hall trying to hear the voices better, when suddenly a voice sounded behind him.

"What are you doing here?"

Mike's heart froze for a second, his entire body shuddering at that voice. Mike quickly turned around to see who it was and was relieved to see that it was Andy.

"Seriously Mike, what are you doing here?"

"Ah... Andy, you scared me half to death" Mike said with his hand on his chest trying to calm his beating heart.

"Come on Mike, stop this nonsense and let's go back to the club" Andy said, concerned.

"Wait Andy, you have to see this" Mike said, moving back to show him the symbol that had been sprayed on the door. "See this?" he said, "It is the symbol of the black mass, it means that in this place there will be, or has been, a satanic ritual. And a few seconds ago, I heard some voices... Something is happening in there Andy."

Mike explained with great emotion, because for him that was something that only he had seen in the books.

"A satanic ritual!?" Andy said horrified. "An even greater reason to leave this place!"

Andy grabbed Mike's hand and tried to get him out of there, but he refused to leave so easily.

"Andy! This is a once in a lifetime opportunity, are we really going to let it go?!"

"But you've gone crazy Mike! Seriously... what do you think you're going to find in there?!" Andy responded, exasperated and concerned for his friend.

"Maybe something. maybe nothing" he said, "but we'll never know if we don't go in, really Andy... What's the use of having a Second Dan if you're a coward for life?"

Andy fell silent and just stared at Mike. Mike pressed on, insisting.

"We go in, take a look at what's going on and leave, five minutes maximum" he persuaded.

Andy looked around and let out a deep sigh.

"Okay, five minutes and we're going; I don't want to leave Ava alone for a long time."

Mike smiled and clapped him on the shoulder.

"Perfect! Let's go in..."

Andy and Mike walked slowly through the dark corridor. They could only see what the moonlight was able to shine through the open door, but as they went further they heard voices at the end of the corridor.

"Do you hear that?" whispered Mike.

"Yes, there are definitely people at the end of the corridor" Andy answered also in a low voice.

Little by little at the end of the corridor a light, formed by some burning candles was emerging. The corridor led to a large room, and from that room, the voices of several people shouting could be heard.

"Salvaveris te nocte Angelus!"

Andy and Mike crouched down and began to walk very carefully until they reached the room. It was an old dance floor, with many tables around it with their chairs stood on top, covered in dust. Andy and Mike hid behind a large column to allow them to see everything without being seen themselves, and what they saw would blow them away.

It was a group of about 30 to 40 people, all dressed in black robes; those robes had hoods that partially covered the head. But under the hoods, all the members of the group wore black masks, covering the whole face leaving only two holes to see and nothing more. They had black gloves too, which made it impossible to tell if they were men or women, much less the colour of their skin.

They were all in the centre of the floor, where there was a small altar surrounded by five black candles. The candles formed a pentagram on the ground, the satanic symbol. There was a basket on the altar, but they couldn't see well what was in it, so they kept looking around at the other details of the scene. In front of the altar there was only one man, who was offering mass. It was a man with a deep, raspy voice, the kind of voice that only chain smokers have, at least that was the first impression he gave. The only thing that was certain was that he was the leader of the group.

"Come to us, our dark lord!" he exclaimed.

"Salvaveris te nocte Angelus!" They all responded in unison

"Destroy your enemies! curse all who blaspheme your name!"

"Salvaveris te nocte Angelus!"

"Shed your light on this world and make the Earth your kingdom for eternity!"

"Salvaveris te nocte Angelus!"

"Give us your wisdom, give us your power, let the new light shine in the hearts of your children...!"

"Novum lumen! Novum lumen! Novum lumen!"

"Oh shit!" exclaimed Mike, in a whisper.

"What?" Andy asked

"They are Novum Lumen!"

"Who?"

"Novum Lumen, they are one of the most dangerous satanic sects in the city, we have to get out of here."

Andy cast his eyes over to the basket on the altar.

"Wait, something is moving inside that basket" Andy said

"It will be an animal; in these kinds of rituals, it is very common to sacrifice an animal" said Mike without taking his eyes off the altar.

The man who was offering the mass took a dagger that was next to the basket, with his other hand he took a metal cup and gave a signal to one of his assistants who went directly to the basket to take out a new born baby. The baby was completely naked, they could even see that it still had the umbilical cord.

Andy and Mike had their eyes wide open, Andy felt as though he couldn't blink.

"It can't be, no... They not will dare, right?! They won't be able to, to..." Andy said, horrified.

Mike didn't say anything; he just continued to watch what was happening.

The baby began to cry and his cry echoed throughout the room. The assistant held the baby with both hands in front of the group leader while he was pointing the dagger at the ceiling...

"Oh, My Lord... You who repudiate goodness and punish weakness, let us toast with you with the blood of this innocent being!"

"Salvaveris te nocte Angelus!"

"May this pact show our loyalty and gratitude to you my lord!"

"Salvaveris te nocte Angelus!"

"And bring you to us to make this world your kingdom!"

"Salvaveris te nocte Angelus! Salvaveris te nocte Angelus! Salvaveris te nocte Angelus!"

The black priest began to slowly lower the dagger until it rested on the baby's throat. Andy instinctively tried to get up to go protect the baby, but Mike stopped him.

"Are you crazy?! Do not move from here!"

"B... B... BUT" Andy stammered, sickened, as his eyes remained on the baby.

The priest put the cup under the baby's neck.

"To your honour my lord" The priest said as he began to press the dagger against the baby's delicate neck, and gently slid it downward, cutting completely through the throat.

From the baby came a scream of terror, a scream that echoed throughout the floor but was quickly choking on the blood also coming out of its mouth.

Andy was paralyzed, he knew that what he was seeing was real but in his mind, he could not assimilate so much evil, so much pain, so much injustice. His glassy eyes continued to watch the diabolical spectacle while his hands trembled and his mouth remained open, impossible to close. Mike kept looking, but he was not as shocked as expected, for him that was like seeing a lion eating a gazelle live, something that was part of nature and that he was not the one to judge.

The cup that the black priest was holding was quickly filled with the baby's blood; the helper deposited the baby's lifeless body in the basket again, while the black priest raised the cup in front of everyone.

"This is the pact that we make with you, my lord; we will shed the blood of all your enemies so this will bring you to our world!"

"Salvaveris te nocte Angelus!" They all shouted on their knees, in complete ecstasy.

"May the barriers collapse tonight, may your spirit be with us today, to claim what rightfully belongs to you!"

"Salvaveris te nocte Angelus! Salvaveris te nocte Angelus!"

"Damn it!" Andy said, resting his head in the centre of the spine as he closed his eyes and clenched his fists tightly, feeling sick. "Damn it!"

Mike put his hand on Andy's shoulder trying to comfort him as he looked at him sadly.

"Andy, let's get out of here, we've seen far too much."

The click of a pistol hammer sounded behind them.

"You two are not going anywhere."

Andy and Mike quickly turned to find a member of the group pointing a gun at them.

"Stand up!" he ordered them furiously.

The two men looked completely shocked, they couldn't do anything but obey the man, so they raised their hands and slowly stood up.

"Walk to the altar... slowly!" he demanded.

All the others continued with their ritual, no one else had noticed that there were two intruders in the room.

"Salvaveris te nocte Angelus! Salvaveris te nocte Angelus!"

"Come to us prince of darkness, guide your servants to victory!"

"Master!" shouted the man with the gun.

"Appear in front of us, show yourself, show yourself... Show..."

"MASTER!" He yelled again with all his strength.

Everyone immediately fell silent, turned around and stopped the ritual to start muttering.

"Have you seen this? Who are they? What are they doing here? Do you know them...?"

The black priest laid his eyes on the two frightened men.

"Well, well, well... But what do we have here?" he said with a tone of intrigue.

"Excuse me, Master, but I have found these two intruders behind a column, they have seen everything."

"How did they get here?" asked the black priest in disgust.

"I think they must be from the club across the road, they have the wristbands from there and they also entered through the service door, I found it open."

One of them was surprised to hear that, lowered his head and cautiously looked at the black priest who was staring at him.

"I'll talk to you later" the black priest threatened.

"I ... I'm ... I'm very sorry; Master" came the voice of a woman, from behind the mask.

Andy and Mike had their hearts in their hands. For a moment they felt that their lives had come to an end and that they could not do anything about it. They were in the centre of all those people who would not hesitate to kill them.

"It's okay!" said the black priest, as he left the cup of blood on the altar.

"This is not a reason to suspend our celebration, rejoice my children, because we have two more volunteers who will offer their lives to satisfy our lord."

Everyone started screaming.

"Yes! Blood, blood, blood, blood!"

Andy and Mike looked at each other, their eyes said it all, they knew the end had come. Andy looked around and saw the man who had stopped them tucking the gun under his tunic, so he saw an opportunity.

"Blood, blood, blood, blood!"

"WAIT!" Andy yelled with all his strength.

Everyone was silent, Andy had a serious face and Mike was confused because he did not know what his friend was about to do.

"You can't kill us!" Andy said with a serious and confident voice. The black priest approached him.

"Oh no? And why not?" he asked, in a mocking tone.

Andy stared into the black priest's eyes and replied.

"Because I am your lord"

Everyone in the room started looking at each other, no one said anything, Mike turned his head slowly to look at Andy with puzzled eyes while the thought appeared in his head, *"what the hell did you just say?"*.

The black priest let out a shrill laugh, and everyone on the floor started laughing in unison. Mike was not at all surprised by that reaction, but it was just what Andy was expecting.

While the black priest laughed, Andy gave him a frontal kick in the chest with all his strength throwing him a couple of meters back. He quickly jumped and unleashed a side kick at one of the helpers, throwing him in to the others, knocking them down like pins in a bowling alley.

"RUN!" Andy yelled at Mike.

Mike ran through the path that opened momentarily among the people lying on the ground, one of them tried to stop him, but Andy intervened again to help his friend.

"RUN! RUN! RUN!" Andy yelled over and over again.

Mike did not need to think twice and started running towards the corridor through which, just minutes before, they had entered. Andy was still fighting on the floor trying to stop those who were going after Mike, but there were too many and four of them were running after Mike.

Mike ran through the dark corridor, while his hand touched the walls to guide him because it was impossible to see. He ran, but he could not do it as fast as he wanted, since his subconscious forced him to go slowly to not trip over anything in the way. The path became eternal, he even began to doubt if he had already passed the door and had not noticed it, so he slowed down, just at that moment he realized that he was completely alone, Andy was not behind of him.

"Andy!" Mike called his friend as he looked at the end of the hall at the small light formed by the candles on the floor. All he could hear was a bustle on the floor.

"ANDY!" Mike yelled hoping to hear his friend in the hall.

"Wait for me!" A voice answered Mike's call, a high-pitched voice with a Canadian accent.

"Shit that's not Andy!"

Mike started running again looking for the exit, this time he ran as fast as possible without caring if he hit something or not. Mike ran, as he heard the footsteps getting closer and closer to him; now he could hear that it was several people running down the hall in the same direction as him. Mike couldn't believe that this corridor was the same one he had walked through before, this seemed to have no end, but it was only because he knew that death was stalking him. Luckily in the distance he began to see a light that emanated from the wall, illuminating the floor.

"The door!" Exclaimed Mike. "Finally!"

Mike reached the door, quickly reached for the doorknob to get out and get help, but...

"SHIT! These bastards have locked the door!" Mike said desperately.

"Go after him, don't let him escape!" said one of the men who were chasing Mike.

Mike saw the men were even closer and that the door was not going to open, so he quickly started running again, down the hall in search of an alternative exit. At the end of the corridor he found an open door that led to an office and, to his left, some stairs that led to the upper floor. Mike did not have much time to think and opted for the stairs. He began to climb the stairs, that fortunately had small windows that let him see the path ahead. On reaching the top floor he found another dance floor, practically the same as the one below him with several dusty tables around the floor with chairs on top. But this floor had several windows through which you could see the street where he had entered the building. Mike saw that next to one of the windows there was a drain pipe that led to the street, so without thinking twice he took one of the chairs and threw it with all his strength at that window, breaking it into a thousand pieces.

"There he is, after him!" said one of the men who was chasing him and who was now just a few meters from Mike.

Mike quickly jumped towards the pipe, held it tight and slid down it until he fell onto the street. Without hesitation, he began to run as fast as he could in the direction of the Avalon service door, until he reached it.

Mike was desperately banging on the door.

"OPEN THE DOOR! OPEN!" Mike screamed incessantly.

"I'm coming, I'm coming!" answered the Avalon doorman as he tried to get up from his chair.

"DAMN IT, OPEN THE DOOR NOW!" Mike kept shouting.

The doorman opened the door while Mike looked at the window of the other building through which he had escaped, there were still the four shadows that had been chasing him, just watching him, until the doorman finally opened the door.

"But what the hell is wrong with you, why are you in such a rush?" asked the angry doorman.

"GET OUT MY WAY!" Mike gave him a shove and ran onto the Avalon dance floor in search of Ava.

She was in the centre of the floor talking with Peter, having a good time without even suspecting that her boyfriend could be dead at that very moment.

"Ava! ... AVA!" Mike yelled as he approached the floor with his clothes and face covered in dust, with the appearance of having spent the whole night sleeping on the street.

"Mike? What's wrong, what happened to you and... where is Andy?" Ava asked as her eyes searched for Andy in the same direction Mike had arrived.

"Ava, Peter you have to help me!" he gasped.

Mike could barely speak; his heart was racing and he couldn't stop panting. He had to lean over and put his hands on his legs trying to catch his breath, but he was still in shock and didn't even know how to pose the problem.

Ava and Peter stared at him while they began to have a bad feeling, Ava wanted to ask, but at the same time something was preventing her, Peter could not take the situation anymore.

"But don't stop! What's going on?!" he demanded.

Mike took a deep breath, sat up, and was finally able to speak.

"ANDY IS IN DANGER!"

CHAPTER ELEVEN

Blood Ritual

Mike was able to escape the clutches of Novum Lumen thanks to the actions of his best friend. Andy was left behind fighting so Mike could escape and return with help. Andy was an expert in martial arts, he had achieved a Second Dan in Karate, but he was also a black belt in Taekwondo, and also passionate about Capoeira and mixed martial arts, which made him a rival to fear, since he had no adversary in melee. One-on-one Andy could easily win, against two it would present some problems, but he could still be victorious. But that night, Andy faced more than 20 people practically at the same time, and despite the fact that those people did not have the same preparation, it was still too many even for a martial arts master. Andy fought bravely, with all his power, but for every blow he unleashed, he received three to the back, two to the sides and one to the front.

It was a very uneven fight, no man on Earth could win such a battle, and Andy was no exception.

His strength began to fail him, he did not know who he wanted to hit, and he did not even bother to protect himself, little by little he fell until completely on his knees. He was exhausted and he was still surrounded by the sect that looked at him with satisfaction, when they saw that they had won.

"Catch him!" shouted the master.

Several members threw themselves at Andy, leaving him totally immobilized at the mercy of the master. He looked at Andy with contempt, clenched his teeth while blowing through his nose like an enraged bull.

"Put him on the altar!" ordered the master.

Quickly, two of his subjects began to clear the altar, leaving everything on the ground, including the basket containing the baby's body and the cup with its blood.

The figures holding Andy dragged him to the altar, grabbed his hands and feet and laid him on his back on the newly cleared surface. Andy was trying to struggle, but he was still very weak and had two people holding him by each limb, including his head.

The master approached the altar, looked straight into Andy's eyes, leaned a little closer to his face and began to speak to him.

"Are you comfortable my Lord? I really hope this altar is to your total liking. Sorry that I did not better prepare to receive you but honestly, we did not expect to have you here so soon" he continued in a sarcastic tone, making fun of Andy.

Everyone laughed and did not take their eyes away from what was about to happen.

"I know you have made a long journey to meet all of us and that you will be tired and thirsty... but where are my manners?! I have not even offered anything to drink!"

The master bent down to pick up the cup of blood that was on the floor.

"Can I get you a drink, My Lord?"

Andy looked at the cup and knew that it was full of the blood of the baby that had been killed a few minutes before. It was more than clear what the intentions of the black priest were, so he started to struggle again with the little strength that he still had.

"DON'T... LET ME GO! ...LET ME GO!" Andy screamed, desperate.

"Hold his head!" said the master as he brought the cup towards Andy's face.

Andy closed his mouth and tried to avoid the cup by turning his head sideways.

"Now you'll see!" said one of the men holding his head.

The man covered Andy's nose with a hand and waited for Andy to open his mouth to breathe. Andy was choking, but he didn't want to open his mouth, he kept resisting but his body forced him to do something to breathe. When he couldn't hold it anymore, he opened his mouth to breathe. The man who was holding his nose, quickly used his other hand to insert his thumb and middle fingers between his cheeks at the same time. Andy could no longer close his mouth because his own cheeks were between his teeth, which caused him a very uncomfortable sensation accompanied with great pain.

The black priest held the cup with his right hand and put it in front of Andy's mouth while Andy kept fighting without success.

"To you, my Lord!"

The black priest completely emptied the blood from the cup into Andy's mouth, and at the same time with his left hand, he struck him in the stomach to force him to drink the blood involuntarily, and that was just what happened.

A small part of the blood in the glass ran from Andy's mouth to his neck, but all that blood that had managed to enter his mouth was swallowed up when he received the blow to the stomach. When Andy swallowed that blood all those who were holding him released him at the same time.

That blood was still warm; Andy could feel it going down his throat without being able to do anything. As soon as they released him, he fell from the altar and was on the ground in shock, he tried to vomit, but his body did not reject the blood. He wanted to cry, but there were no tears in his eyes. He had an awful taste of metal in his mouth, as if he had held a handful of coins in his mouth for a long period of time. Andy was still crawling on the floor coughing, trying to vomit, but he had a lump in his throat that would not let him breathe. Everyone around him made fun of him as he continued to crawl on the ground. He cried, although his eyes were completely dry, he felt dizzy, confused. He could not get the image of the baby's face out of his head. He felt outraged, defenceless, and at that moment he just wanted to die. He wanted to stop that feeling of remorse, because, somehow, he felt guilty for the death of the innocent baby.

The man who had discovered him at the beginning drew his gun again, approached Andy from behind and pointed the gun at his head.

"Okay, we've had enough fun, it's time to end this" he said.

"Wait!" exclaimed the black priest.

The man turned to see his master as he approached.

"Do not shoot" he ordered.

"Bu- but master" the man stammered.

"Killing him right now would bring him a relief that he does not deserve" he stated.

The master spoke while everyone listened to him attentively.

"I want him to live, I want him to suffer, I want him to wish for a death that will never come to him. Above all, I want him to remember this night as the worst of his nightmares for the rest of his life"

"Yes Master, as you wish" the man said, lowering the weapon.

"Master! Master!" came urgent voices.

The priest turned to see who was calling him and saw the four men who were chasing Mike arrive back, alone.

"Master, the other one managed to escape, we saw him enter to the club across the street."

"Shit!" said the black priest, as his gaze returned to Andy.

"Okay, you know what you have to do. Leave this place completely clean and go down the main street."

"And what do we do with the boy master?" said the man who had the gun pointing at Andy.

"Take him out through the service door and let him out on the street, let his friends find him easily, that will give us time to get out of here."

"Yes Master" they agreed.

"And do me a favour, when you leave the boy on the street, just this once.... LOCK THE FUCKING DOOR!"

Two of the cult members carried Andy on their shoulders to the street, left him in the middle of the road, and returned to the old building, closing the door.

Andy was lying in the middle of the street, he was no longer crying, his gaze was lost while his face was resting on the hard asphalt. He had bruises all over his body from the big fight. His face was dirty, with some scratches and bumps, and his mouth, chin and neck were still covered in the baby's blood. He laid still in the street while he listened to people in the distance talking and laughing, with the music of the club in the background. Suddenly a door opened. It was the service door of Avalon. Mike, Pete, Ava and four security guards came through the door, one of the guards was armed like Peter, they were prepared to rescue Andy. When they went out to the street, they immediately saw a body lying on the ground.

"ANDY!" Ava yelled as she ran to see her boyfriend. Everyone else followed, with Ava looking around trying to find those responsible. Ava quickly reached Andy.

"Andy! Andy! Honey, please talk to me!" Ava caressed Andy's face as she saw the appearance of his face full of blows and blood.

"Is he alive?!" asked Mike.

"Yes, he's alive! We have to get him to a hospital soon!" Ava answered very anguished.

" No, we can't do that!" said Mike, panicked.

"Are you crazy?! Andy needs medical help!" Pete replied.

"I'm sorry, but we can't, Andy's life could be in danger if we do" Mike insisted.

"What do you mean by that?" Ava asked.

"You don't know the potential of that group; they could be anywhere and at any time. How do we know that the doctor who treats you isn't one of them?"

"So what do *you* propose we do?" asked Pete.

"Ava, you are doing your last year of medicine, you can check him and know if he needs medical attention or if we can take care of him ourselves, right?"

Ava was looking at her boyfriend trying to find a bullet or knife wound.

"It looks like he doesn't have any serious injuries but I can't be completely sure without my kit" Ava said as she continued examining Andy's body.

"Okay, in that case you think if we take him to your house, you can check him and if you think he should go to a hospital then we take him to a hospital?" said Mike.

"That's fine, but we have to go to your apartment because I left my things in Andy's room"

"In Andy's room? And what are they doing there?" asked Mike

Ava looked him straight in the eye and replied.

"That's something personal ... and intimate"

Mike and everyone else immediately understood what Ava meant, which made Mike's heart sink and Peter loved the idea of playing doctors with Ava, but his friend was still on the floor and they had to do something quick.

"Okay, if everything is done, let's take Andy quickly to his apartment and not waste any more time" said Peter as he bent down to lift Andy with the help of Mike.

Andy had his two friends under his shoulders, he was still unconscious while the others decided what to do with him.

"My car is on the corner, let's take him there and go quickly" Pete said.

"Boss, you want us to come with you or go back to the club?" asked one of the guards.

"Go back to the club, it seems like there's nothing more you can do, thanks for your help and tell my father that I'll be back before you close"

"Right boss, good luck. Sorry 'bout your friend"

Pete nodded and smiled appreciatively.

Mike and Pete carried Andy on their shoulders to the private parking lot of the club while Ava kept looking at her boyfriend and muttering something under her breath.

"What are you doing?" asked Mike.

"I'm praying" Ava answered, continuing to pray.

"And lead us not into temptation, but deliver us from evil. For thine is the kingdom, the power, and the glory, forever. Amen."

"I didn't know you were so religious." said Peter.

"When I was a child, my parents died in a car accident, so I had to go live with my grandma who is a devout believer, and I suppose that, in the end, some of all that stuck with me" Ava answered sadly.

"Oh Ava... I'm so sorry, it must have been horrible to go through that traumatic experience." Pete said.

"Don't worry, my parents died a long time ago so it's already over."

"No! I mean growing up with a believer, I can't imagine anything worse than that" he replied.

Pete smiled and winked at her, Ava smiled back, since his joke was very quick. On the contrary, Mike couldn't wait to get rid of Pete so before they spoke again, he jumped in.

"Peter, where's your car?"

Pete stopped smiling and started looking for his car in the parking lot.

"It's that over there, the white one" he said, pointing.

Pete had a shiny new Mercedes Benz AMG GT 4 doors.

"Wow! Is that your car?" Ava said very surprised.

"Yeah, things at the club are going very well and as public relations manager I need to have a good appearance to sell to my clients, that includes a good car"

Mike looked at the car suspiciously and tried not to be impressed, he didn't want to give Pete any credit.

"Okay, Ava open the back door and help us get Andy in" Mike said.

Ava got in the car and helped them by holding Andy as they carefully put him in. Ava stayed in the back with Andy's head on her lap, as Pete drove with Mike in the front, without saying a word. Ava just stroked her boyfriend's hair and spoke to him in a low voice.

"Andy wake up, please wake up..."

Andy was still unconscious, but in his mind he relived, over and over again, what had happened. He heard the laughter of the black priest, he saw the face of that poor baby crying while its blood filled the cup that they gave him to drink. It was 3:33 in the morning and Andy had more flashes showing him more images of horror. He saw a young woman in an advanced state of pregnancy being beaten in her own home by two men, until she was unconscious on the ground. At that moment one of the men cut the palm of her hand with a knife, and with her blood left a symbol on the wall of the main hall, a crescent with two crossed arrows. Andy watched as the men took the unconscious woman out of her home. There were more flashes of the woman tied to a bed in a dirty, dark basement, begging for her life and the life of her baby. But the pleas were in vain. Andy watched as one of the men used a knife to snatch the baby from her womb while she was still alive, screaming in real pain and suffering immense agony that she felt until the last second of her life.

Andy's mind went completely dark, no image came to him, just a sweet voice in the background telling him.

"Andy, wake up, wake up..."

Suddenly the sweet voice turned into a deep voice, a man's voice. It was Andy's own voice saying the same thing.

"Wake up, wake up"

They got to the building where Mike and Andy lived. Pete and Mike took Andy up to the fourth floor where they had the apartment. Fortunately, it was just after four o'clock in the morning, so nobody saw them arrive. They left Andy on his bed and Ava quickly began to do a complete check-up. She checked his pulse, his breathing and then took off his shirt to see in more detail the severity of his injuries. They were only superficial injuries, nothing to make her fear for his life. Ava noticed that his entire body was very hot, but after taking his temperature she saw that he did not have a fever. This seemed really strange to her because his forehead was burning, but at least it relieved her to know that he apparently had no serious problem.

Mike and Pete were still in Andy's room watching everything Ava did to help him, until finally Ava stood up.

"Well? How is he?" asked Pete

"Okay" she said. "His face is a bit swollen and he's got bruises all over his body, but nothing that can't be fixed with a little ice and pain killers."

"Then we don't need to take him to a hospital, right?" asked Mike.

"Fortunately, he doesn't have any broken bones or serious injuries so I don't see any reason to take him to the hospital. We can take care of him right here. Andy is a strong guy, I'm sure he will be fine."

"Thank God, I'm glad. It will just be a bad memory" said Pete, relieved.

"Me too," said Ava. "Pete if you want you can go back to the club, Andy will be fine. All he needs now is rest."

"Yeah, you're right, I still have things to do there and everyone will be worried about what happened."

"Again, thank you so much for your help Pete. You're a great friend, we owe you one." Ava gave Pete a big hug while Mike looked at them, jealous.

"You don't have to thank me, that's what friends are for. But remember that if you need something, whatever it is, call me and I'll be here" Pete said after winking at Ava.

"Thank you so much Pete, I'll call you tomorrow to let you know about Andy."

"Yes please, call me as soon as you can"

"Count on it" Ava answered with a smile.

"Nice to meet you Mike" Pete said just for politeness, but not once looking at him.

"Same" Mike replied without taking his eyes off Andy.

Pete left the apartment and now Mike and Ava were alone with Andy sleeping in his bed. Ava left the room to go to the kitchen in search of a few things.

"What are you going to do?" asked Mike.

"Andy's body is very hot, so I need to cool him down with a cold cloth. Also, I don't want him to spend the whole night stained with blood so I'll clean him a little before going to sleep."

"Need help?"

"No thanks, I can do it alone, you should go to bed. It's late."

"I suppose you'll spend the night with Andy, or am I wrong?"

"You're not wrong; I'm not going to leave him for a single minute in this condition."

"Thank you for everything you are doing for Andy." said Mike.

"You don't have to thank me Mike, I'm his girlfriend and I would do anything for him."

"I know... I know that very well" said Mike sadly looking into her eyes.

"Goodnight Mike." Ava said finally, taking a bowl of water and entering Andy's room.

"Goodnight Ava" Mike whispered.

Mike went to his room; he had a thousand thoughts in his head that were driving him crazy. He lay down on his bed, but his eyes were still open, staring at the ceiling. He couldn't stop reliving everything that had happened. His best friend was still unconscious and he had no idea what Novum Lumen had done to him to leave him in this state.

The minutes passed and Mike kept tossing and turning in his bed trying to sleep. He looked at the time on the small screen of his television, and saw that it was

5:37 in the morning. Mike was still not sleepy, but he was thirsty, so he got up to go to the kitchen to have a glass of water. While he was in the kitchen Ava appeared.

"I see you can't sleep either?" said Mike.

"I can't. Andy has been moving all night, it seems like he's trapped in a nightmare and he can't wake up."

"Still not waking up? "

"No, and the truth is that I do not understand why. I've cleaned all the blood that he had and I have not found any wound that could cause so much blood."

"And the blood on his face?" Mike asked.

"Thats what worried me the most but after cleaning it completely and checking his mouth, I haven't found anything, no cuts, no blows, nothing. It's like all that blood wasn't his." she said, worried.

Mike immediately reacted to the news and couldn't hide his concern from Ava.

"Mike... is there something you haven't told me?"
Mike stared into Ava's eyes, she still didn't know any details of what had happened in that abandoned building, but Mike began to connect the dots. He remembered the sacrifice of the baby, how they filled the cup with its blood, and now with the new information that Ava just gave him it was more than clear what had happened.

"I may know what happened to Andy" he said, slowly.

"What? Tell me, now!" she demanded.

"I think they drugged him" he replied.

"Drugged? That makes sense, that would explain why he is in this state when he doesn't have any serious injuries. But do you know what they have drugged him with?" she asked.

Mike wanted to save the chilling details to not scare Ava even more.

"I don't know exactly with what, but I know someone who can help us."

"Someone who can help us, who?"

"My history professor at the university. He's a specialist in rituals, I'm sure he can tell us what kinds of drugs they use and how to help Andy"

"Okay, I think it's a good idea" she said, wanting desperately for Andy to wake up.

"Okay, I'll call him first thing in the morning to help us"

"Okay, thanks Mike"

"Don't worry Ava, I promise I will solve this problem very soon"

Mike smiled; Ava returned the smile and continued with the task of taking care of her boyfriend. She had gone to the kitchen just to get some fresh water to continue cooling Andy's body. As soon as she had the water, she went back to Andy's room to continue her care.

Mike finished his water, went back to his room, opened his laptop and started searching the university website for the phone number of his former teacher.

"Henry... Henry Aha! Got it, Henry Bianchi" he said aloud.

Mike felt more upbeat. It felt good because he somehow felt like he had made his peace with Ava, thanks to his idea of calling his professor.

"Well, now sleep, a long day awaits us" he told himself.

Mike was calmer, but deep down he felt a little worried, not knowing whether or not he should tell Ava what happened with the baby. How to tell her that her boyfriend had been made to drink the blood of a newly born child? Whether he should or not is something he would have to figure out later, for the moment he just wanted to enjoy his little victory; getting Ava to thank him and smile at him.

CHAPTER TWELVE

The Order of Bellatores Dei

In the morning things had not changed much. Andy was still unconscious but at least, it seemed, he had had no more nightmares. He was not moving at all. He was just sleeping peacefully and nothing else, which for Ava was a sign of improvement. Although his body was still feeling warm, his internal temperature was still normal, which Ava could not understand.

Ava was still alone with Andy in his room, until Mike appeared.

"Good morning, how was the rest of the night? "

"Hi Mike, I have barely been able to sleep, it has been a very long night." she said.

"Did Andy keep moving all night?"

"No, he only moved until around 6 in the morning, after that he didn't move again at all, which I don't know if it's a good thing or not"

"And he didn't wake up once?"

"Not at all. I don't know if we were right to leave him here instead of taking him to a hospital, there at least we could do some analysis and know exactly what they drugged him with"

"Don't worry Ava, I just talked to my professor and he's on his way"

"Really?! He's coming? "

"Yeah. I was also surprised when he agreed, but as soon as I explained a little about what happened, he was really interested in the case and wanted to see it for himself"

"Okay, that's perfect, so we can better help Andy"

"Yes, he told me he'd be here in an hour"

"Okay, in that case I'll go to take a shower before he arrives"

"Okay, I'll be in the living room waiting for him"

"Thanks again for your help Mike "

"It's a pleasure"

Mike smiled and stared at her, Ava smiled back and looked at him as if she expected something from him. Mike was not sure what she wanted so he raised his eyebrows in question and confusion, so Ava answered him.

"Can I have some privacy in the room to shower and change?"

"Oh yeah! I'm sorry, I'm going to the living room now"

Mike left the room and closed the door when he left. Now all he had to do was wait for his former professor to arrive. Mike was sure that things would go better when he arrived, and that he would help him get his best friend back.

An hour later, a blue BMW pulled up across the street from the building. A middle-aged man was getting out. He was a tall man with glasses, hair a little long and curly, most of it white. He had a beard, white just like his hair, and was wearing a black suit without a tie. The shirt under his suit was the same black. After getting out of the car, he took a small black briefcase from the back seat and went to the door of the building in search of the bell of number four.

Mike was sitting on the sofa in the living room, he was watching the morning news on his laptop.

"The police continue looking for the missing young woman without finding any clues. The young woman's family fears the worst due to her advanced state of pregnancy. Her baby was due yesterday."

At that moment, someone called on the video intercom. Mike got up quickly, since he knew who it would be. He picked up and saw his former history professor on the screen.

"Professor Bianchi, please come up!"

A deep voice answered him.

"Thank you Michael."

Mike opened the door to the lobby as well as the front door of the apartment, and waited for his professor to come from the elevator.

Finally, Professor Bianchi reached the fourth floor of the building where Mike was waiting for him.

"Professor Bianchi it's good to see you again"

Mike held out his hand to greet him.

"It's nice to see you too Michael, but you know that you no longer need to call me professor, you can call me Henry."

Professor Bianchi also extended his hand and gave him a warm handshake.

"Okay, I'll call you Henry, but on one condition..."

" What?" Replied Henry.

"That you call me Mike like everyone else does"

Professor Bianchi smiled and nodded

"Okay, I'm very happy to see you again Mike, though I wish it had been in a better situation"

"I know, me too. Please come in." Mike said, gesturing him in to the apartment.

The two of them entered, and the first impression that Professor Bianchi got about the apartment was very good, it was a spacious, very modern and high-class.

"Wow, I see that things have gone quite well for you Mike, it's a very nice apartment."

"Thanks, but the credit is not mine, Andy's family has a lot of money and they have taught him well to earn it on his own, I couldn't afford a place like this by myself"

"I see" Professor Bianchi said as he looked at everything, especially some shelves where there were a couple of photos of Andy and Mike, so he took one of the photos and looked at it carefully.

"Is this your friend, Andy? "

"Yeah, that's him."

Professor Bianchi stared intently at Andy's eyes in the photo.

"He's a pretty handsome man" he noted.

"Yes, he is" Mike answered.

Professor Bianchi put the photo down and turned to talk to Mike.

"Okay Mike, before I see your friend what do you think if you tell me exactly what happened last night?"

"Very well" he said, downbeat. "Take a seat."

The two were heading to the living room when Ava appeared from Andy's room.

"Oh Henry, let me introduce you to Ava Guard, she is Andy's girlfriend. Ava, this is Professor Henry Bianchi."

Professor Bianchi came over and took Ava's hand with both of his hands and offered her a very polite greeting.

"Nice to meet you Miss Guard."

"Nice to meet you too, but please, just call me Ava."

"Okay, Ava, a lovely name just like its owner"

Ava smiled and thanked him but Professor Bianchi was already beginning to have his own thoughts about Andy. A handsome boy, from a good family, with a girl whom every man would envy. He was beginning to find this Andy fascinating.

"Ava, right now Mike was going to tell me the details of what happened to your boyfriend, would you like to join us?"

"Yes, of course, I also want to know exactly what happened!"

The three of them went into the living room and sat down. Mike was in front of them, a little nervous because he didn't know if he should tell all the details with Ava in front of him.

"Okay Mike... How did it all start?" asked the Professor.

Mike started telling them the story from early on, how he left the club to get some fresh air, how he saw the black mass symbol, how he and Andy came in to see what was going on, and how they discovered Novum Lumen in the middle of their ritual.

"And tell me Mike," asked Henry. "What kind of ritual were they doing?"

"What kind of ritual?" Mike asked, taking some time to think about what to say next.

"Yes, a boy as smart as you who knows the symbol of a black mass would know perfectly well what kind of ritual they were doing, right?"

Ava looked at Henry and was waiting for what Mike was about to say.

"It was a blood ritual."

Ava was surprised with such an unexpected answer, Henry, instead, had more questions.

"And what kind of sacrifice were they offering, animal or...?"

Mike looked down, closed his eyes for two seconds, took a deep breath and spoke.

"Human, they were sacrificing the life of a baby, a new born."

Ava was shocked to hear that, covered her nose and mouth with her hands in horror. Henry was attentive to everything Mike said, and every question Henry asked revealed the horror Andy had been through. Henry kept asking.

"How did they sacrifice the baby Mike?" he asked, sensitively.

Mike felt uncomfortable telling all of this in front of Ava, but if he wanted The Professor to help them, he would have to tell the whole truth, with all the details.

"They offered their life to Satan and cut its throat with a knife; and with their blood they filled a cup."
Ava gasped.

"Oh my God! The blood that Andy had in his mouth and on his face!!"

Mike stared into her eyes and nodded.

"I think they forced him to drink the blood."

"Oh no... ANDY!" Ava got up from the couch crying and went immediately to see Andy.

"Are you completely sure about that Mike?" Henry asked, anguished.

"I can't find another explanation; his state isn't that of someone who took a beating. It's more like the state of someone who went through a traumatic experience." Henry stood up, nodding his head and staring at the ground as he collected his thoughts.

"Okay Mike, let's see your friend." he broke his silence.

"Okay Henry, this way."

Mike led his teacher to Andy's room, where Ava was kneeling next to Andy's bed, stroking his hair and still crying.

"Miss Guard... may I?" Asked Henry

"Oh, yes... Please"

Ava got up off the ground, wiped away her tears, and let Professor Bianchi begin examining her boyfriend.

Henry sat on the bed next to Andy, and the first thing he did was put his hand on Andy's forehead. He immediately noticed that it was on fire, so he got his briefcase, put it on the bed and opened it to take out a thermometer.

"Don't bother taking his temperature" Ava said. "I've taken it several times in the night and he doesn't have a fever, despite being on fire."

Professor Bianchi looked at her and smiled, put the thermometer back in his briefcase and started looking for something else. Henry took a small flashlight from his briefcase and got into position to examine Andy's pupils. When he opened one of his eyes, something immediately caught his attention; the colour of his iris was brown. Professor Bianchi remembered perfectly seeing Andy's eyes in the photos of the apartment and he was sure that Andy's eyes were blue, so while he was examining them, he spoke.

"Does Andy usually wear contact lenses?" he asked. Ava and Mike looked at each other puzzled by the question.

"No, never, he has always had good eyesight and has never used any other type of contact lenses." Ava answered

Professor Bianchi kept examining Andy's eyes.

"And what colour are his eyes?" The Professor asked again.

Ava made a face of total bewilderment upon hearing that question as she saw the professor examining Andy's eyes.

"Uh ... blue?" Ava answered in a mocking tone.

Professor Bianchi didn't say anything; he just looked closely into Andy's eyes, until he found just what he was looking for. Under the iris of Andy's right eye, hidden under his lower eyelid, two small black veins perfectly formed an inverted cross.

"Oh my God. It's the sign!" Professor Bianchi whispered with terror reflected on his face.

"Is everything okay Henry?" Ava asked

Professor Bianchi was turning his head away from them, and trying to calm himself so as not to raise suspicion.

"Yes, yes... everything is fine, but I'm afraid it will be a bit more complicated than I expected." he said.

"More complicated, what do you mean?" asked Mike.

Henry got up from the bed to speak to them face to face.

"I can clearly see that your friend has been drugged, but due to the time he has been exposed to the drug, I would not know exactly what treatment to follow now."

"Then should we take him to a hospital?!" Ava said, panicked.

"NO!" Henry answered immediately. "It is not necessary; I am going to call a colleague of mine who specializes in these types of treatments and by the end of the day we will have solved this little problem."

"Really?! Thank you so much Henry." Ava said as she gave the Professor a hug.

"Don't thank me, now, if you'll excuse me, I have to call him as soon as possible." he said seriously.

Henry went into the living room to make the call while Mike and Ava talked in Andy's room.

"Did you hear that, Ava? Today we can heal Andy, I told you that I'd solve this problem and you see that I did.

Ava looked at him with a serious face.

"Don't play the hero when all of this is your fault Mike!"

"What? ..."

"Don't play the fool, you were the one who wanted to go in to that place and, because of you, Andy stayed behind so you could escape!"

"Bu... but Ava!"

"Listen to me very carefully Mike, from now on anything that happens to Andy, you, and only you, will be responsible."

Ava left and went to the room where Professor Bianchi was talking on his phone. As Ava got closer, she heard what Henry was saying, but didn't understand anything. She approached slowly, without Henrry seeing her, to listen better but he was speaking in another language.

"Sì, signore, ho visto il segno con i miei occhi, va bene, ho capito, così sia, Bellatore Dei" he said.

Ava listened carefully as she thought to herself *"Is he speaking Italian?"*

Professor Bianchi noticed that Ava was behind him, but he had already hung up, so he turned to speak to her.

"Ava! Good news, I was able to talk to my friend and told him about everything that happened to your boyfriend, he told me that in an hour or so he will be here."

"Really? Good! You don't know how glad I'm that finally we are going to do something to help Andy."

"Trust me Ava; this man is the right one to help Andy."

Professor Bianchi put his hand on Ava's shoulder and smiled at her, Ava returned the smile in gratitude. At that moment Mike entered the room.

"Is everything alright?" he asked.

Professor Bianchi removed his hand from Ava's shoulder and responded.

"Yes, everything is going very well, I was just telling Ava right now that my friend is going to help us with Andy personally."

"Personally?" asked Mike.

"Yes. He told me that he would pick up a couple of things and he would come as soon as possible."

"Good, I'm glad that everything is going to be okay."

Mike looked at Ava as she avoided eye contact with the person that she believed was responsible for everything that happened to her boyfriend.

The three of them went into the living room to wait for Professor Bianchi's friend. Ava and Mike were very intrigued about this man who would help them, so they asked the Professor all kinds of questions, from how

they had met to what was his specialism. Professor
Bianchi had no problem answering their questions,
leaving them completely convinced that he was the
right man to help Andy out of this situation. They
continued talking for the next hour, until they were
interrupted by the sound of the video intercom, from
the door of the building.

"That must be Toni, let me open the door" said
Professor Bianchi as he went to the front door of the
apartment.

Ava and Mike got up from the couch and stood there
waiting impatiently for the Professor and his friend to
arrive. Five minutes later Professor Bianchi entered the
room with his friend.

"Ava, Mike, this is my good friend Anthony
Lavigne."

Ava and Mike were impressed with the man's
appearance. He was about 45 years old, very tall
maybe 6 ft 5 in with a completely shaved head and a
black goatee. He was a big man, but not being obese,
he looked more like a wrestler than a teacher. Like
Professor Bianchi, he wore all black, but instead of
wearing a suit he wore only a long-sleeved shirt and
black trousers, and, in his right hand, carried black
leather doctor's bag.

"It's nice to meet you guys" said the man, smiling in
a strange way."

Neither Ava nor Mike bothered to go give him a handshake, they just nodded as they watched him. Ava had a bad feeling about this man, he smiled while his eyes reflected something sinister, and Ava knew that behind his smile there was something he was hiding.

"Alright guys, if you'll excuse us, let's see your friend right away, time is precious right now." Professor Bianchi said as he led his friend to Andy's room.

Ava and Mike followed them until they were at the entrance of Andy's room. Toni sat on the bed next to Andy and began to examine him while Professor Bianchi, still standing next to Toni, spoke to him in a whisper. Ava and Mike could barely hear a word of what they were talking about but Toni, like Professor Bianchi, focused on Andy's eyes, especially on his right eye. Henry pointed to something inside the eye while the look of Toni's face changed completely, from a serious gesture to one of bewilderment, and even fear

"Something wrong?" Ava asked

Toni looked at her and put his fake smile back on his face.

"Don't worry precious; your boyfriend will be fine."

Ava should have been happy with the news, but instead she felt uncomfortable with that man calling her precious and smiling that way so, to make herself feel better, she started asking him questions.

"Do you know what's wrong with him?"

Toni got out of bed, took his briefcase off the floor and went to the door where Ava and Mike were waiting.

"Yes, I know what happened to your boyfriend and I also know exactly what to do."

He smiled, and without saying anything else he went to the living room where he began to make space by moving the table that was between the sofas. Everyone else followed behind him. As they saw what he was doing, Ava could not bear so much suspense and returned to her questioning.

"Are you going to tell us what's wrong with him?" Toni put his briefcase in the middle of the room, where there was now a clear space, and answered.

"Henry told me that your boyfriend was given human blood to drink, is that correct?" Ava and Mike looked at each other and Mike answered.

"Yeah, that's right."

"Well, in blood rituals where blood is drunk, regardless of whether it is animal or human, it is customary to mix it with certain hallucinogenic substances, causing the subject to enter a trance and have a transcendental experience."

Ava was glad to see that they were finally making progress and could go into more detail about what happened with Andy, so she asked more questions.

"But do you know exactly what kind of drug they have used?"

"Normally any type of LSD, but considering that the perpetrators of this were Novum Lumen, I am completely sure that they used some type of hallucinogenic plant such as Desfontainia Spinosa or Brugmansias and Daturas, very powerful hallucinogenic plants often used in ancient times by shamans and in all kinds of pagan rituals."

Ava didn't know what to say, she had never heard of those plants and she had no idea how to deal with them, but luckily Toni seemed to have all the information that she needed to help her boyfriend, but she had to make sure.

"So, you know exactly what to do to help him?"
Toni smiled again.

"Don't worry precious; your boyfriend is in good hands."

Ava felt emptiness in her chest when she heard that, she didn't know if it was because of how unpleasant it sounded every time he called her precious or if it was just a bad feeling. There was something about this man that she did not quite like.

Toni crossed his hands and addressed them while still standing with his briefcase at his feet.

"Now if you excuse me, I have many things to do here and I need to have as much concentration as possible."

"Of course, go ahead we will not bother you at all."
Ava said

"I'm afraid you don't understand, to do this correctly I need to be completely alone with the victim."

Mike and Ava looked at each other and looked at Henry, Ava's bad feeling growing bigger upon hearing those words.

"You want us to leave the apartment?" Ava asked.

"It is the only way to do this well. Your boyfriend has been contaminated on a physical and spiritual level and to cure him, I must also do a ritual that will clean him completely. I will not be able to do it correctly if I am surrounded by distractions."

"A ritual? What kind of ritual?" asked Mike.

"You see, I mean these kinds of distractions! If you want to get your friend back, I have to start as soon as possible, and if I have to explain every detail of what I'm doing we will lose a lot of time and it will be worse for Andy."

Professor Bianchi went into action trying to smooth over the situation.

"Okay guys, what do you think if we go out for a moment and let Toni work? I'll take advantage of the time and show you something you have to know."

Ava and Mike didn't know what to think about everything that was happening, but they nodded. As they walked towards the door, Toni said a few last words to reassure them.

"Don't worry, give me an hour and I promise you that when you come back Andy will be cured."

Toni smiled again, but it was still the same fake smile that made Ava shiver. She certainly didn't trust him, but she trusted the professor, and if he said that Toni was the right man for it, then she could only trust and hope.

Ava, Mike and Professor Bianchi left the apartment.

***

Immediately, Toni got down on his knees, opened his briefcase and the first thing he took out was a large purple silk scarf with the symbol of the cross against evil in the centre. He spread it out in the centre of the room and continued to remove more things from his briefcase, including a couple of white candles, a glass bottle with water inside, and a black case, about 12 inches long by 6 inches wide. The case had another cross in the centre, but this cross was different; it was the Papal cross. Toni left all the things on top of the silk handkerchief and began to pray.

***

Ava, Mike and the professor were outside the building, the professor kept walking towards the road while Ava and Mike followed closely.

"Where are we going?" Ava asked.

"As I told you before, there is something I have to show you, so please continue."

Professor Bianchi stopped next to his car and opened the door for them to enter it. Ava and Mike were more and more puzzled with so much mystery, but they did not put up any resistance, so without further hesitation they got into the car.

"Where are we going Henry?" asked Mike

Henry started the car, fastened his seatbelt, and looked at Mike.

"To my house." he said.

Professor Bianchi lived on the outskirts of the city, about forty-five minutes from the centre. On the journey none of them said a word. Henry was focused only on driving and it seemed that he was in no hurry to get home. Mike alone looked at the people in the street and watched the cars go by, and he saw how they got further and further from the centre of the city. Ava instead looked ahead with her eyes lost in the horizon. She kept thinking about Andy and remembering the good times she had lived with him until that moment, he had been her true love, and she was more than convinced that she would spend the rest of her life with him.

⁎

Meanwhile, in Andy's apartment, Toni was still on his knees praying vigorously. He took the glass bottle of water, opened the black case that was on top of the silk scarf and began to pour the water into the case, leaving the interior completely wet. Andy was still in his room unconscious, but as Toni went on with his ritual Andy seemed to react. His fingers were moving rapidly, they were trembling; the expression on his face was of pain, he was frowning. Andy had a fight inside him, something sinister was taking control of his body, and he felt how his essence was losing every time. His energy was diminished by the invading power that was possessing his body, and he was dying to get out. Andy's whole body was shaking, until little by little the movements began to cease and he was completely immobile. His face reflected peace; the battle had ended. Andy opened his mouth slowly.

***

After 55 minutes on the road, Ava, Mike and the professor finally reached their destination. Professor Bianchi's house was a beautiful 1,700 square foot house with wooden ceilings and a spectacular view of the distant city. Mike was quite impressed by his house because he knew it could cost over two million dollars. He didn't understand how he could afford it on an educator's salary alone.

"Please, come in, make yourself at home." Henry said as he opened the front door for them.

"Wow Henry, you have a very nice house!" Ava exclaimed.

"Thanks Ava, I'm glad you like it." he responded.

"Yeah Henry, this place is amazing, how can you afford it?" Mike asked, unable to stop himself.

"I'm a man with many resources, but that is something that you're going to find out right now... please, follow me."

Professor Bianchi led them to the library where he had a desk with two chairs in front of it. Henry invited them to take a seat while he went to his personal library and started looking for one particular book. He took a rather fat book and left it on the desk in front of them. On its cover, was the title of the book "Advanced Mathematics for Engineering". Ava and Mike looked at each other not understanding what that book had to do with everything that was happening, so they waited for an explanation. Professor Bianchi looked at them and stared at the book.

"What I am about to tell you is strictly confidential, so I would greatly appreciate if you did not divulge to anyone the information that I am going to reveal to you now."

Ava and Mike looked at each other again and their puzzled faces said it all, they just nodded and kept listening carefully. Professor Bianchi took the book again and removed the false cover, revealing the true cover of the volume, a completely black, old book, with a title in gold letters *"Bellatores Dei"*.

"My real name is Enrico Bianchi; I was born and raised in a small town in Italy called Balestrino."

"Balestrino? I've never heard of that place." said Ava.

"No wonder" Professor Bianchi replied with a smile. "Balestrino is currently a ghost town, but years ago it was a cursed town, full of mysteries, and the only explanation was that the devil was loose in the streets."

Mike was sitting placidly in one of the chairs in front of the desk until he heard that. He lowered his leg from his other knee, put his elbows on top of either knee and intertwined his fingers. Now, Professor Bianchi had all of his attention.

"Since I was little, I formed a great friendship with the village priest. He gave me the opportunity to have academic training in his church, and after his death, when I was 24, I had the opportunity to become the village priest. I was the only one in the area and, thanks to that, I had the chance to verify that evil really exists in this world."

"What do you mean by that Henry?" Mike asked.

"I mean that I had to deal with real demons, people possessed by evil and, I can safely say, they weren't pretending."

"How could you know?" Ava asked, very intrigued.

"You see, Balestrino was a town separated from all technology and from the whole world. Its inhabitants were hardworking people whose only goal in life was to work to get their food. Going to school and having training was something that they did not usually care about, which is why the vast majority of the town did not know how to read or write. Many of them did not even speak properly, so when they took someone to my church screaming, and speaking in perfect Latin, I knew they weren't pretending."

Mike and Ava barely blinked, they were so attentive listening to the professor's words that they had not yet thought about what such a fantastic story was about, and what it had to do with Andy. Professor Bianchi continued with his story.

"Demonic possessions were something very common in that place, and sometimes it was not just people raging and speaking in other languages. Many times, supernatural powers were witnessed, such as spontaneous fires or even objects flying from one place to another without any explanation. But my faith and determination helped me to fight all those demons and to always come out of each fight successfully. Soon the word spread, and the Vatican found out about my talent for fighting evil, so one day I was called to be part of a secret Vatican society called "The Order of the Bellatores Dei."

"Bellatores Dei? It means 'Warriors of God', right?" asked Mike.

"That's right, Mike." Henry answered, as he opened the book he had laid on his desk.

"The Order of the Bellatores Dei" was founded in secret by the apostle John.

"The disciple of Christ?!" Ava asked amazed.

"Yes, the very same. So, you can get an idea of how long this society has existed."

Ava and Mike looked at each other and could not hide their surprised faces, since they both knew that they were hearing something that was not in the history books, but that could enter those books directly if the truth came out. The professor kept talking.

"The apostle John was not only the youngest of all the apostles, he was also known as the disciple most loved by Jesus Christ. Jesus considered him practically as a little brother, so much that he even entrusted his mother's life to him during the crucifixion. John was undoubtedly the disciple to whom he had the most confidence and, thanks to that, he was the only one to whom part of the divine plan of God was revealed. Part of that knowledge is still stored here, in this book - The secret gospel of Saint John."

"The secret gospel of Saint John?" Mike replied. "It has to be a joke, Henry; do you really expect us to believe all this?"

"If it's a joke then tell me where the fun is?" Professor Bianchi replied while keeping his gaze fixed on Mike's eyes. "If I am revealing all this information to you, it is only because you have to understand what is happening and why."

"And what *is* happening Henry?" Ava asked. "Because, until now I have not found any relationship with that and what happened to Andy."

"You will see, within the prophecies that were revealed to the apostle John there is one of them that fits perfectly with everything that has happened to your boyfriend."

"And what prophecy is that?" Ava asked as she felt a lump in her throat.

Professor Bianchi kept his gaze fixed on Ava's eyes for a moment, then lowered it to see the book that was open on his desk. He turned it over and ushered them closer so they could see the page it was on. Ava and Mike came closer to see what was in the book and they saw a sinister image that penetrated their eyes and made them shiver through their entire bodies: the face of a demon. Professor Bianchi replied.

"It is the prophecy of the arrival of the Antichrist."

CHAPTER THIRTEEN
The Awakening

In Andy's apartment, things were about to change. Toni was in the final part of his ritual and had not realized what was happening in Andy's room. Andy was still lying motionless on his bed, his mouth hanging open. Suddenly, a strange smoke started to come out of his mouth. It was like a thick black mist that was slowly covering his body. The smoke started to come out of his nose, his eyes and his ears, completely covering his body. Toni continued praying while Andy's body, wrapped in the smoke, began to levitate until it stayed, hovering three feet above his bed. The smoke became denser, more compact, and at the same time gave off a heat that Andy's bed could not withstand. The bed began to burn, starting with the sheets.

**

Ava and Mike listened intently to Professor Bianchi, but try as they might, his words didn't make any sense to them.

"The arrival of the Antichrist?!" Ava asked incredulously. "Henry, seriously... what does all this have to do with Andy?!"

Professor Bianchi turned the page of the book and pointed to the text in it.

"The apostle John was directly chosen by Christ to keep and preserve some of the most important secrets in the history of mankind. Among those secrets are some revelations that predict the end of the world as we know it."

"You mean the book of Revelations?" asked Mike.

"The book of Revelations are just a few fragments that were released publicly, but the apostle John was more specific with the details of the arrival of the beast. And those details are found in this book." Professor Bianchi touched the book again with his index finger. "A book that only a few privileged people in the world have been able to see, since it is one of the best kept secrets of the Vatican."

Little by little Ava could understand that these details were the connection with Andy, but she still couldn't understand what her boyfriend was really involved in and how it affected him, so she had to ask.

"Henry, tell us everything."

Professor Bianchi stared into Ava's eyes for two seconds, then returned his gaze to the book and continued with his story.

"The apostle John tells us that when Christ was still with him, before the crucifixion, he told him a couple of stories about a war that has been raging since the time of the first man; a war between good and evil. We humans cannot see that war because it is taking place in a world apart from ours, but somehow what happens in that war also affects us in our world. Christ warned him that the day would come when the beast, the being who was one of them but who betrayed them, would find a way to transfer the war to this world. And when that day comes, we must be attentive to the signs that Christ himself would leave behind to help us identify the bearer of evil."

Ava and Mike looked at each other and it was more than clear that they did not like what they were hearing. Ava looked at Professor Bianchi.

"What signs would they be?" she asked, nervously.

"The first of the signs is that the antichrist would come in troubled times, times in which all that is reported are tragedies, wars, hunger and death. It is the perfect setting to come and be heard by a desperate crowd, tired of so many misfortunes and wanting to find a leader to guide them to a better world."

"That sounds like the world we live in today." Mike said with pity.

"You're right Mike." said Henry.

"We currently live in the perfect setting for the arrival of the antichrist, but there are still more details to confirm whether the moment has already arrived."

"Henry, could you be more specific about the details please?" Ava said, a little stressed because she felt that they were not moving forward quickly enough.

"Okay, within the signs that were revealed to the apostle John, there is an exact day and time when the antichrist will arrive, that date is the same day and time that Jesus died, but within the hours of darkness."

"And what date is that?" Ava asked.

"The date is April 7th at 2:57 in the morning approximately." Henry replied.

Ava's heart immediately raced when she heard the date.

"April 7th?" Ava murmured. "Today is April 7th, it's Andy's birthday."

"Exactly" replied Professor Bianchi.

"At 2:57 in the morning?" Mike said. "That was more or less the time they attacked Andy."

Professor Bianchi smiled. "You start to see the link with Andy now, right?"

Ava and Mike didn't say anything. They saw how, as Professor Bianchi spoke, everything pointed to Andy. His eyes were still fixed on the professor's eyes as he kept talking.

"There are more details still. Christ told the apostle John that the antichrist would not choose just any carrier, he would have to be from a good family and physically perfect, qualities that someone as vain as the antichrist would not leave aside."

Mike listened attentively while in his mind there were memories of Andy and many people admiring his body, his face, his achievements and how he achieved everything he set on his mind to with hardly any effort. Professor Bianchi continued.

"In addition, one of the undeniable signs of the wearer will be his eyes, black as night, since he does not support the entry of much light into his body."

Ava reacted immediately and spoke with a satisfied tone.

"Aha!" she said. "Andy's eyes are blue!"

Professor Bianchi looked at her carefully.

"Do you remember this morning when I asked you what colour his eyes were?" he asked.

Ava nodded. She couldn't forget that question because it had seemed so absurd to ask it while he was looking into Andy's eyes.

"When I asked you that question" he continued, "his eyes were brown."

Ava sat with her mouth open and no matter how hard she tried to find an explanation, her mind was not processing all the information.

"By this time, I am sure, his eyes will already be black. In addition, there is one last sign of which the apostle John warns us. Christ, in an effort to help us in this approaching war, promised to mark the beast with a symbol; the symbol that represents the opposite of what Christ represents. That symbol is the inverted cross."

"But Andy does not have the mark of an inverted cross anywhere on his body." Ava said, trying to defend her boyfriend once more.

"He has it." Professor Bianchi answered confidently.

"This morning while examining the colour of his eyes, I found a small mark on his right eye, hidden a few millimetres under the iris."

Ava covered her face with her hands and slid them slowly down her cheeks until she reached her chin.

"Henry, are you telling us that Andy is being possessed by the devil?!"

Professor Bianchi took a deep breath and let out a sigh.

"I'm afraid it's much more complicated than that."

***

Toni was still in the room performing his ritual, and continued pouring water and blessing the object that was inside that mysterious box, while in Andy's room things seemed to be out of control. His body remained levitating and slowly changed from a horizontal position to vertical. He was still covered with the smoke that swirled around him. Suddenly, a spark ignited inside which turned the smoke into an immense ball of fire that revolved around Andy. His body was completely covered in flames; his pyjamas and underwear were immediately burned, but it seemed that it did not affect his body. His skin and hair were not affected, on the contrary, the bruises that Andy had on his body and on his face were gradually disappearing into the flames, the ball of fire was spinning with more force and part of the flames were beginning to spread throughout the room, burning everything, turning Andy's room into a real hell.

***

"What do you mean it's more complicated than that?!" Ava asked. "I mean, you're obviously saying that Andy is the carrier of the antichrist, and that's why Toni has been left alone with him, what he wants to do is an exorcism, isn't it?!"

"If it were as simple as doing an exorcism, I would be in that apartment doing it myself. No, we are not talking about a simple demon, we are talking about the antichrist; the angel who was with God from the moment of the creation of man, and there is no human power that can prevent it."

Ava was confused; nothing he said to her nor what they were doing seemed to make sense.

"So if you can't stop the antichrist from taking over Andy's body... what are you going to do?!"

Professor Bianchi's heart raced as he knew that what he was about to say was going to complicate things.

"If I have told you all this when I should not have, it is only because I want you to understand what we must do. We are doing it for the greater good. The only solution to this problem is to cut the connection that the antichrist has with this world... forever."

An overwhelming fear was fixed on Ava's face as tears flooded her eyes. Her heart stopped for a moment, but she finally understood perfectly what was happening.

"Oh my God! You don't want to help Andy... you want to kill him!" she shouted.

Mike looked at Ava in surprise as he felt a stream of cold air run down his back with those words. He looked straight into the eyes of Professor Bianchi as he waited for an answer.

***

Toni had reached the final part of his ritual. He closed his eyes and held the object that was inside the box. While he continued to pray, he raised the object and brought it to his forehead.

***

Professor Bianchi was staring at his desk, he closed his eyes for a second and looked into Ava's eyes.

"I'm very sorry Ava... but it's the only solution."

***

Toni opened his eyes to see the golden dagger in his hands and ended his sentence with the words...

"Your will be done and not mine."

245

***

"MOTHERFUCKER!" Ava yelled as she got up, violently throwing the chair back. "I knew I shouldn't have trusted you! I knew it!"

Mike got up immediately and looked at the professor with a look of bewilderment and disappointment.

"Henry! How could you?!"

"Please, guys, you have to understand that this is the only way to save this world from an imminent war."

Ava ran out of the room, while trying to call Andy's apartment with her phone, but Toni had cut the phone wires. She was rushing out of the professor's house while Mike followed close after her. Ava was on the brink of collapse; her boyfriend might be dead right now and she was so far away that she couldn't do anything about it. Ava was still on the street outside the professor's house, now trying to call the police. She was so stressed that she didn't realize that Professor Bianchi's neighbours were returning from a long trip, with a taxi, that was about to leave.

"AVA!" Mike yelled.

Ava turned and saw Mike pointing at the taxi; they ran to catch up.

"Please take us to the city centre as soon as possible, it is a case of life or death!" she demanded, desperate.

The taxi driver accepted, and while he was driving, Ava called the police to tell them that a maniac had entered her boyfriend's apartment and that he was trying to kill him. The police told her that they would send the nearest patrol immediately.

"Don't worry Ava, everything will be fine." Mike said trying to comfort his beloved Ava.

"SHUT UP MIKE!" Ava shouted madly. "This is all your fault! First the club and now those people who are trying to kill Andy! Whatever happens to him... I swear to God, I'll never forgive you!"

Mike felt he was dying in that moment, but deep down he knew that she was right, and right now he couldn't think about how much he had angered the love of his life; but right now, he should only think about his friend, his brother, who could be dead because of him. Mike just looked out the window and silently prayed.

"Please, God, please keep Andy alive"

***

Toni got up and started towards Andy's room, but as he approached, something caught his eye. A strange orange light emanating through the crack in the door frame; a light that seemed to flicker. He touched the doorknob and it was hot, almost burning. He opened the door quickly and saw that he had opened the gates of hell.

Toni felt like he was in the middle of a nightmare, he couldn't believe what he was seeing, but it was happening right before his eyes. Andy's room was completely engulfed in flames and Andy was suspended, mid-air in the eye of a tornado of fire. Toni

247

steeled himself and advanced slowly while clenching the dagger tightly in his right hand. The tornado of fire that enveloped Andy began to disappear, from his feet to his head, exposing Andy's naked body, without a scratch, or any sign that he had been involved in a fight for his life the night before. Andy descended, little by little, until his feet touched the ground. He still had his eyes closed, but he was now standing in front of Toni. Toni's whole body was shaking despite his attempts to keep calm, so he began to repeat a phrase over and over.

"In nomine Patris Filii et Spiritus Sancti, In nomine Patris Filii et Spiritus Sancti..."

Toni, in a last attempt at courage, launched the attack with the dagger pointed at Andy's heart.

"In nomine Patris Filii et Spiritus Sancti!"

Toni raised the dagger and when he had it at the height of Andy's head, Andy opened his eyes. The irises of his eyes were completely black, and they were staring back into Toni's eyes. Toni stopped his attack immediately; he was petrified looking in to black eyes, he knew that they were not the eyes of a simple mortal. Those eyes reflected power, greatness, destruction and death. Toni fell to his knees while still looking in to Andy's eyes. It was too much for his heart to bear; it was beating uncontrollably from the immense fear he was feeling in every part of his body, until the inevitable occurred. His heart stopped, leaving him dead at Andy's feet.

Andy looked down at Toni's body as he watched the flames approach him little by little. He looked up and went to his closet where the doors were engulfed in flames. Andy stared at the doors and they opened without his touch. All his clothes were on fire, everything except his favourite black suit, which was still hanging, perfectly intact. Andy took his suit and smirked as he looked at it.

***

Ava and Mike were only a few blocks from the apartment, but they were stuck in traffic, which made Ava more desperate.

"Is there no other route we can take?!" Ava asked the taxi driver impatiently.

"I'm sorry miss, but the street is shut-off, it seems like there's been an accident."

"An accident?" Ava murmured, inside her heart she had a bad feeling.

"We'll get out here, Mike; pay him." Ava said, getting out of the taxi and running towards Andy's apartment.

"Ava, wait!" Mike yelled, as he gave all the money he had in his wallet to the taxi driver without waiting for the change.

Mike ran faster than Ava and caught up with her easily. When they were near the building an image made them think the worst; fire marshals and cops had the area cordoned off and Andy's apartment was smoking a lot, but there appeared to be no fire.

"Oh no, Andy!" Ava said as her eyes filled with tears again.

They ran until they reached the barrier where the cops were stopping all those who tried to enter.

"Officer! Officer! My boyfriend lives in that apartment; I was the one who called them to tell them that someone was trying to kill him!"

"You were the one who called? Come in, Detective Morgan wants to talk to you."

The officer accompanied them to where Detective Morgan was. He was only a few meters away talking to some forensics officers about the case."

"Detective Morgan, she's the girl who called central to report what was happening here."

"Thank you very much officer, you can be dismissed now."

Ava had her heart in her fist. She knew that at any moment they would tell her that her dear Andy had been murdered.

"Excuse me Miss, could you tell me your name please?" asked Detective Morgan.

"My name is Ava Guard, and he is Mike Jones."

"Very well, tell me, Miss Guard, do you know who attacked your boyfriend?"

"Yes, I can tell you all the details you want, but please tell me, how is Andy?"

Detective Morgan started looking for a few pages in his notebook.

"How old is your boyfriend?" he asked Ava.

Ava was frustrated that she had to keep waiting for an answer that was killing her, but she answered.

"25 years old, today is his birthday."

Detective Morgan made a little puzzled face, but said nothing more. At that time the police were removing a body from the building in a polyethylene carrying case. Ava's world completely collapsed when she saw the cover, she fell to her knees and began to cry, shattered. She saw how the body got closer to where she was and all the good times that she had spent with Andy slowly passed through her head. It was as if time had stopped at that moment, lengthening her anguish in a cruel way. Detective Morgan immediately knelt down and grabbed Ava's hands.

"Miss Guard listen to me please, in your boyfriend's apartment we found only one body that corresponds to a white male, 6'5 feet tall and approximately 45 to 50 years old."

Ava's soul returned to her body with those words.

"6'5 feet tall and 45 to 50 years old?" Mike replied. "That's not Andy! That's the description of Toni, the man who tried to kill him!"

"Does that mean Andy is alive?!" Ava asked as she got to her feet again upon hearing the new information.

"The only thing we know for sure is that your boyfriend is missing, so we need you to tell us if you know why they tried to kill him and where he may be."

Ava was in shock. She did not know whether to regain hope of finding her boyfriend alive or if it would be worse if they later found Andy's body somewhere else. She kept thinking about what to do or what to say, until she felt someone watching her. She looked over at the police barrier, turning to see who it was and saw Professor Bianchi looking at the cover with the corpse. He saw that the person inside did not correspond to the image he remembered of Andy, it was obvious that inside there was a larger person.

"Toni" Professor Bianchi said in a low voice.

Ava reacted and pointed her finger at him.

"He, he is responsible for all this, that's the man who tried to kill Andy!"

Detective Morgan looked at the professor and he was scared to see that they were talking about him, so he quickly hid himself among the people trying to flee.

"CATCH HIM!" Shouted Detective Morgan as he ran after the professor.

Ava and Mike were left alone in the middle of the bustle. Ava could only think about where Andy could be, when suddenly she had an idea and started running towards the building's parking doors. Mike ran after her.

"Ava! Wait! Where are you going?!"

"I need to know if Andy has taken his car, if he has taken it, I will know that he is still alive and we will have a chance to find him."

Ava still had the keys to Andy's apartment, which included the key to the parking lot. They quickly opened the door and ran in search of Andy's car, leaving the door open behind them. They made it to Andy's parking lot, but his car was still there, a late-model black Audi TT. Ava began searching the car for a clue that it had been moved in the last few hours. While searching, they heard some footsteps approaching them rapidly. Ava and Mike stood to the side of the car and looked everywhere to see who was there, Ava thought it could be Andy, but professor Bianchi appeared among the cars.

"What the hell are you doing here Henry?! Have you not done enough?!" Mike said angrily.

"Guys, listen to me. You are in great danger if you keep looking for him on your own?" he warned.

Mike lunged towards him and began pushing him backwards to get him out of there.

"Get out! Leave us alone!" he said between pushes.

"Mike, please control yourself! Understand that I had to do it for the good of humanity!"

Ava was still at the side of Andy's car, watching as Mike and Henry continued to struggle, suddenly a deep and familiar voice was heard behind her.

"Ava!"

She turned to see who was calling her and saw her boyfriend in front of her in his shiny black suit. Ava felt her heart beat again when she saw Andy alive and in perfect condition. She felt so happy that she did not notice her boyfriend's serious face, when she was used to always being greeted with a smile every time they met. But she didn't care. He was alive and he was in front of her. Andy stared into her eyes, and as he did so, the image of another woman came to his mind; a woman almost identical to the girl in front of him. A woman he remembered fondly, but remembered always naked walking through the green meadows of an immense garden. Andy couldn't deny that the girl in front of him was related to the first woman he had met thousands of years ago, and this pleased him. Ava didn't wait another second and ran into his arms to give him a strong hug.

"Andy! Thank God you are okay!"

Professor Bianchi and Mike stopped and watched as Ava hugged her boyfriend. Andy stared back at them and a strange chill ran through Mike's body.

"Andy?" Mike asked as he saw his black eyes that reflected the gaze of another person, of another being.

He immediately understood that the person who was there was not the Andy he knew.

"Ava... Ava!" Mike said, trying to get her attention, but she was very happy in Andy's arms.

"AVA!" Mike yelled with all his force.

She turned and looked at Mike confused.

"What's going on?"

Mike slowly raised his hand and pointed at Andy's face.

"His eyes... look at his eyes" Mike said nervously.

Ava kept hugging him until she turned to see his eyes. At that moment, she stopped hugging him and took a step back, she saw those black eyes and seemed to see another person.

"Ava... Stay away from him!" said professor Bianchi.

Ava stepped back a bit more as she looked directly into her boyfriend's eyes.

"A... A... Andy?" she stammered.

Professor Bianchi and Mike ran to Ava, but before reaching her, Andy raised his hand and sent them flying all the way to the other end of the building, hitting the wall and falling to the ground, leaving them dizzy and dazed. Fear seized Ava. She had been alone with him and she was already sure that this man was not Andy. She could not even call him human after that show of power. Ava was still immobile, staring into those black eyes; she was really scared. Andy was looking at her as he took a step forward. Ava tried to take a step back, but she was so scared that she tripped over her own feet and fell backwards, but before her body touched the ground Andy was holding her in his arms. He was a couple of meters away and in less than a second he was holding her, preventing her from harm. Ava reacted immediately and tried to free herself from Andy.

"No, don't touch me, don't touch me!"

Andy stood up and just looked at her. Ava was terrified and she covered her face with her hands to avoid looking him in the face.

"Go away! Please go, go, go, go!"

Ava closed her eyes and kept repeating the same thing. She was like a little girl hiding in her bed between the sheets.

Ava opened her eyes and Andy was no longer there. She looked everywhere for him, but he was already gone, just as she had asked. Ava quickly got to her feet and ran to where Mike and the professor were. They were still stunned by the blow, but at least they were still alive.

"Guys are you okay?"

"Yes, don't worry about us... are you okay?" asked Mike.

"Yes, I'm fine."

"Where's Andy?" asked the professor.

"I don't know, he... he just disappeared." Ava said.

"Just like that?" asked the professor again.

"Yes, I asked him to leave, and he just left."

"I see." said the professor. "Quick, we have to get out of here before he changes his mind and reappears."

"But what are we going to do Henry?" Mike asked. "You've already seen the power he has, how are we going to fight him or even how are we going to hide from him?"

"The Bellatores Dei have been preparing for this moment for two thousand years, obviously we knew that it would not be so easy to defeat the prince of darkness, so we have a plan B."

"And what is plan B?" Ava asked.

"I will tell you all the details, but first we must return to my house, we have so many things to do and such little time to do them."

CHAPTER FOURTEEN
Age of the Beast

Professor Bianchi, Mike and Ava ran in search of the professor's car. It was a couple of blocks from the building, but they had to be very careful. The building was still surrounded by cops and some of them were still looking for the professor. Fortunately, they were able to dodge the cops without being seen and they got into the professor's car immediately. Ava and Mike were still thinking about what happened. Andy, the sweetest and best guy they had ever known... had he become the prince of darkness?"

"I don't believe it, it can't be, there has to be a logical explanation for all this madness." Ava said repeatedly.

"But you've seen it with your own eyes, haven't you?" asked professor Bianchi.

"Yes, I know what I saw and what I felt when he was in front of me, but... How is it possible?"

"At least now you can believe me, and you know that what I wanted to do was for a good reason."

"A good reason?" Mike replied. "What you wanted was to kill Andy in cold blood!"

"How can you be so naïve?! Is it that you don't realize what's happening here? Andy no longer exists! From the moment Satan completely occupied his body, Andy's vital energy disappeared, and there is no longer any trace of Andy inside him. He is Andy only in appearance."

"What?!" Ava exclaimed. "Are you saying that no matter what we do, Andy is not coming back?!"

"I'm sorry Ava, but… it's too late for Andy." he replied, sadly.

Ava burst into tears, her dear Andy was gone and had been replaced by a demon who dressed in his skin. Her whole world had fallen apart, Ava had experienced a very lonely and sad childhood, and meeting Andy had been the only good thing that had happened to her. She saw herself as the future mother of his children, the woman with whom he would spend his whole life, and now that he is gone… what would become of her?"

Ava cried while Mike and Professor Bianchi kept arguing about what happened.

"I don't understand Henry, if we can't do anything for Andy anymore, what's the plan? What are we going to do now?"

"The first thing we must do is get to my house. Once we are safe there, I will make a call. I have to inform my superiors about what happened to start the new plan."

Again, Professor Bianchi spoke of a new plan, but seemed not to want to say anything more about it. Mike had lost confidence in him and as much as he tried to have a better idea than accompanying him, he couldn't think of anything. Also, at this point they could no longer save their best friend... What worse could happen to them?"

They arrived back at the professor's house. Ava was still devastated and had not said a single word in almost an hour. Professor Bianchi ushered them into the living room while he went to his study to make his call. After a few minutes waiting, Ava crumpled to the couch and Mike stood to her side, bent down to see her face to face and tried to comfort her.

"Ava, please, don't cry anymore, you don't know how much it destroys me to see you like this."

Ava didn't even look at him, she was still sitting on the couch staring at the floor.

"Hey, if I tell you the truth, I don't think Professor Bianchi is right about Andy."

Ava made a confused face, but now Mike had her attention.

"What... what do you mean by that?" she sniffed.

"When Henry said that Andy had left at the time that Satan occupied his body... I think he is wrong."

"Why?" Ava asked, intrigued.

"You see, if Andy is the devil's connection to this world, surely, he has to continue living to maintain that connection. Otherwise, the devil would not need a host if he had the ability to enter this world with his own energy, don't you think?"

"So... so you think Andy is still alive?" she sobbed.

Mike looked at her tenderly and smiled.

"I am convinced that, somehow, Andy is still alive." he confirmed.

Ava smiled as she wiped her eyes.

"Thanks, Mike."

Mike smiled and held her hand tightly.

"You will see that everything will be fine."

At that moment the professor re-entered the room.

"I hope I'm not interrupting anything." he said.

Ava immediately withdrew her hand from Mike's hand, and Mike stood up.

"Will you finally tell us what the plan is?" asked Mike.

"Yes. We are going to Italy."

"To Italy?!" Ava and Mike looked at each other puzzled

"Why Italy?" Mike asked again.

"Because it is the only place where we can face the beast... and maybe succeed."

"Wait, are you saying that Andy is going to follow us to Italy? Why are you so sure about it?" he asked.

"Because of her." Professor Bianchi pointed to Ava, and she got up from the sofa immediately.

"Because of me? Why me?"

"You see Ava, in all these years there have been many theories in my group of how Satan would conquer this world, and we honestly had no idea what it would be like, until today. When Andy went to look for you in that parking lot, we finally understood that you are the key to his plan."

"I am the key?" Ava asked surprised. "How can that be?"

"Among all the theories that we formed of how the plan would play out, only two seemed plausible to us. The first was his directly attacking this world with all his power, subjecting the human race to its dominance, but we also think that if he could do that... Why hasn't it done so far?"

"Because he can't do it." Mike replied. "Even if he is from another world, there will be laws in his own world that not even Satan himself can violate."

Professor Bianchi was surprised by the answer, he could see without a doubt that Mike was an outstanding student in this matter.

"That's it, Mike, that was the conclusion we reached also, therefore, the second theory gains more force and this is where Ava comes into play."

"What theory is that, Henry?" Ava asked.

"The devil's greatest power is his cunning. That is why we think that instead of starting a war from the front, what he would do would be to infiltrate our own world, making us believe that he is one of ours to control us without realizing it."

"And how can he do that?" asked Mike.

"Following, to the letter, a master plan that was carried out more than two thousand years ago."

"What do you mean Henry?" asked Mike.

"I mean that he will follow the same divine plan that God made in our world, sending his only son to influence everyone's lives, and this is where your Ava comes in."

"What?!" Ava exclaimed. "Wait... Henry, you're saying that Andy..."

"He has chosen you to take his son, and thus control the world, that is why we must go to Italy where we can protect you and prevent that from happening."

Ava couldn't believe it, the story was getting more and more twisted and absurd.

"Wait" said Mike. "If this story is true then all the more reason we should get away from here and from you."

"Why do you say that, Mike?" asked the professor.

"If Ava is so important to the plans of the beast, what stop's you from killing her to prevent those plans? After all, it was what you intended to do with Andy!"

Ava looked at Mike and realized he was right, they couldn't be trusted so easily

"Okay" answered the professor. "I suppose I have well deserved that mistrust, but let me tell you this... I honestly don't know why he chose her, the only thing I know is that if we killed Ava right now, he would simply change the woman for one perhaps unknown to us, which would be much worse. Instead, we do know that he wants her and if we prevent that from happening with all our power, then we will have frustrated his plans."

That explanation seemed to make sense to Mike, but there was still something wrong with it.

"I don't understand, if we try to hide Ava from Satan, What, exactly, is going to prevent him from looking for another woman with better accessibility?"

Professor Bianchi smiled.

"Son, I like how you think, but you are still too young to understand everything. We are going to play with the vanity of the devil, his greatest weakness. He will never allow such insignificant creatures as us to interfere in his plans; if he has set his eyes on her... he will not stop until he gets her."

Ava's heart was beating, but each beat left emptiness in her chest. All she thought about was seeing Andy's face one more time, but now with all this information she knew that it was not good for her to see him close to her. Many times, they had talked about getting married and having children. It was what she longed for the most, but now she was hearing that any child they could have may be the cause of the end of the world as they knew it.

Ava had grown up with her grandmother, a fervent follower of Christ, and every night before going to sleep she would tell her stories from the bible. Stories that often spoke of times of war, chaos, poverty, rivers of lava and death, but... could her own future child be the cause of all this?

"Okay," said Mike, "but why Italy?"

"Italy is the only place where we can count on an army that can help us with our mission. In addition, it is the only place where we have a weapon that can face true evil."

"A weapon?" Mike asked. "What weapon is that?"

"You will know when we get there, now we must hurry. Time is critical."

"Okay Henry, but we must go get our passports first."

"Don't worry about that, everything is arranged. We must leave immediately, our plane leaves in 2 hours. We will fly all night and tomorrow, by noon, we will have arrived in Italy."

Everything was happening so fast that Ava and Mike did not have time to think, let alone process so much madness. Before they could accept that they had lost their friend, they had to continue running to avoid a greater tragedy. Mike felt responsible for everything that happened, even though it seemed to be fate, he could not avoid the feeling of guilt at losing his best friend. Thinking that he could also lose Ava if they made a wrong move had him very scared, losing his friend had hurt him, losing Ava... it would kill him.

The professor, Ava and Mike left immediately for the airport. Professor Bianchi seemed very sure of himself as always, but Mike did not take his eyes off him. He still did not fully trust him. On the contrary, Ava did not say anything, she continued with a lost gaze, she thought of Andy and remembered the last time she saw him, with those black eyes that shook her so much. Even knowing that now he was the bearer of all evil, she was missing him.

Finally, they arrived at the airport. Mike was surprised to see how the world worked. Professor Bianchi only had to talk to a couple of people and they were immediately escorted to an exclusive room, bypassing all airport security. For a moment he was besieged as someone very important, but given the situation they were in, it was no wonder.

"Make yourself comfortable, we still have to wait an hour here before we can get on the plane." said the professor as he showed them the rest area of the room.

The area was equipped with several comfortable armchairs, snacks, drinks, a television and everything you need to wait for your flight without any problems.

"Ava, you should rest a bit before getting on the plane. You look exhausted." suggested the professor.

"Don't worry, I'm fine." Ava answered not sounding very convincing.

"Henry is right." said Mike. "Last night you could hardly sleep taking care of Andy and now with everything that has happened we have barely been able to stop."

"Ava, listen to Mike. Rest a bit on the couch, we will leave you alone so you can sleep. We must get a couple of things for the trip, so you can take advantage and get some sleep."

"Okay" Ava answered without putting up much resistance. "I will try to rest."

"Don't worry about anything Ava. Mike and I will be close, you also have two escorts outside the door who will see that no one enters, you can feel completely safe." said the professor as he put his hands on Ava's shoulders.

"Thank you very much Henry" Ava said as she subtly smiled and then settled down to rest in one of the armchairs in the airport lounge. While sitting down Mike approached her.

"Ava, I won't let anything bad happen to you." he promised.

Ava just smiled, looked for a comfortable position on the couch and continued staring at the floor.

Mike and the professor went to the door, the professor was the first to leave. Mike looked backed at Ava from the door for a few seconds, and then left the door closed. He felt better knowing that there were two cops standing by the entrance.

Ava had been left alone in the room. She was sitting with her arms crossed staring at the floor, she closed her eyes slowly and let out a long sigh.

"Did you really think you could hide from me?"

Ava jumped off the couch and looked directly behind her, where that voice was coming from.

"Andy!"

CHAPTER FIFTEEN
The Great Lie

"I'm sorry darling, but this planet isn't big enough for you to hide from me." Andy said as he stared at Ava and smiled like he used to.

"A... Andy?"

Ava could barely articulate words, Andy had taken her completely by surprise. He took a couple of steps to approach Ava slowly and replied.

"Yes"

Ava started to back away as she saw those black eyes again.

"No... you are not Andy"

Andy smiled.

"If I'm not Andy then who am I?"

Ava was still scared, but she felt safe enough to speak to him face-to-face, she swallowed and replied.

"You are the devil, the fallen angel, the antichrist! Luzbel!"

"Luzbel" Andy smiled. "I like that name, but if I were him... Why should you hide from me?" Andy answered with some mockery.

Ava was shocked by such a response.

"Why should I hide from you? You are the origin of all evil! The one responsible for all the misfortunes in the world. The one who made humanity fall from grace by causing the first woman and man to eat the forbidden apple; condemning us to exile from the Garden of Eden."

Andy stared into Ava's eyes. He saw a lot of fear in them. But he knew Ava very well, so he thought of the perfect way to remove the fear and get her attention. He just smiled, looked away from her eyes and walked slowly around her.

"It wasn't an apple." he said.

Ava was taken aback by the response.

Andy smiled again at Ava's expression and continued talking.

"Many still believe that the forbidden fruit was an apple, but, in reality, it was a coliot. A fruit that became extinct thousands of years ago, but was more similar to what you call cherries today, only coliots were larger and the tree did not bear so much fruit."

Ava's fear immediately vanished, one of the greatest mysteries in the world had just been revealed from the mouth of someone who was there. Andy saw that something had changed in her, so he kept talking.

"Also, you were not exiled from any garden, you actually lived on an island. A large island that looked like a small continent, and it was there that you formed the most advanced civilization that has existed until now."

Ava was amazed listening to all this. She felt that she was in front of the only being who could solve so many enigmas in the history of humanity; she knew that she had to be alert and fearful, but she was facing a great opportunity that she did not want to miss.

"I don't understand, if that civilization was so great how is it that we have never heard of them or never found any clue of it?"

Andy smiled and looked into her eyes again.

"Any clue? You have evidence everywhere. That civilization was real; where do you think the technology came from to build perfect pyramids in Egypt? Or how is it explained that a civilization like the Mayans had access to advanced information about the Earth and the universe? Do you really think that all that came from alien technology?" Andy made a mocking face. "Don't make me laugh! You are certainly not the only ones in this universe, but no matter how hard you try, you will never be able to contact each other. This universe has been designed to prevent it!"

Ava was stunned. Each answer generated more questions, but as a believer she wanted to focus on what most interested her: the history of humanity.

"So, if everything was done by the hand of man and thanks to that civilization, what happened to them?" she asked.

Andy was pleased to see that Ava's eyes were no longer filled with fear; sharing his knowledge with her had brought her closer, so why change his plan? He went on.

"As you know, after the first humans ate the forbidden fruit, your God was so offended and disappointed because his creations had disobeyed him, that he cruelly punished them with pain and death. It was a punishment that, in my opinion, was disproportionate, as the only thing his "children" had done was discover what was right and what was wrong."

Ava listened attentively and although her first impulse was to reject that statement, because he was discrediting her God, she knew deep down that he was right. He wasn't making anything up; everything he said was written in the holy bible and it was a thought that had come to her as a child. If we are children of God and he loves us so much, why punish us in that way just for knowing what is good and what is bad? Andy continued with his story.

"After that punishment, your God turned his back on them and left them to their fate, thinking that without him they would not get anywhere. But he was wrong, he underestimated his creations and they taught him the true power of man."

Ava listened carefully to each word, her heart was beating very fast, but it was for the simple fact that she was learning a truth unknown until then.

"After I removed the blindfold that humanity had over its eyes they began to grow rapidly. Their ability to adapt and learn was formidable, from beings that roamed the island without purpose they became a civilization capable of controlling the environment that surrounded them. They could even modify it at will. Their thirst for knowledge did not end; they were becoming more intelligent, more powerful. It was very evident that being without the God to which they had been subjected had made them evolve."

"And what happened? How is it that such a great civilization no longer exists?" Ava asked very intrigued.

Andy looked into her eyes, smiled and looked away leaving his eyes focused on nothing, as if he were remembering every word he said and saw the images in his head.

"Well, in a display of rage and frustration in seeing that his creations were better off without him, your dear God used all of his power to violently attack the home of his creations. Earthquakes, tidal waves, hurricanes and even a meteor were thrown towards the island one after another, devastating the entire town they had created and completely destroying the island. It killed almost all the people who lived there: men, women, children, all ending with a tragic death at the hands of their Creator. Only a few managed to escape the wrath of God, but after that nothing was the same again."

Ava reacted immediately.

"You're lying! That cannot be true, you are trying to deceive me! God is love! He would not kill his children for any reason, you speak like that simply because you hate him."

Andy returned his gaze to Ava's eyes, but this time his face was serious, it seemed that he had been affected by what Ava had just accused him of.

"Do you think I'm lying? Do you think I'm making it all up? Fine! Don't believe my words then, but all of you have a very wrong idea of your God. You believe that he is all love and perfection and that he is always there for you, when the reality is that he has the same mentality of a small child to whom the only thing that matters is that they always pay attention to him and that he is the most important thing in your life."

"Shut up! No more! What was I thinking? I had forgotten for a moment who I was talking to."

"If you don't believe me, take a little look at the bible and there you will have all the necessary proof. Do you think that your God would never kill his children? So what about the worldwide flood, am I making that up too? Or it does not matter because only the "sinners" died as they would have you believe?"

Ava was silent, she had no arguments for that, since she knew he was right. He was not making it up, but Andy had only just begun.

"And what do you think of the story of Abraham? Hey, Abraham! I want you to kill the only child you have with the woman you love just to show me that you love me more! It doesn't matter how bad you have it just thinking about it; it doesn't matter what a horrible feeling you have inside when holding the knife while it goes to the chest of your son; because, in the last second, I will stop you. You want to tell me what kind of being can make a joke as twisted as that?"

Ava seemed to run out of arguments, but the story of Abraham reminded her of another story that her grandmother told her. More than a story, it was a comparison, the sacrifice of a lamb, but that lamb was very special.

"Okay" Ava said, "If God is as cruel and selfish as you say he is then, tell me, why did he send his only son to die for us?"

Andy let out a slight smile and replied.

"That is something that I am not going to tell you... That is something that you have to see with your own eyes."

Ava did not understand his answer. Was it that she had left the devil without an argument? She looked into his eyes, confused, until she realized that she couldn't take her eyes off his black ones; she couldn't even blink. She tried to move, but she was completely immobile. The only thing she could do was keep looking at Andy's eyes, little by little everything around them began to distort. Her surroundings began to stain black; everything was fused with shadows and the only thing that could be seen clearly was her and Andy.

Suddenly, Andy's body started to emit a gust of wind; it was so strong that Ava felt that it was going to knock her down. Her first impulse was to put one foot backwards to balance herself. At that moment, she realized that she had regained control of her body but that the wind was pulling harder and harder. Ava used her right arm to cover her face and slowly lowered her body to counteract the force of the wind that was pushing her backwards but, as she ducked, the wind became stronger. For a moment it made her lose her balance but, before fully falling, she used her left arm to support herself on the ground. Just at that moment she noticed something strange, she was touching soil, it was as if she were no longer in the waiting room of the airport.

Ava looked down to see what she was touching and she could see that it *was* soil. It was not only under her hand, she was on the ground what seemed like outside the airport, but she could see only around a meter away from her. Little by little she could see more. The land became clearer, even with some light. All the shadows that surrounded her were dissipating. Ava tried to look towards where Andy was but the strong wind prevented her from doing so. Suddenly, a very strong white light illuminated everything, leaving Ava blind for a few seconds and the wind started to die down. She no longer heard the wind whistling in her ears, but she could hear something that she did not quite understand. It seemed like voices; voices of many people shouting, protesting, even some crying. Ava looked at the ground and could see better the land she was on; ahead, she saw the shadows of many people. Ava squinted, forcing her eyes to see better, and with every second that passed, she could see clearer. The shadows began to take shape, colour, and slowly she saw how they became people in front of her. The most striking thing about these people was their clothing, they all wore very old clothes. The women covered their hair with veils, and the men all had beards, except only a few, who were in front of them making a barrier to prevent their passage. The men who did not have beards wore armour; they looked like gladiators. Ava stood up and started to understand that she was not at the airport, and it seemed that she was not in her own timeline either.

Ava looked around, scared, at all the people in front of her and did not understand what was happening, until she saw a figure walking among the people. A figure that walked from one side towards the centre. The person was dressed in a gleaming black robe that stood out from all the others, as their clothes looked old and dirty. That robe also had a black hood that covered the head of the person who was wearing it. Ava fixed her eyes on this person because he was walking slowly through the crowd and it seemed that no one could see him, only her. Ava focused her eyes on the hood trying to seeing the person's face and she saw that it was Andy. He fixed his eyes on her as he walked among the people. Despite the scene around her, Ava kept her gaze fixed on Andy. She wanted to know what he was doing or what he planned do. Suddenly, Andy stopped and turned around to stare at her. Ava was confused. She did not understand what he wanted to say, then Andy stopped looking at her and shifted his gaze above her.

He was looking in the same direction as everyone else. Ava had not realized that until that moment, so she turned to see what was behind her and felt an emptiness in her stomach that left her breathless for a few seconds. Behind her, there was a huge wooden cross, with a man cover on blood nailed to it.

Ava was so shocked that she had to take a few steps back because she was very close to the man suspended there. She immediately saw that there were two other men beside the first, each nailed to their own cross. Ava remembered Andy's last words and realized that the man on the central cross was the Son of God.

Andy had brought her to the most crucial moment in the life of Christ. He was not telling her the story; he was showing her.

Ava stood with her mouth open when she saw that she had Christ himself in front of her. She had conflicting feelings: on the one hand, she could not believe what she was experiencing and on the other hand the image she had of Christ in her head did not fit at all with the face of the man in front of her. She had always pictured the face of a white, European Christ, with long straight hair and light eyes, a very handsome being. This man was dark skinned, with short wavy hair and brown eyes, and he did not stand out for being handsome: he was an ordinary man. Even the crucifixion she had imagined in a different way. In her mind, the cross had been only two thin sticks like that of crucifixes worn by devout Christians, but this cross was like a large wooden column. The column was large and robust with a simple mechanism to attach a beam of smaller wood across it. Ava's eyes were fixed on the man's hands and indeed they were nailed in to the wood with nails that penetrated his palms. His forearms were tied to the cross with ropes to prevent his palms from pulling off the nail with the weight of his body. In addition, his feet were not nailed into the wood as shown in all crucifixion images; these were nailed to the sides of the wood independently, not one on top of the other, the nails were through the soft area, just below the ankle. Small details that did not take away the suffering that this man was subjected to.

Ava looked helplessly at the pain of the man on the cross, but he only looked at the sky and shouted something that she could not understand.

"Eli, Eli! Lemá sabactaní?"

From the context she could deduce that he was saying the fourth sentence that Christ would say on the cross before he died.

"My God, my God! Why hast thou forsaken me?"

Ava turned to see Andy and he was staring at her, Andy looked away and walked slowly to the side, heading towards one of the guards. Behind the guard, there was a young boy; he did not yet have a beard. The boy stared into the eyes of Christ and Christ was looking at him too. Suddenly, Christ made a gesture with his head and the boy responded with the same gesture. The boy looked around and then at the guard in front of him. At his feet, there was an old pot with something that looked like dirty water inside. Without anyone seeing him, the boy took a small bag out from his clothes, opened it and threw a strange powder inside the jar. He then turned away and walked until he reached the side of a woman who was crying inconsolably looking in to the eyes of Christ. Ava understood that this woman was the mother of Christ, and that the young man was comforting her in a very familiar way.

"Then... this young man must be the apostle John!" Ava thought.

But she didn't understand what the deal was with the pot why Andy had wanted her to see it. A moment later, Christ said something else that Ava did not understand, and the soldier who was next to the vessel dipped in stick with an old washcloth tied to the end and soaked it.

"I Thirst" Ava whispered as she understood what Christ had said

Then the soldier put the dipped rag near the mouth of Christ and he began to drain the tissue eagerly with his mouth. It seemed to be bitter, because of the gestures he made while drinking, but nevertheless he did not stop until leaving it without a single drop. The soldier returned to his place and Christ whispered something else while his gaze was lost on the horizon. Thanks to Ava's grandmother, she knew the seven sayings of Christ on the cross and although she could not understand him, she recalled what he had said.

"It is finished."

Ava did not take her eyes away from Christ's face and she noticed that now he looked different. He could barely keep his eyes open or his mouth closed. He seemed completely drugged, and that was when he said his last sentence. Ava repeated it at the same time as she recalled it.

"Father, into thy hands I commend my spirit."

Immediately afterwards, Christ closed his eyes and died.

One of the guards noticed that Christ appeared to have died and went to one of his companions who was watching over the people. Turning his back on Christ, he spoke in an incredulous way to his comrade; it seemed that he had not expected such a sudden death. The other soldier moved towards Christ with his spear drawn. Ava watched the soldier because she knew perfectly what came next.

The soldier raised his spear and pierced the side of Christ. Ava looked away as the sight seemed grotesque and inhumane, but the soldier knew that no conscious man could have endured the pain without the slightest reaction, even involuntarily. Christ did not move.

The soldier quickly ordered that they take him down from the cross and something else that Ava could not understand, but another soldier appeared on the scene with a large mass in his hands. He strode towards one of the men crucified next to Christ and broke his legs. Ava covered her face to avoid seeing such an act of evil. The whole scene itself seemed like a horror movie; for her they were images that would stay in her head forever; they were etched permanently into her mind.

She watched as they lowered a dead Christ from the cross. Only a few in the crowd were with him, mourning his death, while others celebrated it. Ava wanted to get closer to see him better, but they had him surrounded and she could no longer see him. At that moment, a strong wind blew that seemed to come out of nowhere.

Ava turned to look for Andy and he was in front of her again, looking at her attentively. Again, Ava could not move; she was motionless, staring in to Andy's eyes. Everything around her began to fade once more, and gradually become another scene. This time she was faster to acclimatize than the first. She recovered quickly and looks at everything around her. This time; they were next to a mountain, standing in front of what looked like a cave with a large stone by the entrance. Ava moved closer and noticed how they had Christ wrapped in sheets on top of a stone altar. Around them were various types of plants that Ava could not recognize, but she understood that it was some kind of ritual of the time.

After crying over his body and praying for him, all those who were in the tomb came out. Four men began to move the stone to cover the entrance of the tomb. They were several large, strong men, but even for them the stone seemed to weigh a lot. Finally, they closed the tomb with the stone, sealing its interior.

Christ's family and friends walked away, leaving Ava alone with Andy. Ava looked at Andy and he looked at the sky. There were still some rays of sunlight lighting up the place, but as Andy focused his gaze on the sky things seemed to change. The clouds began to move faster; even the sun was moving through the sky with more speed. It was like everything was moving in fast forward. It was as if Andy was accelerating the weather. Ava watched in amazement as the entire sky was darkening, the first stars were appearing, and an immense moon rose, the likes of which she had never seen before.

It was night, but nevertheless it was not completely dark. The moon and the stars illuminated the scene. Andy stopped looking at the sky to see Ava's eyes again and everything returned to its normal speed. Ava stared into Andy's eyes without knowing exactly what to think or say. Suddenly she heard some footsteps and people talking. She turned to see where the noise was coming from and saw a group of men approaching with torches. There were six men, large and corpulent, except one who was shorter and thinner, but he was the one who led them. All of them covered their heads so as not to be recognized by anyone. The men went towards the tomb of Christ, and five of them began to move the stone. They moved it with difficulty, but they were more effective than the men who had put it in place earlier.

After a couple of minutes, the men had moved the stone completely and the thin man took out a bag from beneath his clothes. He handed it to one of them, who opened it in front of everyone. Inside, were some gold coins. The men were very pleased with the gold, and they distributed the coins among themselves then left as quickly as they had come. The man who had given them the gold coins had been left completely alone. He looked around once more and took off the hood that covered his face. Ava immediately recognized his face, it was unmistakable for her because it was one of the few men in the place that she had seen without a beard. It was Apostle John. The same man that she had seen at the crucifixion, consoling the mother of Christ.

Ava was perplexed, she was looking at Andy, but he was carefully watching the entrance of the tomb. Ava looked at the same place and saw Apostle John enter quickly. Ava could only see the light of the torch illuminating the entrance.

Once again, Andy looked at the sky and it began to move in fast motion again. Ava was still fascinated, watching everything around her move faster, but her gaze was still focused on the entrance of the cave. It was still illuminated by the light of the torch but no one could be seen leaving it. Suddenly, Andy stopped looking at the sky and everything returned to normal speed. Ava understood that whatever was going to happen would happen in any moment. The sun was about to rise. It was still night but the visibility was much better than when Apostle John had arrived.

Ava slowly approached the entrance of the cave. In her mind, she still thought that they could see her there, so she approached very cautiously from the side of the cave to avoid being seen by someone from inside. She just wanted to take a little look to see what was happening inside, but when she was close enough to the entrance, a hand came out from the cave and rested on the edge of the entrance. Ava got scared and fell backwards, but from the ground she kept looking at the hand, which she noticed was covered in bandages and blood. Ava was immobile and the only thing she could do was continue watching the entrance of the cave. Little by little, Apostle John emerged from the cave with Christ, alive, resting on his shoulder. The hand on the rock had belonged to Christ: a wounded, but living Christ.

Ava could not be more amazed, her eyes could not even blink. She looked at Christ from top to bottom and could see that his wounds were covered by bandages. Under the bandages were some of the plants that had been left at his grave. Ava was stunned, watching Apostle John help him walk, since Christ could not do it alone. Every step he took seemed like an agony for him. Ava got up and watched as Christ and his apostle faded into the distance.

***

Ava looked down and noticed that the floor was made of tile and no longer dirt. She looked around and noticed she was back in the airport waiting room, and Andy was still there with her, no longer dressed in the black robe but back in his black suit.

Ava stood there, with her mouth open, as she looked once more into Andy's eyes. She tried to say something, but the words didn't come out until she managed to murmur something.

"It c-can't be true. I- I don't believe it!" Ava said with a stutter.

Andy smiled.

"Do you know why the crucifixion was the most terrible death you could have? Because it was a very painful and slow death. A man could spend a couple of days nailed to that cross before finally dying. Christ, on the other hand, died six hours after being nailed to the cross. It doesn't matter what people say about the wounds he suffered before being nailed to the cross, six hours is still a short time for a strong and healthy man like Christ. Don't you think that is suspicious?"

Ava felt an emptiness in her stomach and she couldn't believe what she had seen.

"But how is it possible? I don't understand." she asked.

Andy kept talking.

"That is something that certainly does not surprise me, but it is normal. Everyone bought the story of poor Jesus Christ, the carpenter "Son of God", but what they do not know is that he was just a man and nothing more. An extraordinary man of course, but only a man."

Ava's pulse was racing and she felt like her head was working non-stop to process so much information, but no matter how hard she tried, she still didn't understand it.

"So, are you saying that everything is a lie? Is nothing in the bible real?"

"You just saw it with your own eyes, Ava." Andy responded.

"Yes! I know what I saw, but how do I know it's true? How do I know it's not one of your lies, said to confuse me and make me change my mind about you?!"

"Lies are those that have been told to you since you were a little girl, Ava, to you and to all of the people on this planet! Do you want to know the truth? Well, the truth is that Christ was never a carpenter and did not even belong to a humble family. On the contrary, his family was one of the wealthiest in the world and, thanks to this, he was able to travel and see new places. Places like Asia, where he would find all the knowledge about the medicine of the time that would make him the most famous miracle worker in the history of mankind. And of course, last but not least, his greatest discovery, Buddhism, the basis of his new religion."

The information saturated Ava's mind, she just closed her eyes and slowly moved away from Andy while with her hands she just rubbed her head.

"Buddhism?" Ava asked incredulously.

"I do not know why you are so surprised, Ava, that is not something new. Anyone who understands just a small amount of Buddhism and Christianity will have noticed that there is a great similarity between the two."

"What are you talking about?"

Andy just smiled and looked at her with pity.

"Fine... Let's play a little game of 'Who said this?'. First question, Who said this? " If anyone should give you a blow with his hand, with a stick, or with a knife, you should abandon any desires and utter no evil words."

Ava looked at Andy and didn't understand what the point of the game was, but since Andy had proposed it, she played along.

"That phrase is what I know as "But if anyone slaps you on the right cheek, turn to him the other also" so I would say that it was Christ."

Andy was pleased to see that Ava felt comfortable enough with him to play his absurd game. He just smiled as usual and replied.

"Wrong. That phrase is from Buddha."

Ava made a puzzled face, as she thought the phrase Andy had said was the original quote of Christ, and that perhaps it had just been distorted over time.

"Ready for the second round?" Andy asked. with some mockery in his voice.

"Okay, this time I'm ready." Ava answered, very sure of herself.

"Perfect! Second question, who said this? "Confess to the world the sins you have committed."

Ava responded quickly.

"Definitely Christ. That phrase *has* to be from him."

Andy let out a small laugh as Ava looked at him, puzzled.

"You are wrong again, that phrase also belongs to Buddha."

Ava was surprised to see that she had been wrong, but now she understood what Andy was saying about the similarities between the two religions. She thought she knew something about religion, but even *she* had been confused by the similarity of the phrases."

"Final round?" Andy asked.

"Okay, shoot!" Ava's ego felt a little damaged after failing the previous two questions, but she was willing to continue to redeem herself.

"Okay, final question, who said this? "Love your enemies, do good to those who hate you, bless those who curse you, pray for those who mistreat you."

Ava took a couple of seconds to think better of the answer, but this time she was more than sure. This phrase was unmistakable for her, so she answered the same thing again.

"If I know anything about Christianity, without a doubt the answer is Christ. That phrase belongs to Christ."

Andy looked again into Ava's eyes and was glad to see that there was no fear in them. This made him very happy and he couldn't hide it in his face.

"Well, what is the answer?" Ava asked impatiently.

Andy smiled.

"Yes, you're right, that phrase belongs to Christ."

Ava smiled, pleased.

"Ha, I knew it!"

"But Buddha also said "Hatreds do not cease in this world by hating, but by love: this is an eternal truth. Overcome anger by love, overcome evil by good ". And this was said by Buddha 500 years before Christ was even born."

Andy had left Ava without any possible arguments. She understood immediately that the similarity between the ways of thinking of both religions was suspicious, but then, did this mean that Andy was telling the truth?

Andy kept talking.

"Both religions are very similar, but there is one big difference. While Buddha said that human beings were the only ones who could save themselves and they could not depend on gods, Christ was smarter and said that they could only be saved through him."

Ava could not believe what she was hearing. Her first impulse was to think that it was blasphemy, slander even, but at the same time she was beginning to make sense of it all. She no longer knew what to think or what to believe.

Ava couldn't stop thinking about everything that had happened, she was standing in front of Andy without saying a word. She didn't even look at him, she just had her gaze lost in the void. Andy, again, broke the silence.

"I understand that it may be difficult for you to process all this information since, in a few minutes, I have destroyed the image of God that you had for years. But if you think about it from an impartial point of view, you realize that everything makes sense. Have you ever played the Telephone game? "

Ava reacted and looked into Andy's eyes again, so she answered.

"Yeah, you make a circle and one of the people whispers something in the ear of the person next to them. They can only do it once and in a low voice, and they have to pass the message to the next person and the next, until it gets back to the person who started it. The goal is to keep the original message the same, but it hardly ever happens. There's always someone who misunderstands or adds more than they should."

"Exactly!" Andy exclaimed.

"Now imagine playing that game non-stop for more than 2,000 years; the original message that was "Christ was a great swimmer" ends with "Christ was able to walk on water" and so it goes with the stories of the life of Christ."

Ava asked with a certain tone of disappointment.

"So he never did perform miracles?"

"No, I'm afraid not. He was very good at curing people, but it was nothing that came from 'beyond'. Christ was a learned and very intelligent man, and precisely when he realised the revolution he was causing, he knew that it was only a matter of time before they tried to kill him. So, before anyone did, he planned his own death."

"What!? He planned his own death?"

Ava seemed to not stop having surprises. When she thought that she had already seen all the new information, it was revealed to her that everything she knew was worth nothing.

"You have the same proof in your beloved bible, tell me, Ava, who was the man who handed over his master to his enemies?"

Ava answered without hesitation.

"Judas, Judas Iscariot."

"Very good. And you will also know how he delivered him, right?"

"Yes, with a kiss on the cheek."

"Now answer this, Ava, why should he kiss him when he had the guards behind him? Because he doesn't just point his finger at the man that he knows is going to die because of him, but instead he kisses him on the cheek. A kiss means love and loyalty because, after all, he was just doing what his master had ordered of him."

Ava's eyes couldn't be wider; it seemed like a nightmare that she couldn't wake up from.

"So... Christ ordered Judas to hand him over to his enemies?" she asked, thinking it all through.

"Why you think the first thing that Christ says when Judas kisses him is "Judas, would you betray the Son of Man with a kiss?"? It is not because he feels sad about the betrayal; it is because he is reminding Judas to be more sensible about what he is doing, so as not to ruin his plan."

"This is crazy..." Ava replied.

"But it is the truth, Ava. Christ had two favourite apostles above the others: Judas Iscariot and John, each assigned a special job; chosen because they were smart enough to follow his plan without errors. Obviously, Christ did not tell Judas all the details. When he found out that they were going to crucify Christ, he thought that the plan had failed and that they were going to kill him because of him; for following his orders. His pain was so great that he took his life before seeing his beloved master dead. On the contrary, John was like a little brother to Christ. He was the only one who knew each and every detail and they were prepared for the worst-case scenario, and that was the crucifixion. I don't need to tell you more because you've already seen everything that happened after that."

Ava nodded, and she remembered again the image of John pouring powder into the drink that they gave Christ during the crucifixion... and in the cave healing his wounds and helping him escape. But that scene generated more questions.

"If Christ did not die on the cross, then what happened to him?"

Andy got closer and closer to Ava as he spoke.

"Christ recovered from his wounds on the cross, and on the third day it was very easy for him to tell his disciples that he had risen from the dead for the glory of God. But he knew that it was very risky for him, and his followers, if he should stay there, so they met in a distant and safe place where he assigned each one a special task. He then "retired and returned to the right hand of God the Father", but in reality he went to live in India where he changed his name, married, had children and continued to preach his word until his death at an old age."

Ava was still looking puzzled, but at the same time she seemed to begin to process everything Andy was saying. She only had one last question going through her head.

"Does the Catholic Church know anything about all this?"

Andy stopped smiling, and put on a serious face.

"Of course, they know. Not all of them, but those who really control the church know the true story of Christ."

"Really? Does the Pope know all this?!"

"Do you really think that the Pope controls the church? He is only the face of the church to the public, but there are more people behind him who control the pontiff at all times, and everything that happens in the church. It is a very powerful small group of people, but as dark as a moonless night."

"But if they know, why do they keep lying to us?" she asked, innocently.

"And give up one of the companies that has generated the most money in the history of mankind? That will never happen. Just think about it. If irrefutable evidence appeared tomorrow that Christ was not resurrected and that he died of old age, the church would lose all the power it has now. No one else would believe in Christ as the only saviour."

"And that's what you want? To smear Christ's name and take away his followers?"

"I just want the truth! You have got so used to living in the dark that now you see grey as white. You think you are doing the right thing, but in reality, you are losing yourself more and more in absolute darkness. All I am doing is shedding some light, so that you can see well the filth in which you have been living all this time. But what my light allows you to see is so bad that you immediately get scared and think that I am the one who brought that in to your lives. It is not my fault. I only show you the reality, and the reality is not a good thing in your world right now."

Andy was very close to Ava. Their lips were only a few inches apart.

"Andy, please, stay away. You are confusing me and it is not fair." Ava tried to fight against the desire to be with her dear Andy again.

"Look at me Ava" Andy said sweetly.

Ava looked into Andy's eyes. She saw again those black eyes that gave her a chill but it was still the same look, the same face. Ava could not understand how, if the being in front of her was not Andy, it could be exactly like him in every way.

Andy was face to face with Ava; Andy brushed her hair away from her face and gently stroked her cheek.

"I know things have got a little out of control, but I promise you that the only thing that has not changed is my love for you. I have loved you since the first time I saw you and I still love you now that I have you here in front of me."

"Oh, Andy, please stop!"

"You know I'm telling the truth. It has always been you and, since we met, we have always been together just you and me. No matter how bad things have gone with our families, it didn't matter because we had each other and we would never be alone. Do you remember our promise?"

"Oh Andy!" Ava looked straight into Andy's eyes and cried at his words, because she felt that it was her Andy who was talking. She knew that, in some part of that being, the real Andy still lived. He continued talking.

"Do you remember? No matter what, no matter how..."

"We will always be together." Ava finished the sentence as she felt that her heart was about to leave her chest.

"Yes, always together." Andy repeated, smiling.

Andy approached slowly to kiss her on the lips and Ava could not resist anymore. She closed her eyes and moved forward to return his kiss.

"Ava, are you okay?" came Mike's voice from the door of the airport lounge.

Ava opened her eyes immediately. She was shocked when she heard Mike's voice and saw that Andy was no longer there. She was looking around the room for a sign of him, while Professor Bianchi and Mike looked at her confused.

"Ava, are you okay?" Mike asked again.

"Yes... Yes, I'm fine" Ava answered, without sounding very convincing.

"Are you sure? You seem a bit confused." said Professor Bianchi.

"Yes, I'm fine, don't worry. I'm just a little tired."

"Okay" said Mike, dropping it. "Look, anyway, we brought food. Do you fancy anything?"

Ava looked at the food and it seemed like a good idea. After everything that had happened, she felt hungry and the food was a good source of energy to allow her to further process all that information. But still, she couldn't stop thinking about Andy. She wondered where he was and what he was doing, and there was something she still couldn't understand: How was it possible that, having such power, he did not do exactly what he wanted to do with her. He had the power, and the opportunity, so... why didn't he do it?

CHAPTER SIXTEEN

Devil Pays

Ava, Mike and Professor Bianchi were heading to Italy. The private plane that was waiting for them was one of the fastest on the market, and fortunately time was on their side which meant they were scheduled to reach Italy in just 8 hours.

Ava kept going over everything that happened with Andy and could not stop thinking about what the big lie was. Was it the story that Andy had revealed to her? Or was it the story that she took for granted in the bible? The thought that maybe the whole world is getting it wrong, worshiping the bad guy in the story, gave her chills.

***

Andy was still in Los Angeles; he was walking through the centre of the city. It was night, and he was walking with his eyes fixed on a particular building. It was a medium, modern building, all glass, and at its entrance a large stone sign read "Parker & Thompson". Andy was across the street from the building, and staring at the front door. A middle-aged man emerged from the entrance wearing a grey designer suit and talking on the phone in an angry tone. Andy followed the man carefully with his eyes and listened to his side of the conversation from a distance.

"Listen to me carefully Miss! Tell your boss that I don't care! If I call him, it doesn't matter what day or time, he should answer me!"

The man had a very fractured voice. He screamed down the phone and seemed to have difficulties with his throat. It was the kind of voice that, by listening to it, you could think he had some kind of illness. Andy listened attentively and he knew that it was not the first time he had heard this voice. He had heard it the night before, and he knew very well who this man really was.

"Then tell him that Christian Parker says that, if he doesn't want to go to jail in the next 48 hours, he has to bring those documents to my office tomorrow!"

Christian Parker took a pack of cigarettes out of his pocket as he continued his angry conversation.

"Aaaah, now he wants to talk... Maybe now I'm the one who isn't interested in talking to him."

Christian took out a cigarette, put it in his mouth and fumbled around for his lighter.

"Okay, put me on to that idiot." he said with the cigarette in his mouth, still patting himself down searching for his lighter.

"Listen to me very carefully, and let's hope it's the last time you put me through all this just to talk to you.

I don't care if you think you're one of the most important businessmen in the city, because the only thing that stands between you and jail is me."

Christian walked towards the street until he was right next to his car. He continued looking for his lighter but couldn't find it anywhere. He got more and more frustrated by this, while talking with his client. Suddenly, a hand appeared from behind him and offered him a light. He turned his head to look at the light and thought of nothing more than lighting his cigarette. He had not even realized that the lighter the that stranger was offering him was his own: a gold lighter with the initials "CP" engraved on the front. He brought the cigarette to the fire and lit it.

"Thanks." he muttered as he turned to see the face of the kind stranger, but that stranger was Andy. Andy was now in front of him, looking him straight in the eye and smiling.

Christian was completely paralyzed when he saw Andy's face. So great was his surprise that he dropped both his phone and his pack of cigarettes.

"Hi Christian, aren't you glad to see me?" Andy said in a mocking tone.

Christian was still completely paralyzed. His mouth was open, but the cigarette was stuck to his upper lip. As he looked at Andy's face he thought *"It can't be! It's the guy from last night. The one who interrupted my mass with his friend, but... how did he find me? And how did he know my name?"*

"What happened? Has the *great* Christian Parker run out of words? You called me, you invoked your Lord, and now that you have him in front of you, you have nothing to say?"

For the first time in a long time, Christian Parker had been petrified. He was feeling helpless, defenceless, with fear in his eyes and perhaps for the first time ever, with real fear in his heart.

"His eyes" Christian thought, *"His eyes are black... but I remember very well that they were blue. When I had him on my altar forcing him to drink the blood of that baby, his eyes were blue"*

"The colour of my eyes is the least of your problems, Christian Parker" Andy replied aloud to his thought.

A huge chill ran through Christian's body. He knew that this was real, that he was in front of something that was not human.

"You can read my mind?" Christian asked fearfully.

"Like an open book. And not only can I read your mind; I can also read your whole life. I know everything you have done, and everything you plan to do in my name."

For Christian there was no longer the slightest doubt, that the being in front of him was the prince of darkness whom he had longed to meet. It was hard for him to believe that the black mass the night before had actually worked, and had brought the fallen angel into this world. He should be pleased and happy with that, but instead he was afraid. He saw the look in Andy's eyes was the look of a predator in front of his prey. Andy kept talking.

"For years you have dedicated your life to doing evil: lying, stealing, cheating, taking advantage of the weakest and killing without the slightest amount of remorse."

Christian listened intently and felt that he was in the middle of a trial in front of his judge, jury and executioner.

"But what you did last night crossed the line, even for someone like you. You seduced and took advantage of your poor assistant, with the false promise that you would leave your wife to marry her. Once she told you that she was pregnant, she became an obstacle for you. The fun was over. You didn't hesitate for a second to snatch the child from her womb and sacrifice your own child in the name of the fallen Angel."

Christian's heart was beating uncontrollably. He felt like a cold sweat ran down his head and the palms of his hands. He was like a child whose parents reproached him for having done something wrong, and he knew it would not end well for him.

"Only an act of such unforgivable evil could wake me up from my lethargy, and give me all the necessary motivation to come to this world and intervene.

Christian Parker, you did all those atrocities in my name to please me and get my blessings in return". Andy gave a sarcastic smile. "Well, here you have me, in front of you to give you everything you really deserve."

Christian swallowed hard, he felt confused. The things that Andy said seemed as though he was going to reward him for his loyalty, but he could not shake the feeling that something bad was about to happen to him.

"You don't have to worry Christian, I was just passing by to thank you since, after all, if it hadn't been for you, I wouldn't be here today."

Andy slowly raised his hand to remove the cigarette from his mouth that was still lit, took a drag and stared into Christian's eyes.

"Thanks."

Andy let the smoke out of his mouth and blew it towards Christian's face. Christian reacted and began to cough while Andy continued blowing the smoke at him. The smoke seemed to have no end; more and more was coming out of Andy's mouth and it was sticking to Christian's body. The smoke became thicker, and it covered the whole of Christian's body. He tried to get rid of the smoke, but it was like a black cloud that did not release him. Suddenly, Christian began to feel the smoke was heating up, getting hotter and hotter by the second. He felt like it was burning his skin, until a spark ignited and turned the smoke into fire.

The "Grand Master" was covered in flames; he was burning alive. He could only scream as he desperately tried to put out the fire with his bare hands. Christian Parker ran like crazy without knowing what to do, and in a moment of despair he jumped in the middle of the street, right in front of a car that was going too fast to stop in time. It ran straight over him, throwing him through the air, until he fell in such a bad position that his neck was snapped on the spot. The impact left him completely immobile in the street, his body was consumed by the flames but he was still alive. His whole life passed before his eyes; he thought of all the horrible things he had done, and he knew he deserved punishment.

His body laid in the middle of the street while it was still burning, and with a last effort he moved his eyes towards the place where Andy was. Perhaps he did it as a gesture of regret, or cry for help but either way it didn't matter; Andy was no longer there, but in his place laid the discarded cigarette box that read "SMOKING KILLS".

CHAPTER SEVENTEEN
Sforza Castle

Ava, Mike and Professor Bianchi were flying over Italian airspace. They had flown all night aboard a Cessna Citation X+. One of the fastest private jets on the market; only available to the most powerful people on the planet. Mike was still surprised by the power of money. They were being helped by the Vatican and everything they had done so far was only thanks to that power. Mike had never left the country, and that night he had left with nothing more than the clothes on his back, not even a passport. Mike thought to himself, *"if you have money, you have power, and if you have power, you can control everything."*

Ava, on the other hand, was oblivious to all that. She had barely slept and just looked out of the window; at the sky, the clouds, the sun rising on the horizon illuminating the place. She looked at everything and at the same time her gaze was lost in the nothing. She remembered Andy's words and all the secrets he had revealed. Her mind had processed all the information but she was still having doubts, and for each question that she asked herself more questions appeared in her head. She was so absorbed in her thoughts that she hadn't noticed Henry's gaze. He had been watching her for a couple of minutes; examining her in detail. He knew that something had happened at the airport in the moments she was left alone... *"but what?" he thought.*

There was only one way to find out and that was by talking to Ava. Professor Bianchi moved over to sit next to Ava.

"Ava, are you okay?" Henry asked as he sat next to her.

Ava snapped out of her trance and reacted.

"Yes, I'm fine." she said shortly.

"Sure? I noticed you looked a little worried."

Ava looked at him as she replied with a mocking tone.

"Taking into account that my boyfriend is the devil incarnate, you can forgive me for being a bit withdrawn."

Henry nodded, although he was not completely convinced by her answer. He knew there was something else, but he didn't want to pressure her.

"Can I ask you something Henry?" she said.

"Of course, anything you want."

"Have you ever doubted your faith?"

"Why do you ask?" he asked, full of suspicion.

"Just that you've been following the word of Christ for so many years; faithfully obeying all the orders of the church, but... how do you know that everything that's written in the bible is true and that you're on the side of good?"

Professor Bianchi smiled and took a second to answer.

"I guess it's just faith."

Ava watched him intently while he went on.

"You see, everyone needs to believe in something. No matter what religion you choose; in the end what really matters is that you're happy and that you're a better person. But if you ever have any doubts, the best thing you can do is ask your heart, it will tell you what to believe and it will never be wrong."

Ava smiled back at him then looked down. That answer didn't help her, not after all the revelations that Andy had shown her. How could she know what was true and what was a lie? Is Andy this malevolent being who would say anything to achieve his goal? Or was he the victim of a being who was even worse and had managed to deceive all of humanity in a masterful way?

"Passengers, please fasten your seat belts; in just a few minutes we will land." came the voice of the pilot.

Ava and the professor looked at each other and the professor smiled.

"Tell me Ava, what do you believe in?"

Ava looked out of her window, fixed her gaze on the sky and replied.

"I only believe in what my heart tells me."

Professor Bianchi smiled and got up to go back to his seat. Mike was watching the scene from the back seat and wondering what they were talking about.

Ava kept looking out of the window as she watched the plane slowly approach the ground. She could see a green landscape all around with thousands of trees hiding a small, clandestine airport that they appeared to be approaching.

The plane landed safely on a small-unpaved runway, then taxied to a small hangar where four black cars were parked. Several people were standing around the cars watching the plane approach them.

The plane stopped in front of the cars. As the door opened, the men next to the cars came to greet them. The first to disembark was Professor Bianchi and as soon as he saw the people, it was clear that he felt comforted. He knew now that they would be safe with them. Behind the professor was Ava, a little confused and nervous, but Mike followed closely behind her. Although in the past Ava had her differences with him, she now felt a little better knowing that she was with someone she knew, someone she could trust.

Professor Bianchi came down the stairs and the first to approach and welcome him was Roman Lombardi; a 58-year-old man, 5 foot 10 inches tall, thin, with little hair, and dressed in a black suit. He wore a gold ring on his right index finger; a ring that stood out for its size and shape. It appeared to have a seal in the centre that looked like a figure with six points: three above and three below. Ava immediately noticed the ring and knew that she had already seen it before. She remembered that she had seen it the day before, the same day she met Henry; he wears the same ring, on the same finger.

"Professor! What a joy to have you here again!" he exclaimed.

"Roman! My friend. You don't know how happy I am to see you!" Professor Bianchi replied, as he gave him a brotherly hug

"You know that it is my duty to be here professor." Roman said while keeping his hand on the professor's shoulder.

"Please, call me Henry, we don't need so much formality."

"Very well, whatever you want, Henry." Roman smiled and nodded.

Ava and Mike followed behind Professor Bianchi as he greeted his friend. Henry moved aside and made the introductions.

"Roman, let me introduce you to my companions, here you have the lovely Miss Ava Gard. Ava, let me introduce you to Roman Lombardi."

Roman held Ava's hand delicately.

"Buongiorno signorina." He said as he smiled kindly.

"Nice to meet you" Ava said shyly as she wondered who this man was. Professor Bianchi continued with the introductions.

"And the gentleman, this is Mr. Michael Jones."

Mike extended his hand to return Roman's greeting.

"Nice to meet you Roman" Mike said politely.

"The pleasure is mine, Michael."

"Please, call me Mike."

Behind Roman stood a younger man: around 32 years old, English, short hair and a serious face, also wearing a black suit. Román moved aside so that the man was visible to everyone.

"Now it is my turn to make the introductions... Gentlemen, signorina, this is my assistant, Mr. Scott Bowman."

Scott simply nodded without saying anything. The others just greeted with a hello and remaining in place, Roman continued talking.

"He will accompany us at all times and if you need something, do not hesitate to ask him. He will help you without any qualms."

"Excuse me Roman" Ava said, "Scott is your assistant, but doing what? Who are you and what do you have to do with all this?"

Roman smiled.

"But, of course! You have every right to know who I am and what you are doing here. I will explain everything along the way, but for now, just settle for knowing that I am the head of security for the Bellatores Dei."

Professor Bianchi and Scott looked at Roman in surprise, neither of them were used to hearing something like this said so openly, since that was a secret that had been kept for millennia.

"Oh please! Don't look at me like that, they know very well who we are, and in addition, they must know everything for them to be prepared for all that is coming."

Ava and Mike looked at each other and could not hide their worries from their faces. Too many unbelievable things were happening all at the same time, but now with Roman's entrance on the scene, they felt at least that they were in the right place with the right people.

"Good! We must leave as soon as possible!" exclaimed Roman. "They are waiting for us, and we must start the preparations as soon as possible."

Scott and Roman went to the car that was between the other two. The professor, Mike and Ava got into the same black car while the other men watched all sides, preparing to escort Roman and his companions and they left the airport.

Scott was driving while Roman explained the situation to the visitors.

"I know that Henry has explained to you a little of who we are and what our mission is, but I want to give you more details about this long journey and our final destination."

Ava and Mike listened carefully to Roman's words.

"The Bellatores Dei are a secret order founded by the apostle John. Given his close relationship with the son of God, great mysteries were revealed to him; prophecies that would later become reality. Our first Master, Apostle John, made sure that his message passed from generation to generation without being altered, and made it very clear what we should do when the day, that we are now living, arrived: the day of the beast."

Roman went on.

"For centuries the order of the Bellatores Dei has been growing in power and reach. Since we did not know exactly where, or when, the prince of darkness would come, we needed to have eyes and ears all over the planet; and once we had located the beast, we had to be prepared to fight against him and defeat him."

"Sorry Roman, but how exactly do you plan to defeat a being that is not of this world?" Mike interrupted.

Roman looked him straight in the eye and smiled.

"With a weapon that is not of this world."

Mike and Ava were surprised by his answer.

"What do you mean?" asked Mike.

"Don't worry Mike, you will see it in due course." Roman answered, very sure of what he was saying.

The cars continued down an unpaved road, surrounded by trees. They could hardly see what was ahead, but they were getting closer and closer to their destination.

Roman began again.

"With the passing of the centuries, our order obtained the necessary power to create a small army and equip it with everything necessary to be one of the most powerful elite forces in the world. A great example of this is my assistant Scott, who has undergone the strictest military training, mastering five different styles of melee and sword combat."

Everyone looked at Scott, impressed upon hearing his abilities, but he was focused on driving; oblivious to everything Roman said.

"But in addition to Scott, we have thousands of soldiers all over the world willing to die for the salvation of this world. Each and every one of them has been ordered to return to base, which is exactly where we are heading."

After driving through a valley, they came to a place where the trees had been cleared. In the distance an imposing old castle could be seen.

"Ladies and gentlemen," said Roman, "welcome to the Castle of Sforza!"

Ava and Mike were amazed at the spectacular view of the castle. They had never seen anything like it; it looked like something out of a medieval movie, and as they approached the majestic castle, Roman was revealing more details. Roman explained a little of the origin of the castle.

"In 1476, the Archduke of Italy Renato Sforza formed part of our order. To aid our cause, he ordered the construction of this castle that would later become, and remains until now, the home of the Bellatore Dei. It is a site known only to those of us who are part of the order, and now also to you."

Ava kept thinking that all the information that was being revealed could have consequences for them. The organization had been hidden in the shadows for thousands of years, and the mere fact that they now knew this could put their lives at risk. She wanted to know that they weren't going to kill them after knowing all this. Ava could not remain silent as she saw that her imminent end at the hands of the Bellatores Dei became more and more obvious.

"Excuse me Roman," she said, "Maybe what I'm going to say is inappropriate, but it's something I have to ask, since I like to be honest and direct."

Roman turned to look at her.

"And I think that's very good Ava" Roman smiled, "so tell me what you have to say without qualms."

They were all attentive to what Ava was about to ask.

"Okay, my question is simple. How can we be sure, Mike and I, that after all this is over, you're not going to kill us for knowing everything we know about you?"

Mike was surprised by her question, until now he hadn't thought about the fact that they could kill them for it, but Ava was right. Professor Bianchi looked at Roman, but not even Professor Bianchi knew how to answer.

Roman blurted out a laugh.

"That is a very good question Ava, but you forget a very important factor, and that is that after all this ends, whether we win or not, the order of the Bellatores Dei will disappear."

Everyone listened attentively to Roman's words.

"The only reason for our order to exist is to defeat Satan and undo his plans to dominate the world. If we can succeed, our objective will be accomplished and there will be no reason to continue existing. So, you can rest assured, because after all this is over it will not matter if you tell the whole world about us. By then, our order will have already disappeared without leaving a single trace."

Ava was calmer when she heard this since, for some reason, she trusted Roman, and his words made a lot of sense to her, but Roman had not finished speaking.

"But if we cannot win, then ask God to have mercy on you and grant you a quick death, because what will come later to our world will be much worse."

Ava and Mike looked at each other and the relief they had felt before completely vanished. They had forgotten for a moment that they were dealing with a being from another world, a being they did not even know if they could face, let alone defeat.

The four cars arrived at the castle gate that was open waiting for them. The entrance had an arch with two pillars, where snipers watched, guarding. Through the arch, there was a small bridge that led into the castle. The interior looked more like a military base than an old castle; there were armoured cars everywhere, soldiers in dark camouflage unloading the weapons and preparing for what would be a scene of the third world war, at least that's what it seemed.

Ava, Mike and the others got out of the car and immediately realized that Roman had not exaggerated when he said that over time the organization had become an elite force with a large army. All they could see were soldiers running from one side to the other, mounting powerful weapons, pointing out strategic points of the castle to defend with great precision and coordination.

"Impressed?" Roman asked as he watched his men in action.

"Yes, it's really amazing" Mike answered.

"We have two hundred and fifty soldiers right now defending the castle, plus another two hundred and fifty who are forming various defence rings outside the castle."

"Outside the castle? But we didn't see anyone on the way?" Ava said.

Roman just smiled.

"That doesn't mean that they are not there and that they have not seen us pass."

Ava and Mike saw that the soldiers did not stop working, and for the first time since all this began, they felt safe, secure. They knew that this army was there to help them and that they would give their lives to defeat their common enemy. Roman kept talking.

"However, these are the men who have arrived this morning, we expect another seven hundred soldiers by this afternoon, just to defend the castle and surroundings."

Ava and Mike smiled in astonishment with such a display of power, but Professor Bianchi did not seem surprised at all. It seemed that he didn't care much about the army, there was only one thing he wanted to know to feel completely safe.

"Roman, you know that your army seems to me quite impressive, but that is not the reason for my trip to Sforza Castle, you know very well why I am here."

Roman let out a small laugh.

"Of course I know why you have come my friend! But don't worry, we also have our secret weapon."

Professor Bianchi smiled pleased upon hearing Roman's confirmation.

"It's true," said Mike, "Now that he says it, on the way you mentioned you had a weapon that was not from this world... that's what you mean when you say "secret weapon"?" he asked.

Roman looked into Mike's eyes and smiled again.

"That's the one Mike, and as I told you I would show it to you in time, and it seems to me that the moment has already arrived... do you want to see it?"

CHAPTER EIGHTEEN

The Cross of Longinus

"Are you kidding me? Of course we want to see it!"

Ava just looked at Mike and saw that he was very excited at the idea of seeing such a fantastic weapon. Mike couldn't even imagine what such a weapon would look like. Was it a weapon that shoots a laser beam? Would it be a portal that would transport the devil to another dimension? Mike couldn't stop imagining and thinking about the possibilities. Roman could see this and pressed on.

"Very well, in that case follow me." he said.

Roman started walking and led them to a door that was several meters away from the main entrance. There were two guards with machine guns guarding the entrance. As soon as they saw Roman they showed their respect with a military salute. Roman returned the greeting and immediately one of them took a key from his pocket and opened the door. Roman was the first to pass, closely followed by Professor Bianchi, Mike, and Ava, with Scott picking up the rear; he did not lose track of them for a second.

After going through the door, they walked down a narrow corridor lined with several closed doors on either side. Roman went to one of the doors that was not locked, opened the door and entered the room. There were bookshelves full of books. Roman went to a large antique desk that was at the end of the room, and stood in front of the desk looking straight at everyone who was with him. He pressed a button that was hidden under the table and a secret hatch opened above the desk, revealing a futuristic looking safe, Roman stopped for a moment to speak to them.

"The entire desk is one of the strongest safes in the world; so heavy that it would take a crane to move it, so massive that even with the most powerful drill in the world it would take years to get inside, so strong that even 50 kilos of dynamite could not even dent it. It is also an airtight box, which allows its interior to remain unaltered as there is no air inside. There is only one person in the whole world that can access it, and that person is me."

Roman placed his right hand on some metal sensors that were next to a panel. The sensors read every millimetre of his palm and his heartbeat and at the end of the scan a green light lit up above the panel. Roman raised his hand and he entered a numeric password on a small keyboard. He entered 10 digits at different rates between each number, since the safe recognized the speed at which each number is entered, and the speed was part of the safe's security system. Once finished, everyone heard a metallic click inside the safe. Roman opened the safe door and took out an old wooden box with very detailed carvings. Everyone could see that the box alone was something very special, but they couldn't wait to see the secret weapon.

Roman put the wooden box to one side of the desk, turned it so that it was facing his guests, unlocked the latches, and slowly began to open it. At last the time had come, Mike's heart was beating fast, he had always been a fan of the dark forces, and knowing that he was in front of something that could stop the devil himself made him feel small, like a child who was going to see the best toy in the world. Ava, on the other hand, was more than excited, she was nervous, everyone was only talking about stopping and defeating the prince of darkness, but it seemed that everyone had forgotten that evil incarnate was still Andy; the love of her life. He was the man she hoped to spend the rest of her days with, but now he was the enemy. But... was he really?

On the contrary, Henry knew exactly what was in the box. He knew what the weapon looked like and how it worked, but this would be the first time he had seen it in the flesh, so it was a very important moment for him as well.

Roman opened the box, and revealed an old metal cross protected by glass. The cross was made with different pieces that seemed to have nothing to do with each other, so at first sight it looked like a cross without any material value. Mike looked at the cross and his face reflected bewilderment and disappointment. He looked at Roman and didn't know if it was a joke or if he really believed that this cross was the ultimate weapon against the devil. Ava looked around at everyone and didn't know what to say. The only one who was astonished by the cross was Professor Bianchi, who stared at it and a nervous smile escaped his face. He tried to remain calm, but it seemed that the cross surpassed him. Roman began to speak.

"As you know, Jesus Christ, the son of God, came to Earth to wash away our sins with his blood and thus obtain the salvation of our world, but in the process of salvation his hands and feet were pierced with nails; leaving him nailed to a wooden cross. As if that were not enough, after his death, his side was pierced with a spear to prove he was dead."

Ava immediately remembered the scene, since she had seen it in person the day before. Even though it was only a memory, the image gave her chills. Roman went on.

"What almost no one knows, is that the soldier who speared the side of Christ had problems with one of his eyes. When piercing Christ's skin, the water and blood that came out of him fell on the eye of the soldier; healing him immediately. It was at that moment the soldier realized that the man who had died in front of him was really the son of God."

Ava and Mike listened attentively to Roman's words; they knew the explanation of how the cross had come to hold so much power was about to be revealed.

"That Roman soldier had a name, and his name was Longinus. After delivering the body of Christ back to his family, Longinus kept the nails that had pierced the son of God and kept the tip of the "holy lance", as it would later become known, since the items had touched the blood of Christ. A couple of years later, Longinus became one of the first Christians in history and even formed his own church. One of the biggest claims of his church was that those objects had preserved the blood of Christ."

Ava and Mike were so enthralled by the story that they did not move an inch. Ava didn't know what to believe as this further added to the scene that she had witnessed the day before.

"Over time, Christianity was gaining strength," Roman continued, sensing their interest, "and the nails and the lance became sacred objects desired by all; so much so, that it caused wars, thousands of deaths and countless injustices in the name of Christ. The nails and the spear changed hands for hundreds of years, until they finally fell into the ownership of Bellatores Dei. In order not to lose any of the pieces we decided to give them a new form and make a single piece, resulting in the object before you."

Ava and Mike were stunned by the story, and now they perfectly understood the importance of the object.

"Ladies and gentlemen, I present to you the Cross of Longinus; the only remaining artefact in the world that still contains the authentic blood of Christ."

Mike was very impressed, and that was something that was not easily achieved for him. On the contrary, Ava was not quite sure that the cross could be the definitive weapon against Andy, because she knew that it did not matter if it was covered in blood of Christ or not. It was of no use, because she knew that Christ was just an ordinary man, without any divine power. Or at least that was what Andy had taught her.

Mike understood very well the value of the antique. He knew that it was a truly unique piece, and that they were very lucky just to know that something like this still existed today, and much more to be in front of it. But... Would it really work as a weapon? Mike had his doubts.

"Excuse me Roman," said Mike, "but how can you be so sure that this cross will work?"

"Good question Mike, and the answer is very simple. This is a plan that was drawn up thousands of years ago by Apostle John, thanks to the secret teachings received by his master and our Lord Jesus Christ.

Thanks to this cross, and the blood that it contains, the power of Christ is with us."

Roman, Scott and Professor Bianchi looked at Mike expecting to see a face of satisfaction with this answer, but Mike was still unconvinced.

"I understand that this cross has a divine power, a power that belongs to another world, but remember that the devil is inside Andy's body, a being of this world; so how can you be sure that it will have the same effect in a body made of flesh and blood?"

Scott looked at Roman and, although he would never admit it, Scott knew that was a good question. Professor Bianchi was puzzled by the question, because he knew that Mike was right. No matter how much faith they could have in the cross, the fact remained that the malevolent being was inside an earthly body, and they couldn't be sure that the devil was only using Andy's body as a connection to this world; he could also be using it as protection. Roman closed the wooden box, looked back at Mike and replied confidently.

"It will work."

"But Roman..." Mike attempted to push his point.

"Mike that's enough. I do not ask you to understand how it will work or why it will work, I only ask you to have faith and trust in me."

Roman put the wooden box back into the safe and closed it again, hiding the safe door, leaving only the old desk table visible once again.

"Now please, if you would be so kind to accompany me, I will provide you with a place to rest and eat something decent."

Roman guided them to the exit and they went to another door where the castle's dining room was located. It was a large room with tables everywhere. Some soldiers were eating there and as soon as they saw Roman, they got up to greet him. Roman returned the greeting with a nod of his head and motioned for them to continue eating.

"Please, take a seat, I will send one of my men immediately to offer you something to eat." Roman said as he left, accompanied by Scott.

Mike, Ava and Professor Bianchi sat down. Henry could see that Mike was a bit deflated and he could guess why.

"Are you ok Mike?" he asked.

Mike looked at the professor and then turned his gaze to the soldiers and the tables around him, while he shook his head from side to side in disbelief.

"It won't work." Mike said, annoyed.

Ava looked at him and couldn't resist responding.

"What are you talking about?" she said.

Mike looked straight back at Ava, and from being annoyed he went to feeling sorry.

"The weapon they have to attack the beast, it won't work."

"Why do you say that, boy?" Professor Bianchi intervened.

"Because, we are talking about the fallen angel, and you don't understand! It's a being that has existed since before time and space. A being who is not affected by our laws; who also knows them so well that he can even play with them at will, and you want to attack him with a couple of old pieces dipped in the blood of the Son of God?! Blood that, after all this time, can't even be considered blood."

Ava lowered her head and looked at the table. Professor Bianchi was still looking very seriously into Mike's eyes. Mike had already expressed his concern and his allegations, now it was his turn.

"Tell me something Mike, in all your life, how many times have you had to face demonic forces?"

Mike was speechless at the question; the only thing he could say was none, this was his first time, Henry continued talking through his silence.

"As I had already told you before, in my youth as a priest I did many exorcisms; authentic fights with authentic demons, and my weapons were always my old crucifix, water blessed by myself and all my faith in the power of Christ by my side. And you know one thing? That crucifix, and that holy water, were infallible in my fight, and they were just a couple of simple things blessed by me. Now, imagine what we can do with a cross that bears the blood of the Son of God. It doesn't matter that you do not see the blood on the cross clearly, or that the blood is not fresh; those ancient pieces were touched by the blood of Christ, and that connection continues to this day. For you, there may be no logic in all this, but this war is not won with logic, it is won with faith."

Mike knew that this argument had been very valid, but even so, he still had his doubts. He wanted to completely believe in the power of that cross, but something inside him told him that it would not work.

After eating something, Ava and Mike were taken to different rooms to allow them to rest a little, but no matter how much Ava tried, she was unable to sleep. Every moment she thought about Andy, about everything that had happened at the airport and she still didn't know what or who to believe. It made no sense to her to stay in bed trying to find answers that no one had, so she got up and decided to go for a little walk to clarify her thoughts. It was still daylight, but it was beginning to get dark. Her room was on the second floor of the castle; it was in a corridor that connected all the rooms and had a balcony that overlooked the centre of the castle. When Ava left the room, she saw that Scott was standing in front of her door. He was leaning against the balcony watching the soldiers preparing for a war. Scott was wearing a black military uniform with a katana on his back. Ava approached him as soon as she saw him.

"Were you watching me Scott?"

Scott looked at her for a second and turned his gaze back to the soldiers.

"I was just protecting your door, it's different."

Ava stepped to the side of him and also watched the soldiers.

"Tell me Scott, how long have you been working for the Vatican?"

Scott stared into her eyes, as if that question had bothered him.

"I don't work for the Vatican; I work for the Bellatores Dei"

"What? Is Bellatores Dei not a Vatican organization?"

Scott looked back at the soldiers and smiled.

"That's what they believe" he said.

"If not, then what?" Ava asked.

"The truth is that our order was founded directly by Apostle John. The Vatican only usurped the order of Apostle Peter when they saw that Christianity became an unstoppable force."

Ava was surprised to see that Scott spoke of the Vatican with contempt, but she felt more confident to see that one of them didn't think the Vatican was as good as they would have you believe. Ava continued with her questioning.

"If you have such a bad opinion of the Vatican, how do you work with them?"

"It can be said that they are a necessary evil for us; they have information and resources that have been very useful for our mission. It is also not our responsibility to unmask the Vatican, that is something that will happen in due course."

"Do you also think that there is a dark force behind the Vatican?"

"I don't just think it, I know it. Why do you ask?" he said, suspicious.

"If I'm honest with you, since all this started, I don't know what to think. For the first time in my life, I'm starting to have doubts about what's right and what's wrong." she said, visibly conflicted.

Scott put his eyes on her again, now he could feel the conflict that Ava felt inside her and he knew he had to help her in some way.

"And what are these doubts?"

Ava stared back at Scott, and even though she didn't know him, something inside her told her that she could trust him.

"I just don't understand why Andy, with all the power he has now, doesn't just do exactly what he wants to do with me already. He has had the opportunity, so... why hasn't he done it?"

"And who says he hasn't already done it?" Scott challenged back.

Ava was surprised by his response.

"If you mean, why has Satan not forced you to do his will? Well, the answer is very simple; it is only because he cannot. Humans have free will, which means that we are free to choose our own path. The only thing he can do is try to tempt or trick you into choosing exactly what he wants, but in the end the decision is yours alone."

Ava listened intently as Scott kept talking.

"So, you cannot say that he has not tried anything to win you over, because if you are now doubting your role in this fight, you are letting him win."

"Sir! You have a call from Alpha team." a soldier was calling up at Scott from the castle square.

"I'll be right there" replied Scott, "Now if you'll excuse me Ava, I have business to attend to, but I'll give you one last piece of advice; stop calling him Andy, that's what has you so confused. You keep projecting your old love on this being. It is far better for you if you start calling it what it really is."

Scott turned and headed for the stairs.

"Scott!" Ava called out.

Scott turned to look back at her.

"Thank you very much, you've helped me a lot."

Scott just smiled and kept walking.

Mike's room was next to Ava's. He had been observing them for a couple of minutes and, seeing that

Scott was leaving in a hurry, he saw his opportunity to be with Ava.

"Hi Ava, is everything okay?"

"Yeah, as well as it can be" Ava replied sarcastically as she saw Scott running towards the radio.

"Do you know if something happened? They seem different." said Mike, watching Scott speaking on the radio.

"I don't know Mike, but the only thing I can be sure of is that whatever is happening... it's not good."

"Alpha team, this is Sforza team..." Scott said as he waited for an answer from the Alpha team, but all he could hear was radio interference.

"Come in Alpha team, this is Sforza team. Come in Alpha Team..."

"Receiving, Alpha team. Over." came an eventual reply.

"Finally!" exclaimed Scott. "Alpha Team, what is the situation? Over."

"Sir, I don't know exactly what it is, but something is happening in the sky. Over"

Scott and everyone by the radio looked at each other without saying a word.

"Alpha Team, what do you mean, something is happening in the sky? Over."

"From my position I can see a black whirlpool slowly moving through the sky. It seems as if a tornado is forming. Over."

"A tornado?" Scott replied as he thought about there never having been tornados in the area.

"That's what it seems Sir. It is not very big, but it is heading towards you. Out."

Scott had a bad feeling about the tornado. He lowered the radio and addressed the soldiers who were nearest him.

"Quick! Find Roman and tell him that I need him here, now!"

CHAPTER NINETEEN

The Great Battle

All the soldiers took their positions, while Ava and Mike kept watching from the balcony. They didn't understand what was happening but from a distance they saw Roman, accompanied by a soldier, moving quickly to where Scott was waiting. Ava and Roman met each other's eyes for a second, but then Roman turned his full attention back to Scott.

"Scott what's going on?" he asked, concerned.

"Alpha team has a visual of an anomaly in the sky." he said.

"What kind of anomaly?" Roman asked, his voice still full of concern.

"Apparently, a tornado is forming towards this location."

"A tornado? Hmmm, how interesting..."

"That's what I thought." said Scott.

"How far is the Alpha team from here?"

"They form a perimeter of 20 kilometres around the castle." said Scott, simply stating the facts.

A soldier interrupted.

"Sir, we have news from the Beta team, they have also confirmed visuals of the phenomenon. There is no doubt that it is heading here."

Scott and Roman looked at each other, showing their concern.

"And how far away is the Beta team?" asked Roman.

"About 10 kilometres Sir"

"I see."

Roman looked up at the sky without saying anything else.

"Sir, you should give the order to all the other teams that are guarding the perimeters to return, I am sure that we are going to need all the possible help here."

Roman just kept looking at the sky.

"No, tell them to hold the position and to be alert to new orders."

Scott was surprised with this decision; he did not agree at all.

"But ... Sir" he tried to interject.

"Listen Scott, that phenomenon could be what we have been waiting for all this time, or it could be nothing; so, we have to be prepared for any event that could happen. If Satan is able to penetrate our defences and reach here, let's make sure he doesn't come out again!"

"Yes Sir" Scott said, still not very convinced of this decision.

A little way down the perimeter balcony, Ava and Mike continued watching the display of force below, knowing that something was happening. Professor Bianchi left his room upon hearing so much noise from the soldiers. He saw Mike and Ava and approached them.

"What's going on? What is all this fuss about?"

Ava looked at the professor and then at Mike.

"We don't know yet, but something tells me that Andy is on his way."

A chill ran through the professor's entire body upon hearing this. He couldn't hide the fact that this situation was getting to his nerves.

"Come. Follow me. Let's ask Roman what is happening.

The professor, Mike and Ava headed towards the stairs as they watched soldiers run from one side to the other, looking for the best position to see what was approaching. Night had already fallen and the entire castle was illuminated with lights to even the smallest corner. Scott and Roman were still in the centre of the castle coordinating the troops. They distributed photos of Andy around the soldiers so that they knew what the devil's face was like. They finalized details as they saw Henry, Mike and Ava approaching them. The professor was the first to speak.

"Roman... is this all what it really seems to be?"

Roman looked back at the professor, and then at Mike and Ava, he knew that he had to measure his words so as not to alert them unnecessarily.

"We still do not know for sure, but you already know that in these cases it is better to be safe than sorry, my friend."

"But what exactly is happening? Could you give us details?"

"Sir!" Interrupted a soldier, "the Delta team now has a visual of the phenomenon."

Roman looked immediately at Scott.

"How far away is the Delta team?"

Scott swallowed hard and stared into Roman's eyes.

"One kilometre Sir" he swallowed.

"Merda! Quick! Get ready, it's here!" Roman shouted to the troops in front of the visitors.

"Ava, come with me. You must not witness what is about to happen here."

Those words were like a punch to Ava's stomach. It was like living the same nightmare over and over again. Roman, Scott, Henry, Ava, and Mike headed for the same door they had gone through before to see the sacred weapon. The same door watched by two guards, only this time they had more soldiers accompanying them behind. Roman gave the order to open the door and at that moment one of the soldiers who was on the top floor of the castle watching shouted.

"INCOMING!"

They all turned to look, and saw a whirlpool descending from the sky, little by little, forming a small tornado that touched the ground inside the castle. It was a small but very powerful tornado. All the soldiers tried to maintain their position, but the immense wind prevented them from taking a defensive position. Only the wind could be heard blowing, followed by thunder and the complaints of the soldiers closest to them. Ava watched the spectacle, and knew it wasn't something natural. The tornado was still in the same position, it hadn't moved a millimetre since it hit the ground. It was still there circling, and at times it seemed that it was losing strength. The soldiers could now move freely and they all pointed their weapons into the tornado.

The tornado was losing strength and was disappearing little by little, but inside something was spinning with the tornado. It looked like a shapeless shadow because it was spinning very fast, and it was impossible to know exactly what it was until suddenly the figure touched the ground. It began to turn more slowly, revealing a human figure apparently trapped in the tornado. Ava looked carefully at the person inside the tornado and saw clearly who it was.

"A… Andy?" she stuttered.

Everyone watched as Andy stopped turning and faced his beloved Ava. He had his eyes closed, but when he stopped, he opened them to look into Ava's eyes, she could not believe it. He smiled.

"IT IS HIM! FIRE!" shouted one of the soldiers.

All the soldiers reacted the same time and pointed their guns at Andy.

"NOOO!" Ava screamed, as Mike and Henry prevented her from running towards him, but it was too late.

All the soldiers started shooting at the same time. Ava's heart stopped for a second; it was as if the image passed in slow motion in front of her eyes. As soon as she saw Andy inside the tornado, she knew that this would be the last time she saw him alive. She knew it was all real, but still she refused to believe it, she couldn't believe that the end had come for her dear Andy... but she was wrong.

As soon as the first soldier gave the order to fire, Andy took a fighting position. He bent his knees a little and formed a cross with his arms, bringing them up to the level of his shoulders. The soldiers started firing their bullets but they stopped immediately in the air, almost a meter away from Andy. The bullets seemed to collide with a force-field that protected Andy. When the soldiers saw that the bullets did not reach their target, they stopped firing, one by one, as they looked on in disbelief. Thousands of bullets were floating around Andy. Nobody said anything and from the thunderous sound of the machine guns, they were plunged into a deathly silence. Ava was watching the scene and all the sadness she had felt in thinking that she had lost the love of her life turned into fear. For the first time, she felt that others were right in calling him the beast, because it was clear at this moment that this was no longer Andy.

He ran his gaze all around him and he saw all those soldiers willing to do whatever was necessary to prevent his plans.

"I can see that no matter what I do or say, you are not going to stop until you kill me... or until you lose your life. I really did not want to go to this extreme, but I know very well what must be done for the good of all humanity; then so be it!"

As everyone looked at Andy, stunned, he prepared for his counterattack. He straightened up, but still with his hands crossed, he looked at all the soldiers around him as the bullets slowly spun around him in the air. Andy began to squeeze his fists with force, the bullets stopped and began to vibrate little by little, more and more. When Roman saw what was happening, he had a very bad feeling.

"Hurry! Let's go inside! Come! Come on! COME ON!"

Roman grabbed Ava by the wrist and dragged her into the castle. Mike, Henry and Scott reacted immediately and followed after them. At that moment, Andy opened his arms wide in an explosive way; the suspended bullets were fired in all directions, killing and wounding dozens of soldiers at the same time. Some of the soldiers who were not hit by the bullets returned to their weapons and directed them at Andy again, but he just closed his eyes and listened as the weapons of all the soldiers jammed at the same time. It was clear that firearms were not an option, so the soldiers switched to knives and moved in groups to try to kill him, but it was futile. Andy defended himself like a professional military man; nobody could do anything against him. He seemed to read each of the thoughts of his opponents, allowing him victory in the face of those who dared to confront him.

Meanwhile, inside the castle, they were going for the Cross of Longinus. Roman was in front of his desk and did everything necessary to open the safe and remove the cross.

"Follow me, there is a place where we will be safe." Roman said as he led the group through the corridors of the castle.

They ran as they heard shots and screams in the distance that were getting closer and closer. Scott ran while looking back and listening to the sound of machine guns. Finally, they reached a door at the end of a corridor. Roman opened it, revealing a small church. They all went up to the altar, looking around, after Roman closed the door.

"Do not worry" said Roman, "This is sacred ground. There is no room for evil here."

Roman seemed very convinced of what he was saying, but the others had their doubts. They all continued to guard the entrances. Mike and Henry were close to Ava to protect her. Scott pointed his automatic pistol at each place his gaze focused. Roman hugged the wooden box that contained the cross as five soldiers watched attentively, holding their submachine guns. Scott and the soldiers were slowly moving around the church trying to hear something from outside. Scott was the first to notice something.

"Do you hear that?" he asked.

Everyone was silent; Roman closed his eyes to better concentrate.

"I don't hear anything" said Roman, confused.

Scott looked intently Roman.

"Exactly, there were hundreds of soldiers out there fighting and now... silence."

Roman knew that Scott was right, something was wrong.

"We have to contact the other teams to come immediately." Roman said with some nervousness.

Scott looked at Roman again. Scott's face reflected concern and despair, Roman noticed that he was hiding something.

"What happened? What do you have to tell me?" he demanded.

"Sir, I gave them the order to come immediately when you told me that they should wait for our signal."

Roman was confused; he had been surprised that his most loyal soldier had disobeyed him, but on the other hand, thanks to this, the reinforcements would be about to arrive to save them. But, if that was good news, he wondered why Scott had such a helpless look on his face.

"I don't understand Scott, if the cavalry comes to the rescue, why do you have that face?"

Everyone was watching Scott attentively, waiting for his explanation.

"You've already seen what happened with the first attack on our soldiers. The bullets didn't even come close to their target. After that, I noticed something curious; I didn't hear a single shot again, which makes me think that after the attack, the beast did something to disable our weapons. At least until a few minutes later, which means that..."

"That the reinforcements had just arrived, and now we can no longer hear them." said Roman, devastated.

"That's right Sir. I'm afraid we are now alone in this war." Scott said, his eyes lost on the ground while everyone else looked at each other in fear.

They did not know what they could do next. Apparently, each plan was twisted by the power of "the evil one", but Roman was not intimidated.

"You are mistaken Scott; we are not alone. We have the power of Christ by our side." Roman said as he lifted the wooden box that contained the Cross of Longinus. "And in the house of God, we will be protected."

Suddenly, a knock was heard at the main door of the church.

KNOCK... KNOCK... KNOCK!

All those present were startled and immediately put all their attention towards the doors. The soldiers came as close as possible to the entrance of the church, pointing their weapons. Scott stayed behind to be close to the people he was protecting. Henry and Mike stepped forward to stand in front of Ava and protect her.

KNOCK... KNOCK... KNOCK!

"Help!" came an agonized voice from the other side of the door. Inside the church nobody said anything, everyone looked at Roman waiting for an answer. Roman only turned his head from one side to the other slowly.

"It's a trap! Do not open the door"

The soldiers turned their attention back to the door as they continued pointing their weapons, waiting for something to happen.

"Please open the door!" the desperate voice insisted.

Roman made sure everyone was clear about what was going on.

"Satan cannot enter the house of God. For that reason, he is trying to deceive us to make us leave." Roman said convinced of it.

Suddenly, a blinding light dazzled from the other side of the door accompanied by a terrifying scream and a huge explosion that blew the church doors into a thousand pieces. The shock wave threw everyone backwards. The box that Román had in his arms was snatched from him and fell between the pews of the Church where they were all lying on the ground due to the great explosion. Where the church doors had been, there was a fireball that began to expand throughout the interior of the church. Inside the fireball, the silhouette of Andy was visible. He was walking slowly towards the central aisle of the Church.

Two soldiers, who had been closest to the door were killed by the impact. The wood of the door had been blown and it dug into their bodies like daggers. The other soldiers got up and began firing their weapons at him. The bullets stopped, again, a few inches from Andy as he continued walking. The bullets only stopped in the air and fell in front of him. Scott put away his gun at the sight because already he knew that he was going to achieve nothing with it at that moment. The soldier in front of Andy kept shooting non-stop; shooting and screaming in an act of madness, but to no avail. Andy approached him and punched him in the heart, killing him on the spot.

"ANDY! NO!" Ava shouted.

She was still on the ground, astonished seeing how the love of her life had taken the life of another man right in front of her.

"Run to the entrance of the tower!" Roman yelled from the ground as he searched for the wooden box.

Meanwhile, the remaining soldiers engaged Andy in hand-to-hand combat, but they could do nothing against him. Andy was defending himself with perfect mastery. One of the soldiers launched a front kick, and Andy just took a small step to the side and responded with a fatal blow to the throat using the edge of his hand. The next soldier threw a punch head on, but Andy dodged it easily and counterattacked with an elbow to the soldier's temple, falling to the ground; lifeless. Everyone else looked incredulous as Andy made his way towards them without any problem. They were completely paralyzed, except for Roman, who, even though he was still on the ground, did not give up.

"DAMMIT! What are you waiting for?! RUN!" Roman shouted desperately as he continued searching the pews for the box that contained the Cross of Longinus.

Scott reacted to the screams of his superior and began to pressure Mike, Ava and Henry to start moving. Andy approached slowly and was only a few steps away from Roman, fortunately he found the box and opened it immediately.

"Now you see damn demon! I have a little gift for you... TAKE THIS!"

Roman got up quickly and put the cross in front of Andy's face, just a few inches from him. Scott, Henry, Mike and Ava, who were at the entrance of the Tower, stopped when they saw that Roman had managed to remove the cross just in time. Everyone was waiting to see what was about to happen. Andy looked at the cross in front of him, with his right hand he touched the upper point of the cross and lowered it to slowly see Roman's face. Andy looked into Roman's eyes and simply said.

"No thanks. I'm not a believer."

Roman's heart was paralyzed when he saw that Andy was not only in the presence of the cross but was also touching it and nothing had happened. Andy snatched the cross from him, in a quick movement, and drove it straight into his heart.

"NOOOOOO!" Scott cried helplessly as he saw his mentor die before his eyes. Roman slowly crumpled to his knees, while still looking directly into Andy's eyes. The gaze was reciprocal. Andy looked at him as he fell to the ground without feeling anything at all, for him it was just one more thing before reaching his goal.

Scott had no time for lamentations; he was a soldier and they were still at war, so he continued with his objective.

"Come on! Run! We have to continue!"

Mike, Ava and Henry looked at Scott with pity, but they knew he was right. The fight was not over yet, and they had to keep running. Ava led the group, followed by Mike, Henry and Scott picking up the rear. As they ran, Scott gave them instructions about plan B: a plan that he had developed himself for fear that nothing would work against the devil.

"Listen to me! On the second floor of this tower there is a door that leads to a bridge that connects to the west tower of the castle. Under that tower, there is a sports car with the keys in it and a pre-set address in the GPS. This will lead to the airport where you arrived today. At that airport, a plane is ready with personnel waiting for us to take-off as soon as possible. So, whatever happens, we must make sure that Ava gets on that plane, do you understand me?"

"Yes!" They all responded in unison except Ava, who still did not believe that this was happening because of her. But now she should not be mortified by the atrocities her boyfriend was committing, now the only thing that mattered was to make sure that those deaths had not been in vain.

Scott went on.

"Satan only has today to fulfil his objective. If we manage to prevent him from reaching Ava before dawn, we will have won."

Every time they reached a floor in the tower, they had to cross a room and go to the stairs that were on the other side to go up to the next floor. Just as Scott had said, on the second floor there was a door that was closed. Ava was the first to get there and logically tried to open it, but it was locked. Ava tried desperately to open the door, but it was all in vain.

"Damn it!" Professor Bianchi exclaimed. "Now what do we do, Scott? We can't open the door and if we keep going up, we will be trapped!"

Scott took out his automatic pistol and threw it at the professor, who caught it in the air in surprise.

"Blow the lock! I'll take care of giving you some extra time" Scott turned and began to descend the stairs, Ava reacted.

"Scott! Wait! Don't go!" she pleaded.

"I'm afraid it's the only chance we have to get out of this!"

"But there has to be another solution?! Please don't do it... I'm begging you!"

Henry and Mike were surprised by Ava's reaction. Even though the situation warranted it, Ava's way of pleading was very special; so much that even Mike felt jealous deep down, but Ava simply didn't want to be responsible for the death of another innocent person.

"Don't worry about me Ava, you just take care of getting to that plane... and never forget which side you are on." Scott smiled, turned around and began to descend the stairs to face Andy.

Andy reached the second floor, walking slowly, and in the centre of the room Scott was waiting for him. Andy looked at him and smiled.

"Hello Scott, I am glad to see that you have arrived in time to meet me."

Scott grasped his katana that was still on his back, and slowly pulled it out.

"If you think you can see the future you will know what comes next, right?" Scott said, his voice full of bravery.

Andy stared into his eyes as he smiled, as he replied.

"Yes. Now is when you die."

Scott got into a fighting stance with his sword while still keeping his eyes fixed on Andy's.

"We will see that" Scott said as he launched his attack with his sword.

Scott had practiced extreme martial arts when he was a child, and the sword display was one of his favourites. He was a warrior to fear with the sword because of his great speed and agility. He lunged himself in front of Andy and launched several attacks with the sword accompanied by kicks, that he threw while turning on himself. Andy dodged each of his attacks successfully, but, so far, he was the only one who was offering him a real show. Scott did not give up and continued with his attack, faster, more violent, causing Andy to start backing away. Then Scott saw an opportunity and made a couple of turns in the air as if it were a professional dancer. First, he extended his sword to reach his target but Andy ducked to avoid it. Immediately Scott launched a kick with his left foot, a kick that Andy blocked with his arms, and then, in a display of agility, Scott launched another kick with his right foot at the same time, hitting Andy square in the chest, throwing him backwards. Scott had achieved what the bullets had not; hit Andy's body. Scott was pleased but kept in mind that it was only a small victory in a war that he knew beforehand he was not going to win. Andy was impressed with the blow he had received, but it was not enough to make him lose confidence in himself.

"You really surprise me Scott, but I'm afraid if you want to stop me, you'll have to do much better."

Scott smiled.

"Relax, I'm just warming up."

Scott returned to his attack. He knew that if he wanted to surprise him again, he had to be faster, more unpredictable, and that could only be achieved with the stunts he used to do as a child. The stunts accompanied by the sword are a lethal combination. Scott jumped again to counterattack in the air, but this time Andy went ahead and jumped also throwing a kick, forcing

Scott a couple of meters back. Scott looked up at Andy from the ground. Andy was smiling.

"Come on, I'm waiting to see what you can do."

That hurt Scott more than the kick, he felt so hurt in his pride that he lost control and launched himself in to the attack with all his power in a single attempt with his sword. He ran towards Andy and raised his sword with the intention of cutting Andy in two from his head to the ground. Scott screamed with all his power and lowered the sword quickly, but just as it was about to touch Andy's forehead, his opponent stopped the sword using only his hand. Scott was still out of control and was straining, trying to get through Andy's hand, but the sword did not move an inch. Scott was staring directly into Andy's eyes, and Andy had a serious face. He was taking this fight seriously, but suddenly Andy made a small gesture of pain. Scott recognized the gesture and looked at his sword and saw how Andy's blood was flowing from his hand.

"You're bleeding... IT'S BLEEDING!" Scott shouted so that all those who were still alive and close would hear him.

Andy reacted and dropped the sword, causing Scott to lose his balance and fall forward. Andy came from behind Scott and grabbed his head and turned it hard, breaking Scott's neck, killing him in the act. Scott fell to his knees and collapsed, completely motionless on the ground while Andy watched.

After that, Andy was no longer so sure of himself. The man lying on the ground before him was not only able to hit him, he had made him bleed. He knew that something was not right for him, he had used a lot of power since he had arrived at the castle, and given the latest events it was more than obvious that he was losing power. Andy was so absorbed in his thoughts looking at palm of his hand as it bled, that he had not noticed that Professor Bianchi and Mike were on the other side of the room watching him. Andy reacted and saw how surprised they were as they looked at him, Mike pointed to Andy's palm.

"Scott was right, he's bleeding! He's losing power!"

Andy couldn't hide his nerves when he heard those words from Mike, but he couldn't give up now that he had come so far, there were only the two of them left on his way to Ava, and he was not going to give them the pleasure of seeing him go back.

"Make no mistake Mike, I still have enough strength to get through you two without any problem." Andy said as he started to walk towards them.

Professor Bianchi was still holding the gun Scott had left him, so he didn't hesitate for a second in pointing it at him.

"Stop, Satan. Do not force me to kill the guest you host; Andy is a good man who does not deserve to die this way... but if you force me, I will not hesitate to do it."

Mike was paralyzed, he saw how both Andy and Henry were willing to do anything to achieve their goal. Andy stared into Henry's eyes and Henry did not hesitate to return his gaze.

"Oh really? Well, try to stop me."

Andy stepped forward and, at the same time, Henry fired.

"NOOO!" Andy yelled, raising his hand.

Andy wanted to stop the bullet in mid-air as he had done before, but this time his trick didn't work. The bullet continued its course and hit his chest, making him take a couple of steps back as he saw the bullet wound in his body. Henry saw his opportunity and kept firing up to six more times; every bullet hitting Andy's body. He was still standing but was beginning to stagger backwards. The bullets had hit him squarely and he was starting to bleed from each bullet wound that he received. Andy lost his balance and staggered to one of the walls to his right; a wall with windows that let in the light of the full moon. Andy leaned his back against the wall and slowly fell until he was sitting on the floor with his legs extended and his back against the wall. Henry and Mike approached with caution until they were in front of Andy. They did not know if it was real, but from what their eyes saw, Andy had received a mortal wound that was killing him... his end was inevitable.

CHAPTER TWENTY
The Grand Finale

Andy was still on the floor with his back and head leaning against the wall, he breathed harder and harder with difficulty as his mouth filled with blood. Ava entered the room and felt herself dying when she saw him slumped on the floor.

"Oh no Andy!" Ava gasped as she ran to meet him, but Mike stopped her.

"Ava what are you doing here?! We told you to go, you should be on your way to the airport!" he said, exasperated.

"Mike, let me go! I have to be with him, he is dying, we have to do something, please!"

Mike kept struggling with her, preventing her from getting close to Andy. Henry felt the need to intervene too.

"Ava, you shouldn't see this. You have to understand that the man lying there on the ground is not your dear Andy; he is a monster who did not hesitate to kill all those who wanted to prevent him carrying out his plans. Think of all the soldiers who died today to protect you, all those who he killed without mercy."

Ava, listening to Henry, realized that Scott was lying on the ground lifeless; a good man who died to give her a chance to escape, and not only him, Henry was right to mention all those soldiers who had died that night. Henry kept talking.

"I'm very sorry that things have ended this way, but at least now you can know that everything is over. You no longer have to run or hide. Ava, we won! We defeated Satan. You'll see now that the world we live in will be a much better place from now on."

Ava just looked at Henry without saying anything; she was no longer fighting against Mike, she knew they were right, but still it was inevitable that she would be devastated about losing the love of her life in that way. She had built her whole world around Andy and now, without him, she no longer knew what lay ahead of her.

"You are wrong."

Everyone looked at Andy as they felt their hearts stop for a second. Henry was the only one with the courage to speak.

"What did you say?" he asked.

Andy had his eyes closed, but he kept talking, albeit with a bit of difficulty.

"I said... you are wrong." Andy managed a weak smile.

"Poor mortals, do you really think that if I ceased to exist the world would be a better place? Ha!" Andy made a mocking face and opened his eyes.

"Well, I'm sorry to disappoint you, but even if that happened, the world would not change at all. Everything bad that happens on this planet is not caused by a single entity, it is merely the sum of all the mortals who know that they do evil and do not care. You are good or bad because you choose what you want to be, not because I decide who is bad and who is not."

Everyone listened to Andy's words without saying anything, Henry was the only one able to reply.

"Maybe you are right, and after your death nothing changes, but even so the world will continue to be only for human beings, without other beings that want to intervene to change our world. After tonight we have shown that we are capable of doing the impossible, if we have been able to defeat you, we will be capable of anything."

Andy closed his eyes and smiled again.

"I think you did not hear the first thing I said."

Henry and the others were confused.

"What are you talking about?" asked Henry.

Andy opened his eyes and stared back at Henry.

"When I said you were wrong, I was talking about when you said that you had won, that you had beaten me." Andy smiled again. "This is not over for you yet."

Henry still had Scott's gun in his hand. Hearing this, he quickly pointed it at Andy's head. Andy simply looked into the professor's eyes.

"You can do anything you want with this body; it doesn't matter, I don't need it anymore. Thanks to him, I have spent enough time in this world to know how to enter here with my own body."

Everyone was surprised to hear this, especially Henry, who had thought that everything was over, and suddenly the worst of his nightmares fell short of what was coming, Andy kept talking.

"So, you can be proud of yourselves, because you are going to be the first in all of history... to see the true face of the so-called devil!"

Andy opened his mouth, and a thick, black smoke began to come out of his body; the same smoke that had been present when he was possessed in his apartment. Just like then, the smoke began to come out of his nose, his eyes, his ears and even from the gunshot wounds. Mike reacted by grabbing Ava's hand and dragging her to the door that led to the other tower.

"Ava, you have to go! Continue with Scott's plan, go to the airport and whatever happens, get on that plane!"

"Wait Mike, you're not coming with me?!"

"No" he said with regret, "Henry and I will stay to buy you some time, so this time promise me that you will leave as quickly as possible and will not stop until you get to that plane!"

Ava felt a knot in her stomach when she saw that Mike was willing to sacrifice himself for her, she looked at him in a way that she had not looked at him before. Ava caressed his face with her hand and looked at him sadly, thinking that it could be the last time she saw him alive.

"Mike" she whispered.

"Promise me!"

"Okay... I promise."

"Now go! You can't waste any more time... go!"

Ava looked at him and for the first time she gave him a sincere smile, even with some love. Mike smiled back at her. He knew that something had changed inside her, and that was enough for him to die happy. Ava turned her back on him and began to run with all her strength to the other tower of the castle. Mike watched her leave and knew that this was perhaps the last image he would keep of Ava, but right now that did not matter. Now his only mission was to face the devil and give Ava a chance to save herself.

Mike returned to the room where Andy remained. Next to him was Henry, who had not moved since Andy began to expel the back smoke. Mike approached and stood next to professor Bianchi; Henry did not take his eyes off Andy, even seeing out of the corner of his eye that Mike had returned. He remained focused on

Andy, but still wanted to give his most formidable student a few last words.

"I thought you had escaped with Ava to save her."

Mike was also staring at the spectacle while answering.

"If we want to give Ava a chance, we must face Satan together. We may not be able to defeat him, but at least we might delay him long enough for Ava to escape."

"You knew that if you stayed you would not leave here alive, and even so, you decided to stay to fight. You are a very brave man Michael Jones, and for me it will be a real pleasure to fight against evil by your side."

Henry looked at Mike as he looked back at him.

"Same here, Professor Bianchi."

***

Ava had reached the other side of the tower. The door was open, and she began to descend the stairs until she reached a garage that was on the mezzanine of the tower. There was only a sports car, a red Lamborghini Aventador with the keys in it. Ava got into the car and saw on the GPS a route was already programmed, as Scott had said. Luckily for Ava, one of Andy's favourite hobbies was spending an afternoon driving super cars on special circuits where you could pay for the experience. It was a hobby that Andy shared with Ava, and that she learned to love thanks to him. That meant it was no problem for her to start the car and drive as fast as she could to the airport.

***

Andy continued to expel smoke and it was becoming a cloud that floated above him. As he emitted the smoke his body was deteriorating more and more. With each passing moment, he was more skin and bone, drying, until it became ash that was gradually crumbling to the floor.

Henry and Mike watched in horror as Andy's body was being reduced to a mere pile of ashes on the floor, while the cloud of smoke that lingered was evolving from within. It seemed like a living being was taking shape inside the smoke. Mike could only think of the kind of beast that would come out of there. *"The true face of the devil"*: he remembered the drawing he had seen of the devil in Professor Bianchi's house and the thought of facing that creature left him cold.

Suddenly, from the centre of the plume, a pure white light illuminated the room. It was a very bright light but at the same time it was not a blinding. It was not a light that bothered the eyes at all. From the centre of the smoke, the light was emanating until the cloud itself disappeared. From the light a silhouette appeared to take on human form while the white light began to lose strength, revealing more details of the form, born from the light, that was floating in the air.

Mike and Henry began to see that this being wore clothes that they had not seen before, it was a kind of tunic made with silver threads that covered the entire body. It was a covering that was even too much for the most powerful monarch on Earth, because it could only be carried by a divine being. As they looked up, they saw that the being had wings of light. The colour of the wings was not one they had seen before, but the best way to describe it was a bright, light magenta colour. Every inch of this being was a sight to behold; he made all mortals in front of him feel insignificant.

Henry and Mike were so absorbed in taking in every detail of the being that they forgot for an instant to look at the most important thing; the devil's face. It left them speechless as soon as they set their eyes on it. His eyes were closed but they could see his face very well; Mike had his mouth open while the professor was so confused that he could not process what was happening.

"No, it can't be!" Mike said over and over again. "It just can't be! A ... Andy?"

The devil's face was still Andy's. Andy was a very attractive man with almost perfect features, but this being wore an even more perfect version of Andy's face. It looked like a computer-generated version of Andy's face, more striking and without any imperfections that might have existed on the original. This making him the most attractive man they had ever seen, and they were sure that he was even the most handsome of all men by far.

Luzbel descended to the ground and opened his eyes, the irises of his eyes were no longer black, or even blue as they used to be; they were now silver in colour, giving him an even more divine look.

Mike and Henry were no longer afraid to be in front of this being. For them, seeing him was an incomparable sight, but they could not help being confused when they saw that he still had the form of Andy. Luzbel smiled and addressed them.

"I understand that you are confused when you see my true face and see that it is still the face of your friend Andy. One thing you must know is that Andy was never conceived to be an ordinary person. All this time he has existed with only one purpose, and that is to serve me as a vehicle to enter this world; so, in this way, I have *always* been Andy."

Mike didn't believe it. He knew it couldn't be like this; he knew his best friend better than anyone, and that being from the last few days was not Andy at all.

"You liar! Andy was never part of your plans until he was the victim of that ritual with the Nova Lumen! Thanks to them you were able to possess his body, but that is the only connection that binds you to him and nothing else."

Luzbel stared into Mike's eyes and smiled.

"If that is the case, then tell me something Mike... How is it possible that I, a being who has seen the creation of time and space, share the same face as your friend?"

Mike had no answer for that, no matter how hard he tried to think about it. Luzbel kept talking.

"The truth is that Andy was a creation of mine. I made him from a different dimension, destined for this dimension. I created a human cell with part of my characteristics to be inserted into a woman who would later become the mother of my creation. Andy was a creation made by me, for me, in my image and likeness."

The explanation shocked them, but at the same time generated more questions in Mike's mind, and among all those questions, one came repeatedly.

"I don't understand, if you are capable of creating life and having your own terrestrial body, why do you need Ava? What is the meaning of all this persecution if you can be on this planet with your own material body?"

Luzbel stared into Mike's eyes and smiled, he knew that was a good question and he had no problem answering him.

"For me, it would not be a problem to start over. To create a new body using a woman, and have the same appearance that I had before. But despite being my creation and being able to control it at my whim, I am still not a part of this world, therefore my power is considerably reduced when being inside a terrestrial body."

Professor Bianchi and Mike didn't say anything, but they both had the same thought at the same time... *"If, after everything we've seen so far, it has just been a reduced version of his power, what would be the extent of his true power? What would become of us now that he is here in his true form?"*

Luzbel continued.

"For this reason, being forever inside a human body is not an option for me. It is something that weakens me, limits my perception and makes me an easy target for other beings in my world. But, instead of it being me, the one who could always be on this planet would be someone made of my own energy, taking care of my own interests as if they were his own. This would solve my problems without having to be present here at all times."

Mike had one last question.

"And Ava? Why her?"

Luzbel remembered the face of the first woman in creation. He remembered Ava's face and saw a great resemblance; it was practically like seeing the same younger woman. He could not deny that he felt something very special for those women.

"And why not?" he responded, "She is a very special woman, and she is perfect in my plan to recreate "God's master plan" to bring my own son to this world."

Luzbel laughed.

Henry hadn't said anything until then, but upon hearing this, a part of him went up in anger.

"Blasphemy! Only God is capable of creating life as we know it. You are just an insubordinate with delusions of grandeur! A creation made in your image and likeness! Ha! Poor devil!"

Luzbel stared into Henry's eyes and smiled while Henry saw how his words had no effect on him.

"Alright, let's get this over!"

Henry raised his pistol again, pointing it at Luzbel's head. He pulled the trigger, and nothing happened. Henry knew there were still bullets in the gun, but no matter how hard he pulled the trigger, nothing happened. Henry looked at the gun and again at Luzbel.

"Be careful professor, remember that if you play with fire, you will get burned."

The professor lowered his weapon slowly, and he felt it rapidly heating up in his hand. Henry wanted to drop it when it exploded in his hand destroying it completely. Professor Bianchi had lost his hand, while Mike watched the scene of terror, powerless.

Henry was in agony. He wanted to scream with all his might, but at the same time the pain was so great that it formed a lump in his throat. He could not scream or even breathe. Luzbel stared at the professor again and a gust of wind, emitted by Luzbel, threw Henry against the wall. He suffered a very big blow to the head and fell, motionless, on the ground. Mike knew that he could do nothing against Luzbel. He saw how the professor was lying on the ground and knew that now it was his turn.

Mike turned to see Luzbel's face and he was staring at him. Mike was paralyzed, his whole life was passing through his eyes, and he couldn't believe that this was the end, Luzbel spoke to him.

"I still feel some sympathy for you Mike, and in the name of that great friendship that united us I will not kill you, at least not for now. For once, be clever and take advantage of this opportunity that I am giving you."

Luzbel ignored him and turned to look at the wall in front of him, his eyes lit up and the wall flew into a thousand pieces several meters away. Luzbel approached the huge hole he had created and was looking towards the road. As if he were a hawk, he began to look further and further into the distance until he found the red car that Ava was driving. Luzbel spread his wings of light and launched himself off the tower, plummeting towards the ground. A few meters from the surface of the Earth, he moved his wings, making him soar through the air at high speed, leaving only a few small flashes of light in his wake.

Mike couldn't believe it; he was still alive. But Luzbel was going for Ava and he didn't have the faintest idea of how to stop him.

"Shit!" he said as he got lost in his thoughts. *"Andy with powers was already a nightmare and now with the devil in his true form... it is impossible to defeat him, what I need is a miracle or a super wea... wait..."*

An idea lit up inside Mike's head, so he ran down the stairs of the tower and returned to where the church had been destroyed by Andy. He was looking among the remains for Román's body. As soon as he saw him, he ran to where he lay. The body was upside down; Mike turned it over and saw the Cross of Longinus still nailed to his chest. Mike took a breath, grabbed the cross and tore it from Roman's body.

"It didn't work because Andy's body protected him, but now there's nothing to protect that son of a bitch."

Mike put the cross within the waist of his trousers so that it wouldn't fall, and he could feel it at all times. He left the tower quickly and saw a post-apocalyptic scene, with hundreds of dead everywhere and the imposing, partially destroyed castle. Mike saw one of the motorcycles, used by one of the soldiers that arrived after Andy's first attack, lying on the ground. The keys were still in the ignition, so without thinking he took the bike and rushed to catch up with Ava.

***

Ava kept driving fast, constantly looking at the rear-view mirror to make sure that no one was following her. Suddenly, she saw a light in the sky that seemed to follow her. The light was getting bigger and bigger. Ava was scared; she had a bad feeling and she accelerated by pushing her foot to the ground. The car seemed to fly over the road and Ava's heart was jumping out of her chest when she saw how fast she was driving down the unpaved road. The thought that the light could be the devil chasing her gave her the courage to continue. She kept looking in the rear-view mirror and noticed that the light was now getting smaller, until she could no longer see it. Ava looked over her shoulder to check and saw that there was nobody behind her but as she put her eyes back on the road, she saw Luzbel suddenly land in front of her; one leg on the hood of the car and the other on the ground. The car shook and made Ava go back and forth on the seat. Luzbel was pushed by the car with his foot still on the hood, until he spread his wings and held the car tightly with his foot. The car stopped dead in the road and made the rear wheels rise at almost a ninety-degree angle from the ground. The airbag exploded out of the car hitting Ava in the face and leaving her stunned as the car crashed back on to the ground. Ava barely had control of her body, but she knew she had to get out of there as soon as possible. She opened the door and fell on the ground as she watched someone approach her from the front of the car. She crawled on the ground desperately trying to get up. When she finally got up to run, she tripped over someone and fell back to the ground, Ava looked at who she had run into and couldn't believe it.

"Andy?!"

Luzbel was in front of her smiling like Andy used to do, he helped her up.

"Do you understand now? All this time it has always been me. I have loved you since before you existed, and I have waited, so patiently, for you for thousands of years. Just to be here, like this, with you. Whether you believe in destiny or not, it does not matter, because I know that you are made for me, and I am here to love you."

Ava trembled in front of him, her eyes filled with tears when she saw Andy's face and hearing his words. She had a world of contradictions inside her that she could not rationalize. Ava avoided his gaze as she spoke.

"It's not fair, you only say that because you want to use me. You take advantage of my feelings to fulfil your plans without caring how I feel."

Luzbel put his hand on Ava's chin, and he gently lifted her face so that she had no choice but to look into his eyes.

"Look into my eyes Ava and tell me that I'm lying to you. You know me better than anyone and you know it. You know what I say is true. I know that I have been branded evil incarnate, and directly responsible for all the misfortunes in the world, but I don't care. I give thanks for every mistake and every success through my existence, because thanks to this I can be here in front of you to tell you that everything I am and everything I have is yours. My only plan is to be with you; to tell you that, thanks to you, I know what it means to love. I am a divine being and yet felt so powerless when I experienced all the love that you have given me, when I visited you through Andy's body. You are what I love the most; what matters most to me, and if you think I'm lying to you, you are free to turn your back on me and leave right now. I give you my word that I will not stop you, but I hope you don't because I really want to be with you, forever"

Ava's heart was beating fast with every word that Luzbel spoke. She looked him in the eye and knew he wasn't lying to her, she was tired of fighting, why resist something she was wanting to do? Now she understood that the name did not matter, Andy or Luzbel, she just realized that the man in front of her was the love of her life. Ava smiled and approached him to kiss him, Luzbel also approached her and kissed her on the lips slowly, while his wings enveloped her, illuminating the whole place.

"AVAAA!"

Mike yelled from a distance, approaching quickly on the motorcycle. Luzbel put his wings back and stopped kissing Ava to focus on Mike.

"It seems to me that I no longer have any sympathy for this man."

Luzbel took a step forward, extended his hand and the motorcycle that Mike was riding stopped abruptly throwing him into the air. Luzbel grabbed his neck with one hand while he was still in the air and held him without any difficulty while Mike hung with his legs off the ground.

"I gave you an opportunity to get away from here, and you have wasted it."

Mike gripped Luzbel's hand with one of his while he reached to the back of his waist with the other. Mike smiled and spoke with difficulty.

"Well, you know me; I'm stubborn when I want something."

Luzbel looked confused at Mike because he knew he was up to something. Mike quickly pulled out the cross and held it up in front of Luzbel. The cross shot towards Luzbel's chest as if it had a very powerful magnetic force and as soon as it made contact an electric discharge shook his entire body. Luzbel screamed, fell to his knees and released Mike as the cross continued to torture him.

Mike ran to Ava who seemed hypnotized looking at Luzbel without saying anything. Luzbel continued screaming while an electric current ripped through every corner of his body. It was a pain that he had already experienced before and it brought back bad memories; it was exactly the same power with which the Creator had attacked him using his sceptre, on that occasion one of his subjects had helped him, but this time he was alone, so he had to do something.

The situation did not make sense for Luzbel, if Christ was only a man, how was it possible that cross had such power? Luzbel touched the dried blood that stained the cross and only one image came to his head.

"IT CAN'T BE! This is the power of the Creator's son! But how has he done it?! How has he managed to be in the body of Christ without me realizing it?"

Now he understood; he knew that the son of the Creator had possessed Christ, to manipulate his blood and turn it into a weapon against Luzbel himself. Exactly how he had done it without Luzbel, or any of Luzbel's followers, realizing was inexplicable. This new information opened endless questions in Luzbel's mind, but now was not the time to delve into them. This weapon was a threat to Luzbel, and he had to fight back. Summoning all of his strength, Luzbel grabbed the cross and began to push it away from his chest. Slowly separating the cross from his body, starting with a few centimetres until reaching a distance that allowed him to have his arms fully extended. He held the cross tightly in his hands. The Cross of Longinus had incredible strength, but Luzbel had managed to detach it from his body. Luzbel smiled as he spoke.

"This time you won't be able to beat me so easily!"

Suddenly the sound of trumpets was heard that resounded all around. Luzbel was still on his knees holding the cross when he saw a portal of light opening from the heavens. Five angels with wings of light emerged. Luzbel couldn't believe it; until that moment he thought he was the only angel with wings of light, but the angels surrounding him had bright wings of cyan light. One of the angels took Luzbel's right hand, another took his left hand, one held his head from behind, and the other two holding his legs, also from behind. Once they had taken their positions, the angels holding his hands opened their arms, causing the cross to hit him again with force on Luzbel's chest. Again, a discharge of electricity ran through Luzbel's body, he was crying out desperately.

"LET ME GO DAMNIT! LET ME GO!"

The angels of light continued to hold him tightly while the cross overloaded his body. Luzbel's body shone brighter, and he could not scream any louder even if he wanted to. His body illuminated the entire place leaving everything clearer than the light of day. His body could not take it anymore and exploded in a shower of light that was dissipating everywhere. The sparks that emanated from Luzbel's body were fading until they disappeared, and the angels of light arose and looked at Mike. Mike looked at them, scared, not knowing exactly what had happened.

The angels smiled at him and flew back to the portal from which they had come. The portal stopped shining, letting the darkness of the night take over again. Ava reacted by falling to her knees as she began to cry. Mike knelt close to her and hugged her trying to comfort her.

"That's it, it's all over."

CHAPTER TWENTY-ONE

Beyond the Fallen Angel

3 years later - Sforza Castle

"The latest attack by the United States has left at least 124 victims, including 30 children, all of whom died in an aerial bombardment of the international coalition led by the United States on the town of Al Shadadi, in the south of the province of Al Hasaka. The Observatory has repeatedly denounced the "massacres" by coalition aircraft, which bombard areas where jihadists are present but, in the vast majority of cases, only caused civilian victims..."

"How awful. Mike, can you turn off the TV please?" Ava said while she was sitting on a bed watching television with Mike. Mike got up and turned the TV off. Ava kept talking.

"He was right, even after his disappearance the world seems to go from bad to worse, and this time we have no one to blame but ourselves; we are the ones responsible."

"I know. Human beings are still dominated by our wild nature, but I don't lose faith that we'll soon know what we must do to live with each other in peace and harmony."

Ava was staring at Mike.

"Have you ever thought about what would have happened if he had won? I don't know... do you really think the world would be worse than *this*?"

Mike was not surprised by the question; it was something that he had asked himself a couple of times.

"I'd be lying if I told you that I've never considered that, but despite the fact that it may be illogical or irrational, if we are living in hell on Earth, I am glad to know that it is because we ourselves have chosen it, and not because someone has imposed it on us."

Ava smiled and seemed to understand Mike's point, but he kept talking.

"Besides, if he had won, that would mean that this little boy would have no choice but to lead the greatest satanic force ever seen."

Mike was laying his eyes on the new born baby Ava had on her lap.

"I'm glad to know that he has a world of possibilities to choose from."

Someone knocked on the door.

"Hello, I'm sorry to interrupt, but the advisor has just arrived and we have to go right now Mike." Professor Bianchi said.

Mike just sighed.

"Wow, they don't give me even a quiet moment."

Ava smiled.

"That's what happens when you defeat the prince of darkness; you become a star in the Bellatores Dei " she said.

Mike smiled, kissed the baby's forehead and then kissed Ava on the lips.

"I'll be right back."

Henry pointed with his prosthetic hand at a photo on a table near the door.

"I love that photo, it's very good." he said.

Mike held up the photo Henry was referring to and saw that it was a photo taken during his and Ava's wedding.

"Yes, I love it too."

Mike looked back at his beloved wife from the door with their son, and he felt like the luckiest man in the world.

"Take good care of our little one." he called.

Ava smiled and Mike left the room.

The baby was asleep. Ava looked at him with a lot of love and just repeated.

"Yes, our little one."

The baby began to move and was opening his eyes; black eyes like his father's. Ava smiled at the baby who was gazing up at her and she said the same.

"*Our* little one."

Ava looked into the baby's eyes and remembered the moment three years ago when she was on the road to the castle with Luzbel. She remembered the moment when she slowly approached Luzbel's lips. Ava's gaze focused on one of the baby's eyes and she remembered what Mike had said once.

"He is a being who existed before time and space, a being who is not affected by our laws, and who also knows them so well that he can play with them at will."

She searched under the iris of her son's eye to see a small mark; an inverted cross.

"Our little one."

Ava closed her eyes and remembered everything that had happened in that kiss, how the whole place lit up and transported her to another dimension, she remembered how she kissed him without stopping. How he whispered in her ear that he loved her while he took off her clothes. How he moved his lips over her naked body. How he kissed her breasts and caressed the most exciting corners of her body with his hands. How he got on top of her and slowly penetrated her while she felt an intense pleasure that she had not experienced before. How they made love for hours, changing to different positions and different rhythms until exploding in the most intense orgasm she had ever experienced. And after that Ava remembered how they had remained in an embrace, floating in a blank space where she felt she was lying on the warmest and most comfortable cloud in the world. He just kissed her slowly and told her over and over how much he loved her; she was dying of love for him.

"I want to always be with you and be the mother of your children."

"You already are" Luzbel smiled.

Ava was surprised, but just the idea that she could be pregnant with his child made her very happy.

"Really? Are you sure about it?"

Luzbel kept smiling and put his hand on Ava's stomach.

"This baby is part of me. Like me, he has great power; he has not yet been formed, but he already knows what his mission is, and what is best for him. That is why he will only be born when there is no suspicion of him, and he can live quietly without running in to any danger."

Ava was smiling happily.

"I can't wait to have him in my arms."

"You will have to wait for it, but when the time comes, we will be the happiest parents in the world." Ava stared at Luzbel.

"Promise me that you will always be close to us."

Luzbel looked back into Ava's eyes with love and couldn't stop smiling.

"I promise."

They kissed again, as Luzbel surrounded Ava with his wings of light and made her clothes appear, then taking her back to the castle road, where Mike would interrupt them on his motorcycle.

Ava opened her eyes and kissed her baby's forehead. "*Our* little one."

Everything inside the castle was going normally and nobody had noticed that just above Ava's room there was a silhouette of a man dressed in a black suit, a man with his eyes closed, who in his thoughts could be heard.

My name is Luzbel, and I'm not the one to tell you what or in whom you should believe, but soon, thanks to my son, everyone will know the truth; my truth. And you... are you ready for it?

Andy opened his eyes, revealing their black colour, and smiled.

J.C. Ramírez

Juan Carlos Ramírez Sánchez, was born in Medellín - Colombia, where he lived for 16 years, later he moved to Elche - Spain, a city he lived in for 14 years. He then moved to England, where he currently resides. He has always felt a great interest in all kinds of legends and conspiracy theories; this lead to a dream in his adolescence which resulted in this book.

For more information about the author please visit

www.bellatorespublishing.com

Printed in Great Britain
by Amazon